THE BILLIONAIRE'S TEACHER

BILLIONAIRE NEXT DOOR

ELIZABETH MADDREY

1

WES

"Thanks for letting me crash at your house in the Caymans for a couple of days next week." I reached past Scott for the bag of chips.

"No problem. I like knowing it's getting used. I'm still not sure why you don't just run your dive trips out of it. We're unlikely to want to use the place at the same time, and it would save you all this recon." Scott grabbed the deck of cards out of the center of my dining room table and began to shuffle.

The other guys weren't there yet. Cody was still on his honeymoon, so he obviously wasn't coming, but Austin and Tristan had both texted that they were running late. "You didn't hear from Noah, right?"

Scott shook his head. "Not yet. He'll turn up."

I laughed. "You hope. He's engaged now, remember. And since Megan's in Paris on her honeymoon with Cody, I'm pretty sure the girls' bookstore hangout isn't happening. What'd Whitney say?"

"That they're skipping this week. And next." Scott frowned. "Why would that mean Noah bails?"

"Date night? Duh. I'm honestly surprised you're here. And that Austin is even pretending to come."

"What do you mean, pretending?" Scott clicked the button on the side of his phone.

"How are you married when you're this clueless? Again I repeat: date night. Kayla's free on a Friday. Austin is totally going to skip out early—if he even shows—and do something with his wife." I shot a glance at Scott. "You sure Whitney didn't drop some hints you missed?"

Scott hunched his shoulders. "She knows I'm bad at hints."

"Uh-huh." I reached over and took the cards. "Go home, man. I think we ought to cancel until honeymoon-boy is back."

"Nah. You all still get together when Whitney and I travel. Why—"

"Because the girls have a place to go, too. But they've already canceled. Which means married couples should take advantage of Friday date nights." Scott was lucky God had dropped Whitney into his lap eighteen months ago. I honestly couldn't believe he'd ever have found love otherwise. "Go. I'll let everyone else know we're canceling."

Scott pushed his chair back. "I still think you're wrong. And I'm also not blind to how this gets you out of hosting. Again."

"Hey." I lifted my hands. "I tried to host. It's not my fault it didn't work out. You're here, in my house, aren't you? So it's not as if I have secrets that I'm hiding."

"Fine." Scott scowled. "But you're leaving when, Monday?"

I nodded. I'd thought about heading to the Caribbean over the weekend, but Saturday was our busiest day at the dive shop and Sunday was church. Monday was soon enough. "I'll be gone two weeks. Maybe three. No biggie."

I stood and clapped Scott on the shoulder.

"Ouch."

"Whatever, man. Get Whitney to kiss it better."

Scott snickered and punched my arm. "Have a safe trip. Keep in touch, okay?"

"Okay, Mom."

Scott huffed and headed for the front door.

I got my phone off the table and sent a quick text to the group chat.

> We're calling it. Go have fun on a date night with your SO. Tristan – if you wanna hang, come on by. We can do single-guy stuff.

There. That should handle it.

Tristan wouldn't come. He always had work to do. That was the joy of being a successful independent attorney. Or something. I figured it was more that he was a workaholic than anything.

Of course, it didn't help that he was handling a nasty divorce for a friend right now. Or a friend of a friend. Whatever the situation, all the guys had been surprised when he finally spilled the beans about why he was so cranky. Except Noah.

I'd gotten the feeling Noah had pried it out of him earlier.

When no one immediately replied to my text, I shoved to my feet. I'd clean up all the poker stuff and then...what, exactly?

"One thing at a time." I muttered under my breath as I slid decks of cards into their boxes. I took a few extra minutes to organize the poker chips by color in the aluminum case they'd come in. The other guys always seemed to have no problem just sorting the chips on poker night, but didn't it make more sense to spend the time keeping things organized in the first place?

I shut and flipped the locks on the case closed, then stashed it in the bottom of the china cabinet, which took up the single wall in the dining room that didn't have an opening of some sort. I frowned, like I usually did, at the blank shelves on the top half of the thing. Mom had this grand idea that grown-up furniture would make me want more grown-up things.

Like a wife.

Grandkids for her to spoil.

Unless the cabinet was supposed to magically summon them into my house, I wasn't sure I followed her train of thought, but I also hadn't been able to talk her out of giving the thing to me. Since she and my stepdad had made the trip in a U-Haul specifically to deliver this wooden monstrosity, I really hadn't had much choice.

I sighed. At least it wasn't ugly. I kind of liked the simple lines—Mom said it was mission style. That had launched me down a path of research that ended with me agreeing that I liked the look. But it didn't prompt me to invest in more furniture of that ilk.

Maybe now that money wasn't an issue, I should.

Or I could give Mom the go-ahead and let her take care of it for me.

My phone rang. I laughed as I answered, "Speak of the devil."

"Who are you calling the devil?" The laughter in Mom's voice was stronger than her attempt at censure.

"No one specific."

"That's what I thought." Mom cleared her throat. "Are you standing in the dining room glaring at your china cabinet again?"

I wished, again, that I could believe psychics were real, because Mom had a knack. "How'd you know?"

"It's the only time you call me the devil."

I snorted.

"I'm serious. I'm keeping a list. So is The General."

I imagined the letters capitalized even though there was

warmth and affection in the nickname Mom had for my step-dad. "Well, as long as he's keeping you honest."

"Always." The General chimed in.

"I'm on speaker." I shook my head and wandered out of the dining room to the living room where I plopped onto the leather sofa I'd bought with my first real paycheck. "You're supposed to tell people before they reveal state secrets."

"I don't think your mother's psychic abilities are state secrets, son." The General's gruff voice held a hint of humor. "But I'll keep it in mind. Of course, you're still doing the Jesus thing, aren't you. So you probably don't believe she has the sight."

"I am still doing the Jesus thing, yes." I didn't bother defending it or going further down that train of thought. I'd reached a quiet peace with my parents—all three of them, since Dad and his latest wife had just ended things—when it came to Jesus. I didn't try to force Him down their throats, and they kept their annoyance and teasing to a minimum. Of course, their definition of "minimum" wasn't always the same as mine, but I was still going to call it a win.

"Good for you, honey." Mom's voice was soothing. Of the three of them, Mom was the most open to hearing about it. "We called because I have on my calendar that you're heading to the islands soon and was hoping for more detail."

Right. I'd emailed them about my plans before they were completely firmed up. "I'll fly down to the Caymans on Monday. I'm going to base myself in Scott and Whitney's place there for a day or two, then I hired a boat to take me around to some of the other islands to check out resorts and dive sites."

"A boat? What sort?" The General, for all he was an Army man, loved to sail.

I cringed even though he couldn't see me. "It's a yacht. A small one, but still."

Mom laughed. "For a minute there, I think The General wanted to come along and sail with you."

"I did think about sailing. But I didn't want to be gone quite as long as that would probably take." Plus, I didn't actually understand sailboats, despite The General's efforts. I liked motors. Cars. Boats. Airplanes. They should all have motors as far as I was concerned.

The General grunted.

"You're still going to be gone a long time. Are you sure you can't make separate trips? I worry about your business with you gone."

"Mom." I bit back a sigh. She wasn't worried about the business. She was worried about me. "I appreciate it. I'll be fine. It really does make more sense to hit it all in one fell swoop. Think of it as me saving some fossil fuels by only using the jet on one round trip."

"Well. That's something, I guess." I could hear Mom's frown. "You'll text me some photos, right? Something so I know you're okay?"

"Of course." I hadn't planned to, but it wouldn't be hard to send her proof of life every day or so. No matter how much I tried to remind her, Mom struggled with remembering that I was an adult in my early thirties. Maybe it was because it had been just her and me for so long after she and Dad split up? Even now that she had The General, she worried. "You could come."

"Don't tempt me, boy. Although I'd insist on changing that yacht over to a sailboat. Your mother could use a few weeks of relaxing out on the water."

"No. No way. If I'm relaxing on the water it's going to be on a cruise ship where I barely have to realize I want a new drink before someone is bringing it to me." Mom's refusal made me smile.

The General laughed, deep and throaty. "I guess I know what I need to set up. You want to join us, Wes? We could do a Christmas cruise. I know it'd take you away from your usual beach trip with friends, but we'd sure love to have you."

Guilt tugged at me. I tried to avoid anything that hinted at favoritism when it came to holidays. And yet, the cruise sounded like a good way to spend time with them without having to be around them twenty-four seven. "What if..."

I bit my lip.

"What if?" Mom never had been patient with me when I started talking before I thought things all the way through.

"What if we invited Dad, too? I can pay for everyone. Even put him on a different deck of the ship, if that makes it better. But then—"

"That's a great idea." The General interrupted. "Keeps him from badgering you and your mother about unfair treatment. But we can handle our own cabin."

"Will you let me?" Mom never let me spend anything on her. She seemed to think all the billions were going to disappear as quickly as they'd appeared. "I'd like to do something nice. For everyone."

"I don't—" The General's words cut off with a quiet "oof."

"That would be sweet. Thank you, honey. You just let us know when and we'll get it on the calendar. Do you think your father will have a plus-one?"

I cringed at Mom's words. Knowing Dad, he would absolutely be dating someone. If he wasn't already. With Dad, the possibility was high that he'd been dating someone and that was why he and his wife were no longer together. "If they're not married, she can have her own cabin."

Mom snickered. "Good luck with that."

It was my money. I was prepared to put my foot down. On

the other hand, maybe Dad wouldn't even want to come. "I guess we'll see. I'll let you know."

"Thank you. Be safe. And I'm serious about you sending me some pictures. Words to go with them are a bonus."

I laughed. "Got it. Love you, Mom."

"Love you too, honey. Bye." Mom ended the call before I had to go through the awkwardness of goodbyes with The General. It wasn't that I didn't love him. But he wasn't the kind of man who said those sorts of things. At least not to his adult stepson. I assumed he said it to Mom. I'd given up on anything demonstrative with him beyond a cheerful backslap when we were in the same room. He seemed okay with that.

I opened my to-do list app and made a note to look into cruises for Christmas. Now that I was responsible for that, it wouldn't do to forget. There was a lot of time between now and Christmas—it was barely June—but I was bound to forget during the trip if I didn't write it down.

I opened my texts, but there was nothing new from anyone. Figured as much. Tristan had probably been just as glad for a night off as the couples with significant others. Of course, in Tristan's case, I knew he'd spend the time working. Because somehow he figured that was better than getting a life.

Not like I was one to talk.

Except I still did the dating thing. Maybe it had been tapering off some in the last few months. That wasn't all because of the business. Some was simply because part of me wanted more...substance? That was as good a word as any. And dating apps might bring people together forever in some cases, but it didn't look like it was working out for me.

With a sigh, I hauled myself off the couch. Might as well get a start on packing. Then Sunday wouldn't be any kind of rush.

2

SUNSHINE

I steered the boat carefully into the slip that I'd been given at one of the more elite yacht clubs on Puerto Rico. I would have been happy meeting up at the public docks, but this client had ideas of his own. And he wasn't afraid to insist on them.

Which was fine. It was. He wasn't the first picky rich guy I'd taken around, although usually we just rented the boats. Still, it wasn't unheard of to be asked about a pilot, and in this case, given the boat the guy asked for, I was the natural choice. I knew it. My boss knew it. And even though two of the college guys who'd been hired on for the summer worked pretty hard to get the gig, the boss had come through.

The client wanted the best.

Everyone knew Sunny was the best.

I grinned at my thoughts. Was it egotistical if it was true?

"Ahoy the NeverLand."

I stepped out from the helm and crossed to the port side of the boat that ran along the dock. My eyebrows twitched and I forced them not to lift—but only with effort. The guy hailing me was younger than I'd expected. Maybe some kind of trust fund baby? I hoped not. But I also didn't see how it could be anything else. This boat wasn't cheap to charter. Especially not for a solo and including a captain.

"Ahoy the shore." I smiled and tipped my sunglasses down. He was a good-looking kid. I'd give him that. "I'm not big on the nautical language, though. You Wesley Allen?"

"That's me." The man frowned slightly. "Is Sonny around? I could use a little help with my gear."

This time I couldn't stop my eyebrows from doing their thing. "Let me finish a few things so she doesn't drift off without us and I'll be happy to help."

"Sure." The confused look on his face was hard to read.

I gave a mental shrug and headed back to finish my checklist. The yacht club guys had tied everything off, so that was one less thing that I had to take care of. Nice to have the extra help—especially since the client was paying for it.

It didn't take more than five minutes before I was stepping off the boat onto the dock. The man hadn't moved. He had an impressive ability to be still.

"Ready when you are. Where's your gear?" I started toward land.

It took a moment, but then he fell into step beside me. "I can get it, if Sonny's not around yet. Will he still be ready to go this afternoon? I'm anxious to keep to our itinerary."

I stopped and turned, then propped fisted hands on my hips. "I think we have a misunderstanding and we should go ahead and clear that up now. I'm Sunny—short for Sunshine—and I will be piloting your boat. I'm absolutely ready to sail as soon as we get your gear on board. So there shouldn't be any issues with staying on the approved itinerary unless you have a problem."

"I—" His mouth snapped shut and his cheeks blazed a hot, bright red. "Wow. Stuck my foot in that one. Sunny with a u. Not an o."

I snickered, unable to stop myself. He looked so miserable. And adorable. Like a little lost puppy. "Not the first time there's been a mix-up. We good, Wesley?"

"Wes." His gaze darted to the boat then back to me. He swallowed before nodding slowly. "I guess we are."

I lifted one eyebrow. It was a trick I'd perfected in my twenties after reading about a character who could do it. At the time, I'd considered it the epitome of suave. Now, it was more habit than anything. In this case, though, it served the purpose well enough, because Wes's face reddened even more. "What's up?"

"I just—" Wes broke off and cleared his throat. "You're really okay with being alone on a boat with some random guy for three weeks?"

"Should I not be?"

"What? No. I'm not—you're—" He blew out a breath. After a moment, he nodded. "Right. It's fine. If you're not worried about it, then I won't be."

I frowned, unable to keep the incredulity from my voice. "Are you worried about impropriety?"

"A little?" Wes hunched his shoulders.

I laughed. I couldn't help it. He was adorable. I knew from the paperwork the agency had given me that he was in his early thirties. If he was worried about how it would look sailing with me? "I'm going to take that as a compliment. I'm too old for you. And I'm a consummate professional. There's plenty of room on board, so we should be fine. Besides, we'll be visiting new islands constantly. Once we dock, we'll be schmoozing with dive shops and heading underwater. I think your virtue is safe."

"Okay." Wes's face blazed a fiery red. "You're right. I can get my gear."

I shook my head and started back toward shore. "I can help. I'm stronger than I look."

Wes didn't comment.

I was okay with that. It wasn't that I looked particularly weak. I just got the vibe that Wes had the idea that women should be doing things that were more demure and unassuming than hauling luggage and driving boats. Which, hey, if that was how he wanted to live his life, so be it. It was no skin off my nose. Except, of course, now that he was on my boat he'd have to get over it for the next three weeks.

Hopefully, he'd be able to manage that.

I paused and glanced around the parking lot. There was a small pile of suitcases and diving gear bags being watched over by a man I recognized.

"Hey, Marco." I lifted a hand then turned back to Wes and nodded. "That's yours?"

"Yeah." Wes strode past me and said a few words to Marco that I didn't catch.

"Sunny! Missed you, lady. Where you been hiding?" Marco glanced at Wes. "Did you know you got the best in the business?"

Wes managed a nod. "That's what they said when I booked."

"He thought I was a guy." I shrugged and hauled up the gear bags, hooking them over my shoulder before reaching for the handle of the larger hard-sided suitcase. At least it had wheels.

Marco laughed, loud and long. "You've gotta start telling them to use your full name, Sunny."

I shrugged. "Tried. They can't seem to get it straight. Shouldn't matter what kind of plumbing I have though. Someone asks for the best, they're going to get me."

"Modest, as always." Marco shook his head. "Course, you're right, so…"

"Exactly." I pointed at Marco and winked before turning to Wes. "You ready?"

"Yeah." Wes glanced around. He looked lost and still uncertain. After a moment, his gaze fixed on Marco. "Thanks for the ride."

"No problem. You really are in the best hands with Sunshine." Marco grinned and headed back to the dingy white minivan that served as his taxi. "Later, girl."

"Yeah. See ya." I tipped the suitcase so it was on its wheels and ready to roll. "If you're uncomfortable, I can call the agency and let them know to have a man meet us at the next port. I think Javier's free right now. He's not as good as me, but he's decent."

Wes paused, as if considering.

My eyebrows lifted. I'd made the offer, but hadn't really meant it. Javier was probably free, but with that the case, he was also probably a day into a week-long bender. They'd need to get to him fast and start working on sobering him up if he was going to have to take over for me. And I was going to have to figure out some other way to earn the fee that I'd been banking on from this trip.

Ugh.

I schooled my face and waited, but I prayed with everything I had that Wes didn't change his mind.

Finally, he shook his head. "No. This is fine. I need the best."

I smiled. "You got her. Come on, let's get underway."

I started back to the NeverLand and didn't bother to see if he was going to follow. When I reached the boat, I stepped aboard and lowered the gear bags to the deck before going back for the suitcase. Wes arrived as I finished getting the larger bag aboard.

"Need a hand?" I reached out for one of the bags.

Wes took my hand in his and stepped aboard with his load. I pressed my lips together and narrowed my gaze as I looked at him. He was a client. And a solid ten years younger than me. So anything I thought I might have felt when he took my hand was clearly the product of an overactive imagination on my part.

My husband had died five years ago, and I hadn't been interested in diving into the world of dating again. Not here, in the islands, where so many of the visitors were only looking for a vacation hookup, and the locals? Well, even though I'd lived in the islands for most of my adult life, I wasn't quite local enough.

I could probably find dates among the transplants. But it seemed like an awful lot of work for no good reason. I'd had the kind of love people dream of. It wasn't as if anyone got a second chance at perfect.

And I wasn't going to settle for anything less.

I tugged my hand free and tucked it in my pocket. It seemed nicer than wiping off his electric touch. I jerked my head toward the doors that opened into the galley and salon. "This way."

I grabbed the bags I'd brought aboard and stepped into the enclosed area of the main deck and paused. "This is the salon. Galley here in the back as well. Up is the flybridge and upper helm. Down for staterooms."

"This is nice."

I nodded and started down the stairs. It was nice. In a perfect world, I'd own the thing outright and could run whatever charters I wanted. But this wasn't a perfect world. Not since Luca died and took our dreams with him.

I slid open the door leading to the primary stateroom that filled the bow of the boat. I set the dive bags on the double bed and parked the suitcase at the foot of it. "This is your space. There's a bathroom with shower here."

I tapped the door that closed off the bathroom from the rest of the stateroom. "I'm in the stateroom on the left as you face aft. If you need extra storage, you can use the stateroom on the right. Questions?"

Wes looked around, then shook his head. "Nope. Thanks."

"Of course." I stepped out into the tiny space at the foot of the stairs. "I'm going to go up and get us underway. Get settled and relax. If you want a snack or beverage, the galley is stocked."

"Okay." Wes looked like he had more to say.

I waited a moment, but when he didn't continue, I turned and headed upstairs.

He was either going to get over whatever his issue with me being a woman was, or it was going to be the longest three weeks of my life.

3

WES

I watched as Sunshine—and I was going to just keep on using her full name as long as it took for me to get the image of a gray-haired surfer out of my head—left my stateroom and headed up the stairs.

I probably shouldn't have spent even two seconds admiring her legs, but they were long, tanned, and firm. What was a guy supposed to do?

Mom would probably have a smart comment to make. The General was six or seven years older than her. I was sure she'd probably start making comments about finally getting a daughter-in-law if I said anything about Sunshine to her.

No. When it came to Mom, I'd keep on calling her Sunny.

Speaking of Mom. I reached for the laminated card on one of the shelves and followed the instructions to connect my phone to the wi-fi, then snapped a photo of my stateroom. It wasn't large, but it was certainly luxurious. I tapped out a note letting her know that I'd made it safely to the boat and was now moving on with the itinerary of sailing the islands. I'd sent her the schedule so she could follow along in her mind. Plus, it was never a bad idea for people to know where I was.

The chartering company had the schedule as well. And they tracked their boats. Made sense, given the cost.

I sat on the foot of the bed and gave a little bounce while I looked around. There wasn't much to see. Two levels of shelves ran down the walls on both sides of the bed. Skinny oblong portholes provided light and a glimpse of the water. There were doors with ring-like catches on either side of the cabin. I reached for one and tugged it open, smiling as it revealed a closet. I checked the other side—same thing. Which meant the door with a more traditional handle was likely the bathroom.

I stood and opened that door, my eyebrows lifting slightly at the luxury packed into the small space. There were drawers under the sink for storage, as well as a good-sized shower and a toilet. Everything I could need. And not so cramped that it would be hard to use.

I shut the door to the bathroom and set about settling in. There were drawers built into one of the closets, so I unpacked my clothes into them. The other closet was more for hanging clothes, so I stashed the empty suitcase and the dive gear in there. It was cozy, but it would definitely work.

And I hadn't needed the extra stateroom.

Despite the lack of inflection when Sunshine had mentioned the space, I'd gotten the distinct impression that she'd think less of me if I ended up bleeding over into that space. I was probably imagining it, but I was glad not to need to find out.

I exited the stateroom, pulling the door closed behind me. Unable to resist, I peeked in the door Sunshine said led to hers. It was open a crack, so it wasn't really prying, right? I nudged it slightly, revealing a tidy space. One of the twin beds was wrinkled, as if it'd been slept in and remade. The other was so pristine I didn't imagine she'd even sat on it. There was a small, gold frame on the shelf beside the wrinkled bed. It held a photo of a man, head tipped back with laughter, his hair mussed by the wind.

I nodded and pulled the door closed. Of course she had someone. Why wouldn't she?

Why did I care?

I didn't, obviously. It was simply information to gather and file away.

From her reaction, she hadn't felt anything when I'd grabbed her hand for balance coming aboard. So it really didn't matter what I might—or might not—have imagined. Maybe it was just static electricity.

Unlikely, given the humidity in the air down here, but I didn't need to overanalyze.

I climbed the stairs back to the main deck.

"All settled in?" Sunshine glanced over at me from where she stood behind a console and steering wheel.

"Yeah. Thanks. It's great."

"I've always thought so. The galley's stocked, like I said. Feel free to get comfortable. We have about ten hours of sailing ahead of us before we get to our first stop." She kept her eyes shifting between the view ahead of her and the instruments on the console. "If you need something, let me know."

It sounded like a dismissal. Was it meant as one? It was just the two of us on the boat. Did she really expect that I wouldn't want to talk to her the whole time? I wasn't the world's most outgoing person, sure, but I wasn't one of those people happy to sit in silence for hours on end. Especially not when there was someone right there to talk to.

I ran my hand over the top of the table on my way to the galley. "Can I get you something? Soda? Water?"

"I'm good. Thanks."

I fought a sigh as I crossed the deck and opened the fridge. It was, as she'd said, stocked. It wasn't big enough to last the whole trip. Resupply would, obviously, be part of what she did while we were in dock. I'd assumed she would go diving with me. But maybe she just made introductions and then went off to do her thing?

It didn't matter.

I snagged a soda, closed the fridge door, and popped the top. I considered, briefly, sliding onto the banquette behind the table, which was bolted to the floor. But no. I didn't need to start off the trip antagonizing Sunshine.

I headed out onto the uncovered portion of the deck. The breeze from being underway was refreshing. The time in the Caymans and on Puerto Rico before getting to the boat had me second-guessing my decision to come in the summer. It was hot. And thick.

On the flip side, it would be hot and humid back home in Virginia, too. It wasn't as if I'd given up cooler temperatures to come down here. The top deck provided shade for half of the space out here. I considered the lounge chairs, but the ladder leading up was too tempting to not explore.

I carefully climbed up to the top level and couldn't stop my grin. The water surrounded us on all sides. I could see the island behind us, rapidly shrinking as we headed away from it. An American flag snapped in the wind off the back of the boat. There was another driving station up here, as well as built-in lounge seating.

For a moment, I was tempted to sit in one of the chairs facing the helm, but I quickly dismissed that thought. I wasn't going to do anything to disrupt Sunshine's ability to get us to the next port safely.

Instead, I settled in the corner of the seating that ran down one long side and across half of the shorter side. There was a triangular table bolted into the floor at this section of the seating, so I set my soda down, leaned back, and dug my phone from the pocket of my shorts. I took some pictures and texted them to Mom.

The messaging app chimed. I tapped to accept Mom's video-call request.

"Hi, honey. Oh look at that water."

I laughed and spun the camera a little so she could get a better view. "Not bad, right?"

"Not at all. I'm glad you have wi-fi."

I pointed the camera back at my face and nodded. "Satellite internet has come a long way."

"I guess it has." Mom squinted at me. "You haven't been sleeping well."

"I've been busy. I'm sleeping fine." Both were true to varying degrees. I didn't know what Mom was seeing, but I also didn't want her to worry. "The dive sites in the Caymans are all set. And if I can use Scott's house as a base, it's even better. But I did find a resort that would work with me to keep the cost down if necessary."

"I don't know why you're worried about keeping the cost down. It's not like scuba diving is an inexpensive hobby."

I blew out a breath. Mom was right. I understood it on some level. At the same time... "I guess I just want people to be able to dive somewhere other than the quarry, you know? If I can keep the cost down, then everyone can dive where there's more to see than trout and sunken cars."

Mom laughed. "You're a billionaire. Why not buy an island?"

"Oh, sure. I'll get right on that." As if islands were routinely for sale. Weren't all the habitable islands already countries? Or owned by people with family wealth?

"I'm serious. I was poking around on my phone and there are websites devoted to listings for the rich and famous. You could afford one. Then you could really keep the cost down."

I shook my head. Owning an island? That sounded like a lot

of work. I'd have to have an air strip. And it'd have to be private flights—although I guess we could charter from whatever international airport was within a reasonable distance. And—no. What was I thinking? "I'm not buying an island, Mom."

"Okay. It was just a thought. Have you dived today?"

I shook my head. "Today's been all about getting underway. There is diving in Puerto Rico. Obviously. But everyone has those trips."

"Hmm."

I frowned at Mom. "What's that mean?"

"Nothing. Honestly."

I didn't believe her. But I knew her well enough that I understood I wouldn't be getting anything more out of her on the subject. It was probably just a rehash of the discussion we'd been having since I started talking about leading dive trips. I don't think we'd ever see eye-to-eye on it. "All right. Well. I should go. The satellite internet works, but it's not free."

Mom laughed. "It's good to be a cost-conscious person. Thanks for letting me see your face. Don't forget to send me pictures."

"I won't. Love you."

"Love you more." Mom blew a kiss and the call ended.

I shook my head and set my phone aside. I reached for my soda and leaned back against the cushions, letting the breeze and the motion of the boat relax me.

"Wes?"

I hadn't intended to sleep, but apparently I had. I blinked open my eyes. "Hi. Sorry."

"It's fine. Thought I'd check that you have sunscreen on. I'd hate for you to start off the adventure with a burn." Sunshine smirked.

Sunburn probably wasn't something she had to worry about. Not if the golden bronze tan of her skin was any indication. If the sun did anything to her, it was relegated to bleaching streaks of blonde into her hair.

I, on the other hand, could and did burn. If I was careful, I could tan, but it wasn't my skin's default. "Yeah. I slathered it on before getting in the taxi. Appreciate the thought, but I'm not careless."

She nodded. "Good to know."

I winced at her clipped tone. "Sorry. I don't wake up well. I really do appreciate you looking out for me."

After a moment, Sunshine shrugged. "All part of the service. Are you enjoying things so far?"

Now she was all chatty? Shouldn't she be driving? There was probably some kind of autopilot now that we were on a plotted course and away from the traffic near port. If I didn't want her questioning me, I probably ought not to question her. Especially since I had no idea about driving a boat. "Yeah. I sent some photos to my mom. Then she wanted to chat, so we did a quick call. It's nice that there's internet."

"It can be, for sure. But sometimes the best part of being out on the ocean is taking the opportunity to disconnect." She smiled as she said it.

I decided she wasn't trying to make a jab. "Disconnecting is good. I've made some strides in that direction in the last year."

Sunshine tipped her head to the side.

Was it an invitation? Why not. I cleared my throat. "I used to work in software. Government contracting, actually, which is about as boring as it sounds. But ever since I learned to dive— actually, even before I learned but when I was itching to give it a try—I've thought running a dive shop, taking people on trips, all of that would be the best ever. Now I get to."

"That's a big change from software."

I chuckled. "You have no idea."

Her gaze shifted toward the front of the boat, and then back to me. "I picked up some red snapper this morning. And some conch salad. I've got the makings for a nice, fresh fruit salsa. Hungry?"

As if the words triggered something, my stomach rumbled.

She laughed.

My gaze shot to her face at the sound. It was...wow. I cleared my throat and pushed away the errant thought that she was beautiful with the sun glinting off her hair and that wide smile. "I could eat."

Sunshine jerked her head toward the ladder. "Come on down and help me prep some lunch, then."

I scooted out from behind the little table. Sunshine had already gone down the ladder in an effortless manner that left me a little awed. Of course, this was her living. It made sense that she was comfortable on the boat. But still.

I did what I could to avoid looking like an uncoordinated land lubber as I followed her.

She was already in the kitchenette. She pulled containers out of the fridge and set them on the table. "You want to grill the fish?"

I shook my head and raised my hands, palm out. "Oh, no. I'm not going to be responsible for that."

"You don't grill? I thought all men had a thing about manning the flames."

"Not this one." Did it diminish my masculinity? Cody loved to grill, and because of that, the rest of us rarely got a chance. Scott had a grill that I suspected he used more frequently now that he was married. Or maybe he let Whitney use the thing. It wasn't as if he grilled for the rest of us. But the other guys in our little gang? To my knowledge, none of the rest of us even owned something that could pass for a grill.

"Huh. I'll make a note." She set the fish aside and pushed some fruit toward me. "You can chop?"

"Sure. Is there a knife?" I glanced into the small kitchen space. I hadn't seen cooking tools anywhere, but everything was probably put away so it didn't slide around as the ship rocked.

"Of course." She pulled open a drawer and withdrew a chef's knife. She put it on the table and gestured to it. "You know what dicing is?"

"I do." I guessed, given that I didn't grill, she now wasn't sure if I could exist in the kitchen. "I can cook. I just don't grill."

Her lips twitched. "Sorry. I wasn't sure. Dice up the mango, papaya, pineapple, and avocado. You can put them in this."

I took the bowl she extended. "Got it. That's the fruit salsa?"

"The start of it. When you've done that, we'll add a spicy pepper or two and some lime juice."

"Spicy is good."

"Yeah? Then we'll add two. Seeds or not are up to you." She dug around in the fridge until she found two long, skinny green peppers. "Don't touch your face or eyes after you chop those."

"Got it." I'd made that mistake before. It was the kind of thing that only happened once though. My eyes watered from thinking about it. I moved around the table and sat. There was a cutting board that I hadn't seen her set out, but I pulled it, the fruit, and the knife closer and got to work. "Do you enjoy cooking like this?"

"It's better than going hungry." She unwrapped the fish. "I don't hate it. I like a real kitchen when I have the chance. Or a restaurant where none of the prep or cleanup is on me."

I laughed. "I like that last option myself. Or, if I can't justify the expense of eating out all the time, I get those meal prep deliveries. At least it means I don't have to think about what to cook all the time."

She looked up from seasoning the fish. "If this is out of line, let me know, but why would you worry about the cost?"

"What do you mean?"

She gestured to the boat, still holding a spice jar in her hand. "You can afford this. And me. For three weeks. Unless you've been saving up for a long, long time, that means worrying about money isn't something that should be high on your to-do list."

My face burned. Unfortunately, I hadn't started on the chiles yet, so I couldn't blame that. "All right. I guess that's fair. But I don't want to be one of those rich guys who doesn't think about it. That might not make sense."

She shot a long, considering look my way before nodding once. "Maybe."

I contemplated asking what that meant, but I wasn't sure I really wanted to know. There was more I could say on the subject. The guys—all of us—had a lot of conversations about using our billions in a way that honored God.

Maybe running a dive shop and taking people on cool trips didn't immediately sound like that was what I was doing, but I definitely considered it a calling. A ministry, of sorts, even.

I'd never felt closer to God than under the ocean, surrounded by His creation. I didn't think it was possible to dive and *not* be awed by all that God put into the earth. When I was diving, the words of Psalm 8 always played through my mind. *What is man, that thou art mindful of him?*

It was easy to lose sight of that in the day-to-day.

It was impossible to miss forty feet under water.

4

SUNSHINE

We arrived in the British Virgin Islands last night a little ahead of my anticipated schedule. It was nice to clear through with the authorities and get settled at the dock while it was still light out.

Wes had gone ashore for dinner. He'd invited me, but I was content to make a sandwich. I was only there to drive the boat and introduce him to some of the dive operators I knew. I'd just as soon keep our relationship as professional as possible. The lines would blur—they always did when it was a smaller group on the boat with me—but it was still important to make sure the line between employee and friend didn't get crossed. I'd watched too many acquaintances get stung when they forgot what the relationship was supposed to be. Boat operators in the islands were a tight-knit, gossip-fueled community. Once someone got a reputation, it was next to impossible to change.

As a single woman, I couldn't risk my livelihood. And I didn't want to spend the rest of my life fending off advances because someone had heard I offered different services along with driving the boat.

I blew out a breath and finished getting ready. Today was a

new day. Part of my job was to take Wes around. So that was what I'd do. If he wanted to dive, we'd do that. I was happy to go or stay ashore if there was a group he could join.

I smoothed the comforter on my berth and gave one final look around the small cabin. I prided myself on being neat. Even though this was my personal area, I never assumed that the guests wouldn't poke their heads in. Curiosity was a natural thing.

Content that it would pass as professional, should Wes decide to take a glance, I kissed my fingers and lightly touched my husband's photo, then crossed to the door and headed out. I paused in the small space near the stairs up to the main deck and listened. There weren't any audible snores coming from the main berth. But I also didn't hear any sounds of someone moving around. It was early yet, so that wasn't completely unexpected.

I climbed up to the main deck and took my first deep breath of the ocean air. There was nothing like it. I closed my eyes and drew in another deep lungful then let it slowly out. I made a quick check of everything at the helm—it was all as it should be —then crossed to the kitchen to start some coffee.

While Wes had been at dinner last night, I'd taken a quick trip to the market for fresh fruit and some *pan de Mallorca,* a sweet bread that made a fantastic breakfast. At least in my opinion. Hopefully Wes would agree. If not, there were some nice little cafés nearby that would have hot options.

"Morning."

I glanced over from staring at the coffee maker. "Morning. Coffee's underway."

"Thanks." He crossed the deck and stepped out onto the uncovered portion, then tipped his face up to the sky.

The early morning sun glinted off his hair, and something in my belly quivered. I looked away and swallowed. He was good looking. I wouldn't deny that. At least not in the privacy of my own thoughts. But he was also younger than my younger brother. And it felt...disloyal to my husband to even notice.

The coffee finished brewing and I took the carafe and filled two big mugs as I fought the urge to look back over at him. "Do you take anything in yours?"

"I can fix it."

I startled. I'd been so studiously ignoring him, I hadn't noticed that he had come back into the kitchen. "Okay. There's half-and-half in the fridge. And some vanilla creamer if you like that."

"Sugar?"

I watched his lightly tanned fingers curve around the handle of the mug, and had to swallow again as my imagination took off on its own. I cleared my throat and forced myself to look up and meet his eyes. "Couple of kinds in the top drawer."

"Great. Thanks."

"Sure." I sipped my coffee and slid out of the way. Distance from him felt more necessary than air right at that moment. I could get the fruit and bread out when he was finished doctoring his drink. "I have a light breakfast available here. Or I can suggest some places nearby for something hot, if you prefer."

"What do you have?" Wes pulled open the drawer and his eyes lit up. He grabbed two packets of the raw sugar I stocked, tore them open, and dumped them into his mug.

"Fruit and sweet bread." I paused. Said like that, it didn't sound like it was going to set anyone up for a day of diving. I tended to like a heavier midday meal, and I hadn't asked his preference.

"That'll work. Probably better for me than a donut." Wes raised his mug to take a drink.

I set my coffee down on the table and scooted around to the

fridge. Wes didn't move immediately. I had to give him a long look before he shot me an impish grin and moved to sit at the banquette.

I shook my head and got out the container of sliced fruit. The bread was wrapped and stashed in the cabinet above the sink. I got it, and then plates and forks, and carried it all over to the table.

I put a plate in front of Wes before taking my own. Suddenly, I was less interested in the fruit than the bread. Carbs were always my go-to for emotional eating. And I was absolutely not going to investigate exactly what it was about Wes that sparked that craving.

Oh, who was I kidding? No investigation necessary. The man —boy. I really should keep in mind that he was a solid ten years younger than me. Maybe even more than that. I'd have to look up his birthdate on the rental paperwork. Maybe keeping that number in the front of my mind would help me avoid concentrating on how long it had been since I'd seen such a perfect specimen of man.

Was it disloyal to my deceased husband to notice?

I frowned and reached for the bread.

"You okay?" Wes was watching me with open curiosity.

"Yeah. Sure. Of course." I had a feeling the smile I offered was sickly, but there was nothing I could do about it. I pulled one of the buns off the loaf and reached further into the bag for the packet of powdered sugar that accompanied the treat. I opened it and tapped out a generous hill of the white confection onto my plate, then tore off a hunk of the bright yellow bread, dipped it into the sugar and popped it in my mouth.

Wes watched me. I couldn't decide what he was thinking. Maybe that was a good thing. I dipped another hunk of delicious carbs into the sugar. "What?"

"I don't think I've ever seen someone eat bread like that."

I nudged the powdered sugar toward him. "Try it before you knock it."

With a shrug, Wes dumped some of the powder onto his plate and reached into the bread bag to grab a roll. He studied it for a moment before tearing off a piece, dipping it in the sugar, and eating. "Mmm."

"See?" I set my bread down on my plate and reached for the fruit. I pried up the top and scooped some onto my plate. It wasn't what I wanted, but I also didn't need to stuff myself with bread just because of Wes.

"I apologize for doubting you."

I snickered. "Stick with me, kid. You might learn something."

His eyes flashed. "I'm not a kid."

"Someone's testy." I held up my hands. "My bad."

He shook his head and continued eating.

A joke about needing a nap was on the tip of my tongue, but I bit it back. There was no need to irritate him on purpose. It was good to know that he was sensitive about the age thing though. That was definitely going to help me keep my thoughts in line.

Or so I told myself.

I forced myself to eat the fruit I'd scooped onto my plate, then stood and carried my dirty things over to the kitchenette. There was a small dishwasher, so I loaded them in and left it open for Wes. "When you're done, can you clean your spot? Then we can head ashore and I'll get you started on some intros. If you want to dive at any of the spots they like, I can take you out, or, if they're running a group and you can tag along, I'm good with that, too. Just let me know your preference."

"You don't want to dive?" Wes glanced up as he reached into the bag for a second piece of bread.

"I'm happy to, like I said. I just don't know what you prefer."

He frowned. "I'd like you to come along."

I waited to see if he'd expand on that. When he didn't, I nodded. "Then I will. Let me know when you're ready."

I didn't wait for him to say more, but headed down the stairs to my room. I opened the door, stepped in, and closed it with a quiet click. Then I leaned against it and closed my eyes. This was day two and I was already having problems. How was I supposed to make it three weeks?

I'd been praying he'd want space when we stopped on the various islands. I did enough moving between them that I could always occupy myself for the time he needed to scout and dive. I would've been fine just hanging out on the boat, for that matter. I had a freshly stocked Kindle and plenty of sunscreen.

But no.

Apparently, when he'd hired a driver and a guide, he'd planned for that to mean constant companion as well. And since that was absolutely something the charter company would support, it was going to be up to me to figure out how to deal.

So that was what I'd do.

I blew out a breath and moved to my bunk. I reached for my tablet and quickly turned it on. Of course it needed a minute to connect to the wi-fi, because why wouldn't it? When I finally had internet, I opened the browser and went to the company portal to dig up the info on Wes's age.

I'd been right on. Ten years.

I couldn't pretend he was my kid. But my youngest brother was only four years older than him, so maybe I could treat him like a surrogate kid brother. That should keep any belly quivers under control.

Shouldn't it?

I logged out and set the tablet back on the shelf. Kid brother. I pictured my youngest brother, his wife, and their triplets. I could do this.

There was a knock on my door. "Sunny?"

"Yeah?" I crossed the small space and opened the door. Then stepped back. Why was he so close? Kid brother, girl. "Ready?"

"I am if you are. Should I bring my dive gear?"

I shook my head. "We'll come back for it. Let's go schmooze the operators first."

Wes stepped out of the way and gestured to the stairs. "After you."

I wanted to argue, but bit my tongue. My brother would never have let me go first. How was I going to be able to keep our relationship on the right foot if Wes refused to play by the rules?

5

WES

I had to give it to Sunshine, she knew the island as advertised. If she had this kind of knowledge—and this number of contacts—at every stop on our planned trip? I had my whole job basically done for me already.

I glanced longingly at the little sidewalk café as she led me toward our next destination. My steps slowed.

She stopped and looked over her shoulder. "Coming?"

"Lunch?" I pointed to the empty tables under umbrellas. I was sweating. And hot. And hungry. And I could probably drink six gallons of water.

Sunshine laughed and the sun glinted off her hair in a way that made me catch my breath.

"Soon. Promise. I have a better spot in mind if you can hold on." She tipped her head to the side. "You look peaky. Need water?"

"Only like I need air." It pained me to admit how out of shape I felt next to her. I could justify that she lived down here and so was used to summer in the islands, but the truth was, I was soft. I liked air conditioning. A lot. Plus inside there weren't bugs.

"Hang tight." She ducked into the café. I watched as she strode to the upright cooler, her long, tan legs eating up the ground. She picked up two big bottles of water and carried them to the cash register, where she greeted the guy—clearly a local—with a flirtatious grin.

I couldn't catch what they said, but he made her laugh and my teeth ground together. At least in there, the sun couldn't work its magic on her hair.

Oh man.

I forced myself to look away and study the traffic. Summer wasn't the height of the tourist season down here. It was so hot. So humid. And okay, sure, islands and equator and blah blah. I definitely wouldn't be bringing groups down here in the summer, no matter how much better the prices were.

"Your water, sir." Sunny gave a wink as she pressed an icy cold bottle into my hand.

"You're a lifesaver." I unscrewed the top and took several long swallows. "Heaven."

"Gonna make it?" She opened her own bottle and took a delicate sip.

"Now I will." Probably. My physical thirst, at least, was handled. I couldn't do anything about the way everything in me responded to the sight of her in shorts and a tank top with skinny little straps. She hadn't dressed like that to torture me. Everyone I saw was dressed basically the same. Too bad I'd never had a sister. Then, maybe I'd have some way to reframe my thoughts, because thinking about her age—or the photo of the guy in her cabin—wasn't doing it.

What was ten years, really?

And maybe she had a brother?

"Great. Let's get going." She took off again, though I noticed her steps had slowed enough that I could keep pace beside her.

I took another swallow of water as we turned the corner. "Where are we headed again?"

"Best ceviche on the island. Also where the local dive guides hang out. Figured we could handle both, in case you decided to go the local route rather than the resort option." She tipped her head to the side. "Should I have run it past you first?"

I shook my head. "It's a good idea. I was sticking with resorts because we'd need a place to stay anyway. And food. That kind of thing."

"Sure. But there are other ways to get all of that and fill up on some local flavor in the meantime. Plus the prices, hospitality, food, and schedule will all be better. And you're pumping more into the local economy rather than into some corporate chain's pockets."

My eyebrows lifted. Talk about passionate. I probably shouldn't mention—or even notice—how her eyes had brightened as she spoke, showing off the hint of gold around her pupils. "Sold. Does that hold for every island or just here?"

Sunshine laughed as she started to walk again. "I have contacts of both sorts just about everywhere."

"Been down here a while?"

Her nod was curt.

Oops. Did she think I was making a dig at her age? I wasn't. Or, at least, I wasn't trying to. "Should I apologize?"

"Hmm?" She glanced over, her forehead furrowed. "You're fine. If I was new, I wouldn't have the contacts you need."

"Sure. That's true." Apparently, I was bad at small talk. Who knew? It had never been an issue before. Then again, I couldn't remember a time when I'd been so motivated to find a point of connection with another person. Especially one who was throwing out clear "no trespassing" signals.

Which I should respect. Of course I should.

No matter how awkward it was going to make the next three

weeks on that small boat, with long stretches of sailing between the islands and only the two of us. Maybe...no. I dismissed the idea as soon as I had it. There was no way she was finding herself attracted to me and working to fight it. I could tell when a woman was interested in me. Sunshine definitely was *not* giving off that vibe.

"Here we are." Sunshine ducked under a drooping awning and skirted between rickety glass-topped tables with metal chairs tucked up against them.

"Sunny! Girl, where you been?" A tall, solidly built woman with ebony skin stood and moved away from the crowded table, arms open.

Sunny embraced the woman. "Working. You know how it is."

The woman laughed, deep and throaty. "Always said you work too much."

"What else am I going to do?"

The woman's face fell and she nodded once. "True enough. Been a while, though."

Sunshine simply shrugged.

I hovered behind Sunshine, unsure of what I should do. I didn't understand whatever had passed between the two women. And as much as I might like to, I got the distinct feeling that questions wouldn't be welcome.

Sunshine cleared her throat and her voice came out overly bright. "Speaking of work, this is Wesley Allen."

That was my cue. I scooted to the side and held out my hand.

"Wes, this is Corinna. If you ever need diving advice, she's the one to look for."

Corinna laughed again. Her grip of my hand was strong and cool. "Good to meet you. Come sit with the gang."

Sunny had already dragged two more chairs over toward the table, and the group of people huddled there were shifting to absorb them into their ranks.

I hovered on the edge of the group as they took turns greeting Sunny, exchanging high fives and fist bumps, along with jokes—some more creatively risqué than others. She laughed, rolled her eyes, and outright dismissed some of them as she took her seat.

After a moment, she glanced back and met my gaze. Her eyebrows lifted and she patted the back of the empty chair. "Come on and sit, Wes. Everyone, this is Wes. He runs a dive shop outside DC and is looking for all the best places to bring groups to dive."

"Nice. You'll get the hookup with Sunny there. But if you're staying near here, be sure to get in touch." The kid—and I felt dumb thinking of him like that, but he looked like he was sixteen with his shoulder-length blond hair and scruffy, laid-back posture—flicked a business card across the table.

I picked it up, scanned the words, and nodded. I tucked it into my pocket. "Thanks."

"You diving today, Sun?" The kid spoke again. "I've got a private, just two, in an hour or so. You could come along."

"Where are you taking them, Joe?"

Joe. I filed his name away. The card had only had the company name on it and no one seemed excited to introduce themselves. Then again, I was the only newcomer here, so maybe it hadn't occurred to them that it would be polite.

"Ceviche for two." Corinna reappeared and set an enormous bowl of fragrant fish and citrus in front of Sunshine and me. She added a basket of tortilla chips to the table and went around to resume her seat. "Eat and talk. See if you can keep Joe from taking his newbie divers to the wreck."

"Oh, Joe. You aren't." Sunshine frowned. She dipped a spoon into the ceviche and loaded a chip, then expertly popped it into her mouth without dripping the juice all over herself.

I wasn't convinced I'd be able to eat as gracefully, but I could give it a try. I scooped a smaller portion than Sunny had and managed to catch the juice with my thumb as it dripped down my chin. The contrast of sweet and sour and salty flavors exploded in a happy contrast on my tongue.

"What? They want to see a wreck. They've got the advanced cert, so they should be fine." Joe shrugged. "Not like there are sharks or anything."

Corinna snorted.

Others in the group chuckled.

"Joe." The quiet censure in Sunny's voice stilled the group.

He sighed and looked away. "Fine. We'll go to the glass-bottom instead. Happy?"

She nodded. "I am. And your divers will be, too. You know it's a better excursion."

"I guess." Joe's face was close to a pout. "At least it still quali-fies as a wreck. But it's not a treasure dive."

"Did you promise them a treasure dive?" Corinna's words held a warning that I didn't understand.

I glanced between Joe, Corinna, and Sunny, obviously missing something.

Joe held up his hands. "No. Of course not. That would be illegal."

Ah.

"See you remember that, or I'll put the word out."

"Aw, Corinna. Come on—"

"No." Corinna cut Joe off. "We have a code. You agreed to it when we added you to the group. If you want to break the code, we can revoke your membership."

Heads around the table nodded.

"No. I keep the code." Joe's shoulders hunched.

I was completely lost. A glance at Sunshine netted me a tiny headshake. So I didn't ask. If I posed my questions later, would she answer? I honestly couldn't say.

Either way, Joe's response had eased the tension around the table and the casual conversation resumed.

"So you going to come along, Sunny? Make sure I'm swimming the straight and narrow?" Joe's teasing words held an edge.

She glanced at me, eyebrows raised. "What do you think? It'd be a good spot to take your groups. It's not a hard dive, but it's got a lot of beautiful fish and a small sunken boat that often draws harder to find species. It's down about forty, maybe forty-five feet."

I nodded. That was a good depth. It didn't feel like you might as well be snorkeling, but it wasn't so deep that you needed extra training. "Sure. Is it beach or boat?"

"Boat. We can meet Joe out there." Sunny looked over at him. "An hour you said?"

He nodded. "About. Island time."

"Do your clients know that?" Sunny tipped her head to the side.

Joe frowned. "You've changed since your husband died, Sunshine."

Corinna punched his arm. "Watch yourself."

"What? Am I wrong?" Joe rubbed his arm where he'd been hit. "When Luca—"

"Enough." Corinna interrupted, but not soon enough to keep Sunny's face from losing all its color. "Idiot."

"Sorry." Joe muttered as he pushed his chair back with a loud screeching noise. "Guess I'll go get things ready. Will I see you there?"

I looked at Sunny. She was staring down at her hands. I tentatively touched her arm. "We can dive somewhere else. Or not at all."

That jolted her out of her thoughts. "No. It's a good site, but don't wait for us. I'm not sure what else our schedule holds."

Joe's face flushed but he nodded once and left.

"I'm sorry, Sunny." Corinna reached across the table and squeezed Sunshine's hand. "Why don't you dive the Pot instead? Avoid him altogether."

Sunshine loaded another chip with ceviche. "We'll see. I need to show Wes the good spots for his tours. The Pot's advanced."

I wanted to say something comforting. Encouraging. But I didn't know what that would be. Maybe silence was the better choice. I scooped some more of the ceviche for myself and told myself to that it didn't matter who Luca was.

Except I knew.

She had his photo in her stateroom.

And that meant she was not just too old and out of my league. She was still in love with her deceased husband.

That should have been enough to convince me I needed to move on.

But it didn't.

6

SUNNY

I reached behind myself for the ribbon attached to the zipper of my wetsuit and tugged it up. If I was diving for pleasure, I'd probably skip the wetsuit and simply wear my swimsuit. But with Wes...it felt like neoprene was the smarter choice.

I picked up my buoyancy control device, BCD for those of us who dive, flippers, mask, and snorkel and headed up to the main deck. I made my way over to the swim step and set my gear down. I'd strapped air tanks there and took the opportunity to work them free and lay them gently on the deck.

I glanced over toward the stairs. Wes was taking his sweet time getting ready. Not that we were on a clock. We could always head back to the dock here for the night if he wanted. Or I didn't mind sailing through the night and making some progress to our next port of call. Wes didn't seem overly concerned with keeping to a strict schedule, and that worked well with the idea of island time.

I gave Joe a hard time about it, but he wasn't wrong. Everything moved a little slower—a little more easily—here. It was one of the reasons Luca had wanted us to stay and make it our home.

I hadn't objected.

Of course, I would have followed him to the ends of the earth without needing any justification for it. Because Luca himself had been my home. And now that he was gone? I was...rudderless.

I pushed the thoughts away. They were ridiculous. I was a forty-three-year-old woman. I shouldn't feel adrift like a kid just out of college with no idea how the world worked. Even if it wasn't unreasonable, now wasn't the time. I had a job to do here. I should get to it.

I stood one of the tanks up and slid the straps of my BCD over it, then tightened them down. I hooked up the hose to my regulator, spun the handle to set the air flowing, and took a couple of deep breaths through the regulator to ensure it was working like it should. Satisfied, I laid the tank, now with my vest attached, back down.

I was ready.

Where was Wes?

For that matter, where were Joe and his set of clients? Hopefully, he hadn't decided to take them to the deeper wreck dive after all. There was talk of treasure hunting there. If old forks or the odd key could be considered treasure. Maybe it gave people a thrill to show something like that off and talk about having rescued it from the ravages of the ocean and time.

Never mind that it was illegal.

Never mind that, rightfully, it belonged to someone else.

Finders, keepers was the battle cry of the treasure hunter, and most of the time they got away with it.

Those who tried to fight for the right thing often ended up in the hospital. Or worse.

"Sorry. I didn't mean to take so long." Wes crossed the deck quickly and dropped his fins and mask. "My mom called."

I smiled. "Is she worried about you?"

"She's my mom, so yeah. But mostly she wanted to tell me some news about my dad before he got to me."

My eyebrows lifted.

"It's complicated. They're not together. Dad...I love him. But he's got some problems. And he'll always try to spin it so it's someone else's fault, you know?"

I laughed. "I know several people like that. Yeah. Good times."

"Anyway, she wanted to warn me that he was probably going to be coming around—metaphorically—looking for some cash."

"Ah." Thankfully, neither my parents nor Luca's had ever done that, but Corinna had some stories from her own family. It was part of why she'd finally moved to the islands and essentially cut contact with them. "Will you give it to him?"

Wes shrugged. "I'll let him make his pitch, but probably not."

I tipped Wes's tank up so it was standing and kept a hand on it. He obviously had plenty of money. I hadn't done any sort of research on him—the company frowned on it, for one, and I really didn't care—but our charters weren't cheap. Usually, I had groups that maxed out the occupancy and only took a couple of days. Something that made a split a reasonable enough undertaking if people saved up. But he'd scheduled three weeks, with me at the helm, all alone. So, yeah, he had money.

Wes squatted and fixed his BCD onto his tank. He turned on the air, inflated the vest a little, and took a quick breath through his regulator. After a nod, he leaned it back down beside mine. "Did you want to wait?"

"Not unless you want to. I can show you around, same as Joe. And..." I paused, frowning as I turned to scan the ocean around us. "I suspect he got mad and decided to stick with his original plan."

"The treasure dive?"

"Yeah."

Wes scowled. "Can you report him?"

"Not really. Technically it's in international water. So it gets murky. Who do I report it to? I can assume I know what port he'll return to and maybe have someone waiting to try and check things out, but it's easy enough for him to lie. At this point, if he's willing to take people to rummage around a shipwreck, I don't think lying about it is going to be out of the question." I was frustrated, too. Luca and I used to do the good Samaritan thing. He was convinced that if enough people made a fuss, eventually word would get out and everyone would somehow realize they needed to stop. His optimism was something I'd loved about him.

Even if it was stupid.

"I'm sorry." Wes laid his hand briefly on my shoulder.

I was glad for the wetsuit, because even with it, I had to fight the urge to shiver. Which meant it was all in my head. And that was ridiculous. It was probably also responsible for my gruff voice when I spoke. "Yeah, well. Can't win 'em all. You ready to dive?"

There was a tiny beat of space where he looked at me with concern before grinning widely and rubbing his hands together. "One hundred percent."

We both bent and reached for his tank-BCD combo and our hands brushed. Dang it.

"I've got it." Wes slid one of his arms into the BCD and hitched the tank up while getting his other arm through in a motion smooth enough that I realized he was definitely a well-practiced diver. At least as far as getting gear on.

While he closed his vest and checked his dive computer and

gauges, I got my own BCD on and did the same. Convinced I was as ready as I was going to get, I stepped down onto the swim step and sat on the deck. I pulled my goggles over my head and let them dangle around my neck as I put on my flippers.

Wes sat beside me and did the same.

"Ready?"

He nodded.

I put my goggles in place, popped my snorkel in my mouth, and stood. I circled my index finger and thumb and took a big step out into the water. I dropped down under the surface for a second before the air in my vest popped me back up. I spit out the snorkel and treaded water while I waited for Wes to join me.

When he was in the water, he flashed the OK sign back at me with his thumb and index finger.

I reached around behind my neck for the group of hoses connected to my air tank, found my regulator, and put it in. A quick exhale to clear out water and I was ready. I pointed my thumb down, waited for Wes to return the motion, then began to slowly let air out of my BCD, letting gravity and the weights integrated into the system pull me under the waves.

This was my favorite thing.

It was as if all the cares and worries of the world stayed above the water. So now, as I descended, I just had to focus on my rate of descent, clearing my ears, and enjoying the beauty of God's creation.

Curious angelfish darted over to investigate our bubbles and the bright splashes of color on the sides of our wetsuits. As we neared the reef, I slowed my descent even more until I hung suspended at the best depth to move around without having to make a ton of adjustments.

Wes overshot slightly and it took him a minute or so to tweak his buoyancy to match my depth. He flashed OK. I returned the gesture and signaled in the direction that we needed to go if he wanted to see the sunken glass-bottomed boat.

I wasn't sure that he cared about that, but it was a nice path through the area that would show off the animals who made their home here. And he could get a feel for the current, such as it was, at this dive site.

Wes swam beside me. I appreciated that he didn't lag behind or zoom ahead. And he had a good mastery of the kicking technique needed to propel himself through the water without stirring up a lot of the ocean floor. As dive partners went, he was the closest to ideal that I'd had since Luca.

My mind shied away from that comparison.

Instead, I focused on breathing easily and admiring the fish. A flash of color made me pause and reach for Wes's arm.

He turned and I pointed to the green snout of a moray eel that had darted back into its hiding place as we swam by.

Wes's eyes brightened.

It was almost more interesting to watch him watch the fish than it was to see them myself. He had a visible appreciation for everything around us, despite the scuba equipment he wore. I couldn't explain it—years of diving with groups had honed the instinct. It was something in the eyes. And the speed that he swam. Wes was enjoying being down here, not simply zipping from one thing to the next to say he'd done it.

I waited until he made eye contact again and we swam on, the warm water surrounding me like a gentle hug.

As the main section of this reef began to wane, the bump of the sunken boat appeared in front of us. It wasn't a large boat—when it sailed it had probably held ten or so tourists huddled around a giant pane of glass in the bottom to see the fish that they were too nervous to snorkel with.

At least, that was why I assumed someone would take a tour like that. Maybe it was unfair. But the water here was so clear, people didn't have to scuba to enjoy the underwater sights. And snorkeling was something even the youngest could master.

Even still, these types of excursions were popular. And this one, at least, had provided some new foundation for the reef to grow into and an interesting spot for divers.

I paused beside the boat and gestured for Wes to go ahead and look around. There was nowhere I couldn't see him today. The water was clear and undisturbed by other divers.

I eased up a few feet so I could look down on the wreck. Wes was peering into the hull. I wrinkled my nose. I hadn't explicitly said not to go in it, but I hoped he wouldn't. For one, there was nothing all that exciting inside. And two? I hadn't checked that he actually had a wreck diving cert. For something like this, it might not be technically necessary, but I didn't like the idea of someone deciding to just go into closed-off spaces without knowing what they were about.

Thankfully, he backed away and continued circling the boat. After a moment, he glanced from side to side, then rolled over and faced up. I felt the sizzle of connection with him as our eyes met. He gestured for me to come closer, then pointed.

I swam down to where he was and followed his finger. A young sea turtle stared back at me. I wished for my underwater camera. I tilted my head. Was his fin caught in something?

I moved until I had a better view. The turtle's back fin was caught in some netting. That netting hadn't been here the last time I was at this site. Granted, that had been several months, but local dive operators were good about cleaning up trash they found when they were down with a group. And it was illegal to try to capture or kill while diving in these waters.

Maybe the netting had fallen overboard by accident. Or washed out here and snagged on the rocks, then trapped the turtle. I shouldn't speculate. What I did need to do, though, was free the turtle's fin.

If he'd let me.

I drew my dive knife and considered the problem. It would be best to get all the net off the fin, if possible, rather than simply freeing him but leaving the net attached.

I reached slowly toward the fin with my free hand and slid a finger under the net. Good. It was wrapped but not too tight.

Wes watched, concern evident in his eyes.

Using my fingers to protect the turtle's fin, I sawed carefully at the netting. It gradually pulled apart.

Wes reached around and tugged away the rest.

Free, the turtle glanced back, then swam away.

I sheathed my knife and breathed a contented sigh.

Wes was pulling the net free from the rocks and boat and balling it up. I appreciated that he realized we couldn't leave it to snag some other creature. I took the opportunity to give my gauges and dive computer a quick check. We'd been down for twenty minutes. We should probably make our way back to the boat and surface. My air was fine, but men tended to go through theirs faster.

I tapped Wes on the shoulder and held up my air gauge. He nodded and looked around. I let my gauge go and reached for the netting so his hands were free. He pulled the gear forward and checked his air, then flipped it so I could see. He did, in fact, need to start heading back.

I pointed back the way we came.

He mimed a deep sigh but shot me an OK with his fingers.

I fought a chuckle, adjusted the air in my BCD, and started back toward the NeverLand.

We took it slow. Neither of us was in a place where we'd be better off surfacing and swimming back on top of the water using our snorkels. So we might as well enjoy another trip along the reef.

When my compass indicated that we were where we should

be, I stopped and gave Wes a thumbs-up, indicating that we should head toward the surface. He returned the gesture and we both began inflating our BCDs and kicking slowly toward the surface. I appreciated that he didn't seem to be in a race to the top, either. It was easy for us to stay below our rising exhaled bubbles, a rule of thumb to help divers avoid serious injury, or even depth, from decompression sickness.

Wes and I broke the surface of the water in tandem. He pulled his regulator free and grinned at me. "That was awesome. I swear that turtle said thank you."

I laughed, the action spitting out my mouthpiece. "I'm glad you spotted him. Or her."

"Me, too."

Something about the way he looked at me sent a shiver—the good kind—down my spine. I reached for my snorkel. "Don't know about you, but I could go for a snack."

I didn't wait for a response. I just put my face in the water and swam the rest of the distance to the swim step of the boat.

Getting back on the boat after diving was the worst part. I always preferred when there was someone waiting on board to lend a hand, so I hauled myself out of the water and quickly unfastened my BCD and laid it down, then worked my feet free of their flippers. I was hopping to my feet when Wes's hands curled around the edge of the step.

"Take off your BCD and I'll grab it." I reached down.

Wes tugged his goggles down around his neck. "You don't have to—"

"All part of the service." I prayed my smile was cool and professional. I had to do something to put some distance back between us.

A line formed between his eyebrows, but he worked the catch on the BCD and shrugged one arm out of it. I reached down and grabbed the now empty armhole and pulled as Wes worked his other arm free. When he was clear, I heaved it onto the deck, fighting the urge to groan as I did so. Why were things so much heavier on land than in the water?

Of course I knew the science, but I couldn't stop the thought anyway.

Water rushed over my feet as Wes hauled himself up on the swim step. He stood up with a grace that I envied. "Thanks for the assist. Getting back in the boat is always the worst."

I laughed. "I thought the same thing."

His fingers grazed the back of my hand as he reached for the hoses on his tank and let a little more air into the BCD. Then he cranked the valve closed and lifted the equipment like it was weightless.

I shifted out of his way, collected my fins, and joined him on the deck of the ship. We worked in easy silence to stow the tanks and rinse the gear with some of the fresh water on board. It was the kind of simple companionship Luca and I had enjoyed.

I cast a glance at Wes and pressed my lips together. Why did he remind me so much of my deceased husband? Was it God's way of letting me know that I needed to dig myself back out of this hermit-like bubble I'd created for myself in the last five years?

Or was I just blinded by perimenopausal hormones and the first good-looking guy who'd been around in a while?

7

WES

The past three days had been a fantastic combination of diving excursions and sailing between islands. I loved seeing the differences between the various places. And the similarities, for that matter. Much of the diving was the same —there was a reason so many people dove in the Caribbean— but it was all worthwhile.

I'd made several connections with resorts. I'd also found locals on each island who appeared to offer better trips all around than those resorts. For cheaper. And that was all thanks to Sunshine. She knew where to steer me and who to introduce. Honestly, the charter company was undercharging for what I was getting out of this.

I took one last quick look in the mirror before heading out of my stateroom and climbing the stairs to the main deck.

Sunshine was already in the little kitchen area. She glanced up and smiled at me and my heart nearly stopped.

Which was ridiculous. For so many reasons. Reasons I absolutely should not have to keep reminding myself of. Even so, I ticked them off mentally: she was a good ten years older than me, there was someone in her life if that photo in her room was to be believed, and finally? We were only going to be around each other for another two and a half weeks. Her life and livelihood was in the Caribbean. Mine was not.

With that stern warning to myself fixed at the front of my mind, I nodded politely, and studiously ignored the sundress that fluttered around her knees and the skinny straps that highlighted the golden tan of her shoulders.

"Morning. There's coffee and fruit. We still have plenty of time to make it to church." Sunshine scooted out of the kitchen and took a seat at the banquette with a mug in her hand. "I hope you'll like the service. I always try to hit this one up when I'm in the area."

"I'm sure I will." I'd taken a look at the church's website last night. Their theology was sound—at least if I went by what they said on their "We believe" page—and really that was all I cared about.

I filled a mug with coffee and added cream and sugar. I'd quickly learned that Sunshine made her coffee considerably stronger than I ever bothered with at home. Which meant I added more to it. She never said anything, but that didn't stop me from wondering what she thought. Did it diminish my masculinity that I didn't drink it black?

Not that she drank hers black.

Of course, no one would accuse her of being masculine.

And I needed to stop. Immediately. Because it could not—would not—matter what she thought of my coffee drinking habit. Or anything about me. I was her client. Period.

I felt my face morph into a scowl as I scooped fresh-cut fruit into a bowl and carried it and my coffee to the table.

Sunshine looked over and her eyebrows shot up. "You all right?"

I wasn't going to try to explain the way everything about her got under my skin in all the right ways. I shook my head. "Tired, I guess."

"We can skip the afternoon dive, if you want. Honestly, it's not anywhere close to one of the best in the islands. I only added it to the list because you wanted to stay an extra night and go to church." Sunshine watched me over the rim of her mug.

I speared a chunk of fruit and bit in, letting the tangy and sweet blend together in my mouth. There was a part of me that didn't want to skip the dive. Swimming beside her under the water with just the sound of my breathing and the ocean was a painful intimacy I wasn't in a hurry to miss. But that might be the exact reason I should agree. "What would we do if we didn't dive?"

She shrugged. "Start out for the next island? Unless you need more time on shore."

"I think we saw everything yesterday."

Sunshine laughed. "We did. But I also know if you're not used to this much time on the water it can be nice to have dry land under your feet for more than a few hours. I'm fine with that, if that's what you need."

"I'm doing okay." I chewed another couple of bites. "You're sure this dive site isn't worthwhile?"

"It's not *not* worthwhile. It's as good as the places we went yesterday. But it also tends to have more tour operators, so it can get crowded. Depending on how good the divers are, that scares the fish."

That was definitely not the sort of location I wanted. "Let's skip it."

"Okay." She glanced at her watch. "Probably have another five, maybe ten minutes before we should leave. This church isn't on island time."

Island time was a recurring theme I was finding as we traveled from place to place. Most of the diving and hospitality contacts did their best to adhere to the actual clock, but not always. It only took one weak link in the timing to leave Sunny and me twiddling our thumbs for half an hour.

I could admit in the quiet of my own thoughts that I didn't mind the extra time with her.

But I still didn't want to walk into a church service late when I was a visitor. I hurried to finish my coffee and fruit. Sunshine took my dishes and carried them to the sink over my protests and then we were busy making our way down the pier to where a scooter waited.

"What's this?"

Sunshine took one of the helmets off the handlebars and offered it to me with a grin. "More authentic transportation than a car."

I tipped my head to the side. "Where's mine?"

She just laughed and fastened the chin strap of her helmet, then straddled the scooter. "Hop on, Wes. Or don't you trust me?"

There was a teasing edge to her tone that I was almost convinced I'd made up simply because I wanted to hear it. But there was no mistaking the glint of something—humor? Challenge? Both?—in her eyes as she waited, watching me.

I settled the helmet on my head and, squashing my misgivings—and boy, oh boy, did I have misgivings—threw a leg over the back of the scooter.

Sunshine started the tiny machine and I imagined it wincing under our combined weight. Neither of us were large, but we were still grown adults. I rested my hands against her waist. Surely that would be enough? I was trying, desperately, to minimize the contact points between us.

I was failing. Miserably.

"You're going to want to hold on better than that." Without

waiting for me to respond, Sunshine tugged one of my arms and drew it around her waist.

The force pulled me forward and before I could think about it, my other arm followed suit. And now? Now there was nowhere that we weren't touching. My legs pressed against hers. My chest pressed against her back. I was surrounded by her scent and the fireworks that exploded in my skin everywhere we touched.

With a raucous laugh, Sunshine kicked off and we zoomed through the parking area of the marina and out onto the streets.

Sunday morning was, apparently, a quiet time here. There were some people out walking or opening shops and restaurants, but the majority of the short drive was devoid of people. It was as if we were driving through an enchanted town.

I smiled slightly as my imagination took off. I was going to blame Sunny's proximity for any and all flights of fancy. There was no other reasonable explanation.

Ten, maybe fifteen, minutes later, Sunny slowed, signaled, and turned into the parking lot in front of a low-slung building with a large veranda across the front and a boat ramp leading up to the main doors. It wasn't the type of church building I was used to, at all, but the sign on top made it clear that we were exactly where we planned to be.

She parked the scooter in a line of similar vehicles— although ours was by far the least dinged-up of them—then reached up and took off her helmet. She twisted and met my gaze. "You can let go now."

Right. I quickly moved my arms and slid off the scooter. Only when I was safely not touching her did I unfasten my helmet.

She held out a hand for it. "What'd you think?"

"Of the scooter?"

She nodded.

"It's better than walking?" I really didn't know what she was after, but that seemed like a reasonable answer.

Sunshine laughed, throwing her head backward as she did. "I guess I'll take it. Ready to go in?"

That was another question I didn't know how to answer. It was time. That was clear from how the few people in the parking lot were making beelines toward the front door. But was I ready? Probably not. New churches were always hard for me. It was why I didn't usually bother when I was on vacation. Everyone would look. Probably stare. Ugh.

I shrugged. "They're about to start."

She tipped her head to the side, nodded once, and gestured to the ramp.

I waited while she hooked the helmets on the scooter before she started toward the door. I fell into step beside her, hurrying my last step to get to the door in time to tug it open for her.

"Thanks." Her comment was quiet as she brushed past me.

I swallowed. Why did such a tiny touch cause the same reaction as sitting pressed up against her on the scooter did? It made no sense.

The question churned in my brain as I shook hands with the greeters and followed Sunshine to a row of chairs. Thankfully, she chose something near the back. I'd never loved sitting front and center. Back home, we usually congregated in the front half of the worship center on the right side. It was closer than I preferred, but at this point, the location was pretty well ingrained in the group. I didn't see it changing.

Of course, it wasn't as though I'd said anything to anyone about it. Knowing them? They'd all be willing to move. But I hated making it about me. That wasn't the point.

Didn't mean I couldn't be excited that someone else seemed to share my preference. Especially as one-off visitors.

I wasn't sure what I expected, but the service really was a lot like the one at home would have been. I knew the songs. The pastor, in cargo shorts, a T-shirt, and an unbuttoned short sleeve plaid shirt over it, had a good message from the book of Job. I got the impression they'd been parked here for a while. They were just getting to the end though, where God answers Job's questions.

Or sort of answers them.

The problem of evil wasn't something that I tended to dwell on, though I knew it was a problem for a lot of people. Maybe it was because I'd been headed so far down the wrong path when God found me—thanks to the guys in the group—and dragged me kicking and screaming into His mercy and grace. I'd been a reluctant convert, but much more because it seemed too easy. Too good to be true.

When the final song ended, Sunshine practically jumped to her feet. "Ready to go?"

I blinked and stood. "Uh. Sure. Are we in a rush or can we get lunch before we head back out onto the water?"

"Lunch is fine. Actually, I know a great place closer to the marina, if that works for you?"

I nodded.

"Great. Let's go." She spun and her long strides carried her through the doors into the lobby before I'd made it to the end of the row.

What was that?

"Thanks again for joining us today." The pastor was practically blocking my exit, his hand extended. "Will you be in town long?"

I shook his hand. "No. We're actually heading out after lunch."

The pastor's eyebrows knit together. "Have you seen the weather forecast?"

I shook my head. I'd been leaving all of that to Sunshine.

She was the expert. And I'd hired her to handle getting me from place to place. "I'm sure the captain has it all under control."

"Okay." The worry didn't ease from the man's face, and a tiny knot of concern rooted in my stomach. "Be safe. Enjoy your time in the islands."

"Thanks." I forced a smile that felt tight on my face and headed out into the sun. I blinked at the glare and glanced toward where we'd parked the scooter.

Sunny lifted a hand. She was already straddling the thing, helmet fastened under her chin.

I hurried down the ramp. "Are you okay?"

"Yeah. Of course. Hungry." The helmet made it hard to read the expression on her face.

I took the straps of my helmet and fastened it in place, then climbed on behind her. This time, I didn't hesitate, just hooked my arms around her and braced myself against the onslaught of feelings that accompanied the action.

Sunshine backed the scooter out of its spot and then took us quickly—maybe too quickly—out of the parking lot and back onto the streets into town. The wind rushing past would have made conversation impossible even if I'd had an idea of how to bring up whatever was going on with her. Because she could say she was fine as much as she wanted, I didn't believe her. Maybe five days wasn't long to have known her, but if this was a normal part of her personality, I should have seen hints of it before. Shouldn't I?

It wasn't long before she pulled the scooter to the curb in front of a small café with colorful umbrellas open over tables on the sidewalk. I eased off the back and unbuckled my helmet, mouth already watering at the spicy scents emanating from inside.

"Smells amazing." I drew in a deeper breath.

"Food lives up to the hype." She flashed a grin my way as she reached for my helmet and hooked both of them over the handlebars of the scooter. "Come on. We're early enough to get a table in the shade."

The café was already doing a brisk business, but there were still tables with shade from more than the umbrella overhead. Since the heat and humidity had already made their presence known as well, I was definitely on board with whatever help we could find to keep the temperatures cool. Or cool-ish. True cool wasn't an option.

I followed Sunny to a table. She plopped down in one of the chairs looking out at the street. I hesitated, then sat beside her, taking in the same view. I wasn't sure I could handle sitting across from her and focusing on her face—and her tanned shoulders—right now. Not until my system settled from our proximity on the scooter.

"What's good?" I plucked one of the plastic-coated menus from beside the umbrella's pole and scanned the offerings.

"Everything."

I glanced over.

She held up her hands. "Promise. I've never had something that I didn't love here. Most of the time, I just ask the server to bring me what's best today."

"All right." I put the menu back. There was enough food on the boat that if I didn't end up enjoying lunch, I wouldn't starve. It wouldn't the be the first time I made a meal out of snacks. More than likely, it wouldn't be the last time either.

I'd barely finished the thought when a teenage girl appeared at our table with a grin. "Sunny!"

"Hi, Martina." Sunny rolled the "r" and the girl's name took on a whole new flair. "What's good today?"

"You always ask that. I told Mama you were here. She's working on something special for you." Martina's gaze shifted to me. "Should I make it two?"

I nodded, even though I didn't think she was actually addressing me. "Why not?"

Martina beamed then turned back to Sunny. "I like this one. We have a new *fresca*?"

"All right. Let's give it a shot." Sunny looked at me. "There's only been one I didn't like, you game?"

I shrugged. "Let's do it."

"I'll be right back." Martina hurried away.

"What was the one you didn't like?" There were a handful of restaurants back home that played around with house-made *frescas*. At least I knew what I was getting into with that.

"They mixed pineapple and passion fruit. It wasn't my thing. Others seemed to like it though, so I can't even say it was bad. Just not a drink I found refreshing and pleasant."

I nodded. "I'm not sure I could pick out passion fruit on a dare."

"It grows down here. Like a weed, in some places. You can't beat fresh like that, but for me, if there's passion fruit, I don't want any other flavors mixed in. It's strong enough on its own."

I didn't have to answer because Martina returned with two tall glasses filled with ice and a vaguely green liquid. Straws poked out of the drink, paper still covering their tops.

"Be sure to tell me what you think." Martina placed a glass in front of each of us.

Sunny tugged off the straw wrapper and took a long sip. She tipped her head to the side and closed her eyes. After a long moment, she swallowed. "Heavy on the lime. Is it papaya?"

"Just a touch. There's one more in there." Martina watched Sunny with dancing eyes.

Obviously, it was going to be tricky. Or, at least, the girl hoped to stump Sunshine. Curious, I took the wrapper off the top of my straw and sipped. The icy blast of tart and sweet in perfect balance was delicious. And refreshing, as advertised. I got the lime that Sunny mentioned, but beyond that I had no idea. And I was just fine with that. I didn't need to know what was in something to enjoy it.

"Star fruit." Sunshine set down her glass and met Martina's gaze. "Tell me I'm wrong."

"I can't. But Mama will be impressed. Maybe annoyed. She thought for sure she would get you with that one. Your food's almost ready."

When Martina had moved away, I looked at Sunny. "Star fruit?"

"It's green, star-shaped—"

"I know what it is." I interrupted before she could get further in the description. "We have them in the supermarket at home. I've even bought them. They're interesting."

Sunshine laughed. "That's code for you don't like it."

I took another sip of the *fresca*. "I like them in this."

"I'll see if we can take the recipe home. It'll give you a reason to buy them and think of the islands."

"All right. The guys would probably get a kick out of it at our next poker night."

"Tell me about them?"

I gave her a curious look.

"What? You don't talk about your life at home. I'm curious."

Well, that was a two-way street. It wasn't as though Sunny talked about her life at home. I didn't even know which island she considered home. The charter company I'd booked through was based in Puerto Rico, but I hadn't gotten the feeling that she considered it home. Then again, maybe I hadn't known her well enough then to tell.

I smirked inside. Not that I knew her all that well now. It had only been five days. Five days of being together nonstop, certainly, but it still didn't mean we should expect to know all there was to know about one another.

I took another sip of my drink. "We've been friends since college. Things have been shifting a little lately. We're all in our thirties and starting to settle down, I guess."

"Natural. But not you."

I raised my eyebrows. "Why not me?"

"No ring, first off." Sunny pointed to my bare hands. "And also, men who are in serious relationships don't tend to book three-week solo vacations."

"It's not a vacation. I really am working. But your point is still valid." I was able to get away to do this because I didn't have anything keeping me in Virginia. If I was honest with myself, that fact was also one that had pushed me to take the trip in the first place.

I was about to start describing everyone, beginning with Scott, when Martina returned with two huge plates covered in a jumble of seafood preparations and a pile of what looked like a fruit slaw.

"Enjoy." Martina set the plates down with no explanation and hurried away when another table hailed her.

"Smells good." I leaned over the plate and breathed in. "Can I pray?"

I don't know what prompted me to extend my hand, palm up. But the look Sunny gave me before she slid her hand into mine did crazy things to my heartbeat that I was probably better off not analyzing.

8

SUNNY

I missed a lot of what he said in the prayer because I was dumb and put my hand in his. Driving the scooter this morning had been exquisite torture. I'd known it would be when I opted for the scooter over a cab. But I was tired of trying to keep my thoughts professional. I was only human. And it had been a long time since I'd had a man's strong arms wrapped around me like that. It hadn't hurt that Wes's chest was firm and muscular. I'd noticed that when we dove. Or, more accurately, when he peeled his wetsuit half-off after diving. I dragged my mind away from *that* train of thought before I did something that was going to embarrass both of us. Or drop back into the bad mood that had been the result of sitting next to him in church, unable to concentrate on the sermon because I was wrapped up in him.

Wes squeezed my hand and I yanked it away with a muttered, "Amen."

My cheeks were hot, and probably a blazing red that no amount of tan would hide. Great. Just great.

Wes picked up his fork and poked at one of the fried lumps on his plate. "Any idea what this is?"

I eyed my own meal and found a similarly sized chunk. I speared it and popped it in my mouth. "Mmm. Conch. You'll love it."

With a nod, Wes ate the bite he'd been poking. "It's good."

"Do you have to know what everything is before you eat it?" I couldn't live that way. There were too many things that tasted amazing but were utterly ruined if someone explained what it was and how it was made. Take pretty much any sort of land-based meat. How did anyone spend time thinking about the process of slaughtering and prepping a chicken and then dig into a dish made out of it? Maybe if I'd grown up having to do it I'd be fine. As it was, I was content to eat what I was given and not think too hard about the rest of it.

"I guess not. Sometimes a little mystery is good."

I pointed my empty fork at him. "Exactly. Now, tell me about your friends."

A smile flashed across Wes's face. He shoveled a bite of fruit slaw into his mouth and chewed.

I took it for the thought-collecting measure that it probably was and attended to my own food. Hopefully, he wasn't going to try to turn this on its head when he was done. I'd been introducing him to the bulk of the people I still considered friends. It didn't bother me that they were mostly business acquaintances. Luca had been the one who made friends easily. I was content to come along for the ride. Left to my own devices, I could make casual relationships and maintain them. And I could handle business relationships. But the deeper friendships? Those continued to remain outside my ability to nurture.

Wes swallowed. "Scott is probably the linchpin of the group. He's the one who...collected us, I guess you could say. He's the reason I have the money to do the scuba thing—the reason all of us in the group are able to pursue our dreams, honestly."

I nodded. He had been careful to avoid mentioning money,

but here again I realized that he definitely fell into the "more than I'll ever manage in a lifetime" category. Which was fine, of course. Money didn't fix the world. I'd seen that firsthand when Luca died. He had plenty of insurance—it was simply a good business decision when you worked a job like ours—and so while I'd been given quite a bit of money when he died, I would rather still have him.

Wes continued to eat steadily as he talked. "Anyway, Scott was made the guardian of his cousin's child when she died. Then he ended up marrying the nanny."

I laughed. "You're kidding?"

"Nope. Whitney's great though."

I shook my head. "I didn't think that happened in real life."

He grinned at me while he reached for his drink. "You and me both. Still, they're pretty happy together. As are Austin and Kayla. They were friends and teachers at the same high school. Then Austin finally got up the nerve to ask her out. Now they're running a tutoring center together."

"Can married couples not teach in the same school together?" If they both still loved teaching—which sure seemed to be the case if they were doing tutoring now—why had they left the school?

"Probably. There were some problems that meant they needed to leave. Rather than looking for a new school, they opened their own thing." He shrugged like it was no big deal.

I frowned slightly. What kind of problems? More to the point, why was I so invested in Wes's friends?

Even as I thought the question, I knew the answer. I was invested because I was invested in Wes.

Not. Good.

"Next up is Cody, I guess." Wes chuckled. "I'm kind of going in the order they all fell in love."

"That's not the usual order you'd go in?"

He shook his head. "Nah. I'd say I'm closer with Cody and Noah than the others. Not by a lot, mind you, but maybe by enough that I would've mentioned them first if I was having the conversation two years ago."

I glanced down at my half-finished plate of food and gave it a tiny nudge away from me. A flicker caught my eye and I reached for my phone. "Hang on a sec."

"Sure." From the look he gave me, he was curious, but he also didn't press.

I appreciated that. I stood and carried my phone outside of the bounds of the café eating area then tapped to call back the main charter number.

"Oh, thank goodness."

"Hi, Zee. What's urgent?"

The receptionist, and my favorite person at the chartering company, cleared her throat. "Are you watching the weather?"

"No. I'm having lunch."

"Girl. You need to check it out. There are two storms forming south and east of us. They're saying it looks like both will end up being named."

"You know that doesn't mean anything. There are a lot of variables—"

"And most of them right now are sending that storm in your direction. The boss wanted to be sure you knew and were keeping an eye on it. He's not saying you have to hunker down—yet—but you know the drill."

I nodded. I did. And I took safety seriously. "I'll pull up the maps and see what's what. Thanks for the heads-up."

"You think he's overreacting."

I sighed. "Zee, I think I have his newest boat and the wealthiest client we've had in a while, so he wants everything to be perfect. He was in a sweat from the moment the reservation was made and I don't think he'll fully breathe out until the job is finished."

Zee cackled in my ear. "You're probably right. Keep an eye on it anyway, okay? I'm more concerned about you than anything else."

"Appreciate it." And I did. Zee was the closest thing I had to a mother figure down here. My own mother hadn't approved of Luca. Hadn't approved of us living in the islands. Hadn't approved of me not running home when Luca died. Basically, Mom just didn't approve. And Dad valued his sanity more than any urge to disagree with her. Fair enough. He had to keep living with her. I didn't.

"Expect me to check in a few times once we know what's going on."

I snickered. "Roger that. Later, Zee."

I ended the call and headed back to the table.

"Everything all right?" Wes had finished his food in the short time I'd been away. The man could sure pack it in with a singular focus.

"Yeah. Technically, it's hurricane season, and there are already some storms forming. I'd like to get back to the boat and give them a look. We might be better off rerouting." There were options. Good ones. We might not hit all the islands that he'd initially listed when he made his reservation, but I could still make sure he left with lots of contacts and dive trip possibilities. From what I gathered, that mattered more to Wes than a strict adherence to his itinerary.

"Okay."

I tipped my head to the side. "Just like that?"

"Yeah. You're the expert when it comes to this. I trust you and will follow your lead." Wes tossed a balled-up napkin onto his empty plate, then glanced over at mine. "You want to get a box for that?"

I looked at the food. I probably should. Just because I couldn't stomach the idea of eating it right now—the worry from Zee reaching out so persistently was starting to build—didn't mean I wouldn't regret it later. "Yeah. I'll go get one and take care of the check."

"I can—"

I waved Wes back into his seat. "You already did. I'm just a conduit."

He laughed. "As long as it's not coming out of your personal pocket."

I wasn't going to analyze how that made me feel. Because it was confusing. Instead, I made my way through the tables and into the little café. I went up to the counter and snagged a box off the stack that sat beside the register.

"You're leaving already?" Martina's mother turned from where she manned a cooktop and wiped her hands on her apron. Her brows knit. "We have some good desserts."

"Sorry. I need to go check on the storms."

"Ah." The older woman nodded and punched keys on the register.

Islanders understood. Just as they also understood there was little, if anything, to be done about it. If the storms were going to hit, they were going to hit. Evacuation wasn't always possible. Even in the situations when it was, most would rather ride it out than flee. Storms were as much a part of life here as the sunshine and ocean. And all were unpredictable.

I handed over cash, including a good tip for Martina. "Thanks. It was delicious."

"It's good to see you. Come back sooner than you did this time. Okay?"

"I'll see what I can do." I leaned across the counter to kiss the air beside her cheek. "Stay safe."

"You as well." Martina's mother turned back to her cooking.

My phone chirped an alert at me as I passed through the door and back into the outdoor seating area. I dug it from my pocket. Nothing that Zee hadn't already warned me about, just the app catching up with alerts. I still needed to get back to the boat and spend some time looking at path predictions.

"Ready?" I set the to-go box on the table, picked up my plate and slid the food on it into the box, then flipped the lid closed.

Wes scooted his chair back and stood. He picked up his drink and took a last long pull on the straw, draining it. "Now I am."

We went back to the scooter and I tucked the container of food under the bungee cord strapped across the tiny shelf at the back of the ride. Wes might end up partially sitting on it, but that was fine. It'd taste just as good squished as not.

Neither of us spoke as we put on our helmets and drove to the marina.

Concern about the storms wasn't enough to keep my body from noticing every square inch where Wes touched me. It was all I could do to focus on the road instead of arching against him like a cat.

Thankfully, it wasn't a long trip.

I parked the scooter and texted the owner that it was back in the agreed-on spot, then hurried down the dock to the boat. I didn't even check to see that Wes was following. I needed to check the weather.

And a little space from him would also be a good idea. Anything to get my traitorous body under control.

Wes seemed to understand. Maybe he needed the same? No. That was ridiculous. I knew what I looked like. And okay, sure, I wasn't breaking mirrors or sending small children running when I walked into a room, but I wasn't being scouted to model for...anyone. Not even AARP, which was certainly the more likely demographic for me than any other magazine out there.

I snorted quietly as I hurried to my cabin and my laptop.

I bit my bottom lip. There were definitely two storms and they were watching a third area that looked troubling. It was early in the season to have so much activity. Did that mean the whole summer and fall would be one storm after another? So many of them fizzled out before they got to the islands. Or they took a turn and just rampaged in the ocean. I was fine with either.

I drummed my fingers on my leg before grabbing my phone and dialing Zee.

"Two calls in one day, I'm flattered."

I rolled my eyes even though she couldn't see it. "You called me, so the first one doesn't count."

Zee's laugh was deep and rich. "Whatcha need, hon?"

"Advice."

"Well, now, you know I love telling people what to do. You came to the right spot. But before I suggest action you're never going to take, why don't you get a little more specific?"

I sighed. Zee was at the forefront of people pushing me to date. She was more pragmatic about it though, not supposing I'd find a second happily ever after. She just thought I needed male companionship to release some of the stress she swore I carried around with me.

Reminding her that I was serious about my relationship with Jesus—which meant sex wasn't on the table—didn't do more than elicit a quiet hmmm.

"The weather? Remember how you got me all worked up about the storms?"

Zee scoffed. "I didn't get anyone worked up. But if you're feeling that way, I'm just going to point out—"

"Stop." I couldn't stop the exasperated chuckle. "The weather. Would you divert? We'd been planning to sail down the east side of everything to keep it simple. I should go ahead and reroute, right? Put some islands between us and the storms?"

"Hmm." Keys clacked on Zee's side of the call. "I probably would, yeah. And I'd go ahead and plan to skip Barbados and Tobago all together."

I nodded. We weren't scheduled to be that far south until closer to the end of our trip, but the new route would make getting over to them more of an issue. "All right. I probably will end up skipping one or two of the islands up here, too, since their major marinas are on the east side."

"That seems wise. You didn't need me."

I heard the unasked question in Zee's tone. Why had I called her? "I needed to double-check that I was thinking clearly."

"Oh?" Zee drew out the word.

"Fine. Yes. He's attractive."

"And loaded."

"Zee."

"What? You think I don't search up the single men who want a solo trek with my girl?"

I pressed my lips together. I'd specifically not done a web search on Wes. It wasn't my business. "You didn't need a web search to know that. You can just look at our invoice."

"Mmhmm. What if I told you we could have tripled our fee and it wouldn't have made him sneeze?"

I blinked.

"Your silence is talking for you."

"Stop it. It's not my business."

"Okay. Fine. You don't want to know. I respect that." Zee waited a beat. "I'm just going to say it starts with the second letter of the alphabet."

"Zee!" My mind reeled. Surely she didn't mean billion. But of course she did. And there was no way I would have been able to get her to keep that piece of information to herself. Now that I had it, what was I supposed to do with it?

Forget.

Put it away.

Because it didn't matter.

"I'm just saying," Zee said, "even if he was ugly it might be worth it."

"Zee. What's gotten into you?"

Zee laughed. "I just think it'd be a treat to see my girl on the arm of a *billionaire*. Think about it."

I probably wasn't going to be able to avoid thinking about it now. But I also wasn't going to tell Zee that. "You know I'm not interested. I had Luca. And that's enough for one lifetime."

I glanced over at his photo and my heart panged. We should have had so much more time together.

"Honey, you know I loved Luca, same as you. But it's been a lot of years. You're young yet. You deserve to live."

"I am living." My voice was firm.

Zee knew me well enough to stop pushing. "Okay. Make sure you update your plan in the system so we have your new route."

"I will. Thanks, Zee."

"Mmmhmm. Be safe."

I ended the call and set my phone beside me. Then I hunkered down and got to work plotting a new course that would, hopefully, keep us out of any storms.

I watched Sunny disappear below and tucked my hands in my pockets. She obviously needed time to figure out what we should do, but I wasn't sure how to make myself useful. If that was even possible.

Maybe all I could do was stay out of her way.

I climbed to the top level and looked out over the island, then turned to watch the ocean. It was hot, but on the water there was a breeze that made it bearable. Birds flew overhead, calling out to one another as they did whatever it was birds did with their lives.

What would that be like?

Even now that I had my dive shop, I woke up every morning with a list of things that I needed to accomplish during the day. I was glad that they were now things I enjoyed doing—even the less delightful tasks, since they went into running the shop.

My phone rang. I glanced at the readout and wrinkle my nose. Ignoring it wouldn't do any good, but I just didn't feel like dealing with my dad right now. Guilt and a tiny bit of hope that this time it might be different made me answer.

"Hey, Dad."

"Wes, my boy!" Dad was in full salesman mode.

I cringed. "How was church this morning?"

"Good, good. I like this new place that Glenna is taking us to. The pastor's great. He gets it. Today he was reminding us that we were children of the King, so it was our destiny to have everything we asked for. Good stuff."

Oh boy. I wasn't going to touch that. I should be glad he was going to some kind of church. Right? Although maybe staying home was better than getting his head filled with whatever that was. I cleared my throat. "And Glenna? How's she?"

I meant "who's she," but Dad could read the subtext.

"Ah. Right. I was going to email you about that. She's great. I met her at a coffee shop a couple of weeks ago and we just clicked. It was fate."

I couldn't count how many women my dad had considered fate. I also wasn't going to try. "It's nice that she's encouraging you to go to church. Maybe the two of you could try out some of the places on the list I sent you a few months ago."

"Come on now, Wes. Don't be a drag." Dad's tone of voice made me frown. Why did it always seem to feel like I was the adult in our relationship?

Oh, right. Because mostly I was. "Just a suggestion."

"Yeah, well, I thought you'd be happy that I was even bothering with your Jesus stuff."

I closed my eyes and bit down hard on my tongue. I didn't know if a prosperity gospel church was better than no church at all. Did they even preach salvation there? Because that was where Dad needed to start.

"Anyway, it all kind of ties together with the reason behind my call."

"You weren't just calling to check in? Or to talk about the Christmas cruise idea I floated?"

Dad scoffed. "Hard pass on the cruise. I don't want to be

trapped on a boat with that woman and the weirdo she married. But if you're bailing for the holidays, maybe I'll plan to take Glenna somewhere nice. Just the two of us."

"Okay." It was the safest response I could dream up. I didn't have any delusion that Dad and Glenna would still be an item at the holidays. That was six months away. Dad's relationships just didn't last that long. "Thanks for understanding."

"You're a grown-up, Wes. You get to do what you want. But if you did want to make it up to me, I have an idea."

Oh boy. Left the door wide open for that, didn't I? "Oh?"

"And it's really why I called. I've got a line on a startup company that's going to do big, major things. They just need some cash influx, you know? And since you've got all that money sitting around, I figured you could hook them—and me—up. What do you say?" Dad was back to his friendly salesman persona.

I wanted to say no. I wanted to shout it loudly in hopes that he would, finally, understand that I wasn't his personal ATM. But I also didn't want to burn a bridge with him and ruin any possibility that at some point I might be able to get him to see how much he needed Jesus.

I cleared my throat. "Do they have a prospectus or something that they're using for their other venture capital applications?"

"Come on, Wes, it's not that formal. Not yet. Just some friends with good ideas who need cash to get started."

"I see." And I did. "Maybe I could meet with them—and you—when I'm back in town. You know I don't do business without a good understanding of what I'm investing in."

"Investing...oh, no, I wasn't thinking like that. It was more like you gift me the money and I invest it. You wouldn't be associated with it at all."

"You don't want me to benefit from it down the line? If it's a great idea, I definitely want to be part of it. I just need—"

"Not happening." Dad's voice was firm. "Not with these people."

"I don't understand, Dad."

He sighed. "Yes, you do. You're just so high and mighty you always have to make me explain. Get me to grovel."

"I don't want you to beg. That's not what I'm after at all."

"Right. That's why you can't just give me money when I ask." Sarcasm dripped off Dad's words. "I need cash, son. Two mil, three would be better."

I shook my head and sank down onto one of the cushions. "No. I can't."

"Won't."

"Fine. Won't. How did you already blow through the five million I gave you last year?"

"Not your business what people do with a gift they're given. Didn't I teach you anything?"

I pinched the bridge of my nose. Dad always felt obligated to all the details of my life—spending included. Guess he didn't feel it went both ways. "I guess it doesn't matter. I'm not giving you money."

"Wes."

"Dad."

I waited, listening to his barely controlled ragged breathing on the other end of the call. I closed my eyes. The beautiful blue of the ocean wasn't enough to distract me from the headache brewing behind my eyes.

"Fine. I guess you made your choice."

I wanted to ask what choice he thought I'd made, but I was also pretty sure I didn't actually want to know. "I'm sorry to have to say no."

"You don't have to. You're choosing to."

"You're right. I love you."

"Pfft. Sell it to someone who's buying."

The call ended. I imagined on the other end of things, Dad was raving about missing the old days when he could slam down a phone and get a satisfactory jangle of the bell in the handset. That was a rant I'd heard plenty as a child. Dad was a champion at hanging up on people.

I'd only been on the receiving end since cell phones were invented, but Mom had stories. One where he'd smashed a handset down so hard it had shattered.

Dad and anger were good friends.

I drew in a deep breath and let it out as slowly as I could. I got the anger thing from him. It had consumed me in high school and some of college. Until I'd met Noah and Cody and been dragged into their circle.

And then dragged to Jesus's feet.

I could only be grateful that He'd pursued me when I'd wanted nothing more than to run the other way. Was He chasing Dad? Or Mom and the General? It didn't seem like it most days. But then, I wasn't sure it had been visible to others when I'd been on the receiving end. So I'd just keep praying and trying to be an example. What else was there to do?

I couldn't have said how long I was sitting there, half-praying, half-feeling sorry for myself when the engine rumbled to life. I opened my eyes and watched as we moved away from the dock. And then I remembered the storms and the concern of the pastor and the reason we'd hurried away from the café before Sunshine had a chance to finish her food.

I pushed to my feet and crossed the top deck to the ladder leading down. I was getting better at descending quickly without falling the last few feet. That had to be a good thing, right?

Sunny sat at the helm.

"What's the verdict?" I slid past the dining table and came up beside her.

"I had to alter our plans. You'll still end up with the same number of dive contacts, so I'm really hoping you won't mind."

"I don't. Especially if the alternative is trying to ride out a hurricane in this thing. It's a great boat, but I'm not sure that's an experience I'm excited about." I didn't really want to ride out a hurricane in any kind of boat. Or ship. Or on land, if I was perfectly frank. In Old Town, we would, occasionally, get the outer arms of hurricanes as they whipped up the East Coast. That level of rain and wind was more than plenty for me.

"Smart man." She checked her displays and adjusted the controls. "We'll shift to the west side of the islands as we head south. It means cutting out some of the spots that jut out to the east."

I nodded as I tried to pull up a mental picture of the map of the region. There weren't many islands that we'd be missing with this change. At least not if I was recalling properly. "Seems reasonable."

She glanced over her shoulder at me and flashed a grin. "I'm glad you think so. I'm getting a little pressure to choose a marina and hunker down until we know what's going on."

I winced. I didn't really want to do that. On the other hand... "If that's the safest thing to do, we should do it. I can always reschedule and we can pick up where we left off."

Sunny shook her head. "I don't think it's warranted. Not yet. We might get to that point in the next seventy-two hours. I'm keeping an eye on things."

"Okay. I trust you." And I did. She was the expert here, so I definitely wasn't going to try to second guess her.

"Thanks. If you start to get seasick, let me know. We're probably going to be hitting some water that's got some teeth to it."

"Good times."

She laughed, clearly picking up on the dread in my tone. "Like I said, let me know. I'll do what I can to keep us calm."

I watched as she made some adjustments on the controls, then swiveled the chair to look directly at me. "Tell me about Cody."

"Cody?" I frowned. Why was she asking about him?

"You got interrupted at lunch."

Oh. Right. Dad's call, even with the advanced warning that he'd be reaching out, had thrown me. I'd forgotten I was giving Sunny a rundown on my friends back home. I glanced around and finally gave up. I moved over to the bench that ran along one side of the deck, and sat. "Cody's great. He and Noah both work for a big Christian nonprofit. Cody ended up falling into event planning and has now realized he loves it. And that first big gala he planned ended up bringing him and Austin's sister, Megan, together."

"Are Cody and Austin good friends?"

I nodded. "Definitely."

Sunny smirked.

"What's that for?"

"Nothing."

I considered pressing, but her expression didn't give me much hope that I'd be able to get a straight answer out of her. I gave a mental shrug. "After Cody is Noah. He's probably the one I'm closest to. He just got engaged to his..." I trailed off. How was I supposed to describe Jenna? She and Noah were friends. But they were exes. Kind of. And then there'd been that whole backup date thing.

"His...?"

I laughed. "I'll go with friend, I guess. But it's more complicated than that."

"Love always is."

I tipped my head to the side. "Spoken from experience?"

"Oh no. We're not talking about me. You're telling me all about your friends. Honestly, I'm surprised you have so many."

"Wow."

Sunny's hand flew to her mouth as she laughed. "That came out so different than I meant it."

"Uh-huh." I crossed my arms.

"Seriously." Her shoulders continued to shake but she did manage to keep her laughter quiet. "I'm sorry. Truly. I just meant it's got to be hard when you've got so much money."

I arched a brow. "Does it?"

She groaned. "Ugh. Dang it. Zee."

"Should that make sense to me?"

"Probably not. No." Sunny glanced down at the controls on the helm for a moment then back to me. "Zee basically runs our outfit. You booked with her. Probably."

I nodded.

"So when I was talking with her about the weather and our plans changing, she happened to mention that I needed to be extra cautious because it wasn't going to look good to shipwreck a billionaire." She shrugged. "I'd already figured you were rich. But also, wow."

I couldn't quite stop the bark of laughter. "That's about how I feel about it."

"Sorry. It really doesn't change anything. And I won't bring it up again."

"No. It's fine. It's not as if it's a secret." Or, not really. I'd love if it could be one, but that wasn't particularly possible for all we tried to stay out of the public eye. "As for my friends, I guess you could say we're all in it together."

She was quiet a minute. "To be clear, you're all billionaires?"

I nodded.

"Wow." She cleared her throat. "Okay."

I waited to see if she had more to add, but she stayed quiet.

"Last one in the gang is Tristan. He's a lawyer. Serious. Keeps to himself a bit more than the rest of us."

"Closet serial killer?"

I snickered. "No. Well. Probably not."

Sunny grinned at me. "Lawyer, huh? Bet that comes in handy."

"It has. Many, many times. Something's up with him right now though. We've all noticed, but he's being cagey."

"And you're letting him get away with it?"

Her words echoed the thoughts I'd had numerous times. "For now, yeah. But I suspect we'll gang up on him pretty soon if he doesn't spill. He talked to Noah a bit in the spring, but we're not convinced it was the real scoop."

"Sounds like a good group. Have you talked to them since you've been down here? I don't see you on the phone much."

"I haven't. Sent some texts. Photos." I shrugged. We were friends, not stuck in one another's pockets all the time. "I guess I should update them about the change in our plans so they don't worry. Now and then they can all have moments where they act like old ladies."

Sunshine laughed. "But not you, right?"

"Of course not." I puffed up my chest. "I'm the stoic, manly type. Haven't you noticed?"

Something flashed in her eyes—appreciation? Nah. Couldn't be that. It was gone before I could analyze it.

"Super manly." Sunshine made an exaggerated fanning motion and her voice dripped with sarcasm. "So hot."

I clutched a hand over my heart. "Ouch. You wound me, woman."

A beep from the controls cut off any reply she would have made. I watched as she concentrated on the displays. When it became clear that she needed to focus there, for whatever reason, I slipped back out to the ladder and climbed up to the top deck.

After taking a seat and spending a moment enjoying the breeze and the view, I dug out my phone and checked the time. Church should be over back home. The gang might even be together having lunch, although more and more, the couples were looking for Sunday afternoons to be couple time. Family time.

I didn't blame them. Mostly.

It just stank not being in a relationship. Or even dating. Before all the money, I'd been the one in the group who always had a date. Or two.

Now?

Well, we tried to stay out of the public eye, but we'd had enough publicity that I'd been burned one too many times when it came to the dating apps. Or even chatting up a nice-looking woman when I was out. Once they got that look in their eye and started to hint around to determine if I was *that* Wes Allen, I was done.

Besides, I was busy enough with the shop.

At least, that was what I told myself.

I tapped Noah's contact and settled back as it rang.

"Wes? Hey, man. How's the Caribbean?"

"Hot." I smiled as something in my chest settled with Noah's friendly greeting. "Diving's good though. How's Virginia?"

"Also hot. And sticky. Like every June. Guess you didn't escape the weather with your trip, did you?"

"Not so much." Although the ocean breeze when we were underway kept the humidity down. "But I've made some great contacts. Changed up some of my tentative plans. I'm glad I did this. Still wish you—or the rest of the group—could have tagged along."

"Yeah, sorry about that." Noah even sounded sorry, which was more than the other guys had when they'd begged off.

"I get it. What's the news?"

Noah laughed. "News? Did you forget how things work around here? It's just the same grind, day by day."

I snickered. It definitely could be that way. "You love it."

"I love parts of it. I've been working a lot with Jackson Trent at the office to get my idea for Ballentine's new undertaking off the ground. That has been incredible."

"That's great. I'm looking forward to hearing more as you get it set up. How's everyone else?"

"Same as ever. Tristan was planning to check up on you today or tomorrow. At church he mentioned he'd seen an article about some hurricanes forming?"

I nodded. Leave it to Tristan. "That's part of why I called. We're rerouting because of them."

"Your captain doesn't think you should park and wait them out?"

"Not yet. She seems really confident that we'll be safe if we move to the west side of everything. I trust her to know what she's doing. I've already learned a lot from her." Sunny had even had some good suggestions for my form that helped me use my air slower when I was diving. She was a good teacher.

"Her? I thought you had some grizzled old guy named 'Sonny' or something."

I chuckled. "Yeah. Her name's Sunshine. Sunny for short. It was a moment at the initial meeting."

"Oh?" Noah's voice held a hint of teasing. "A moment, eh?"

My face flamed. "Not like that. She's older. It's not—"

"Ah. So grizzled old lady."

"No. She's not grizzled." Far from it. I got a mental flash of Sunny in her swimsuit as she peeled away her wetsuit, and swallowed. "Or old. Just older than me."

Noah must have sensed some of my thoughts. "Hmm."

"Don't 'hmm.' I said it's not like that." Why had I thought it was a good idea to call anyone back home? Ugh. Time to get off the phone.

"But you want it to be."

"It wouldn't work. Her life is here. Mine's up there. Plus did I mention she's like ten years older than me? If she thinks of me as anything other than a paying client, it's as a younger brother. An annoying one." That was what I was going to tell myself at least. Because all of those were perfect reasons why nothing would work out anyway. And I didn't want to ruin the rest of my trip because I got a weird idea and then made it awkward. Besides, she hadn't given me any indication that she was interested.

Noah cleared his throat. "You hear yourself, right?"

"Noah. Just drop it. Okay?"

He sighed. "Fine. You didn't push too much when I was figuring things out with Jenna, so I guess I owe you that much."

"This isn't like that."

"I heard you."

I could practically see the smirk that accompanied Noah's words. "Whatever. Just tell everyone I'm fine, would you? I'll keep the group chat updated if we make any other changes in the itinerary."

"Will do. We'll be praying you stay safe."

"Thanks. Later." I ended the call and dropped my phone on the seat beside me.

Why had Noah suggested the idea of something more happening between Sunshine and me? Well, fine, he hadn't put the idea there—I'd had the idea. But I'd been doing a great job of keeping it firmly in the ridiculously impossible category.

Now, after talking to Noah, I could only wonder, *What if?*

10

SUNSHINE

I hopped off the boat onto the dock. It was early. The sun was just peeking over the horizon, flaring out in deep reds that made it impossible to stop the sailor's chant about weather from repaying in my head.

I was taking warning.

But I was also keeping a firm eye on the trajectory of the storm and I honestly believed we were going to be fine. All but one of the computer models had it veering north in the next twelve hours. So while it had strengthened to a strong tropical storm, by the time it hit hurricane strength, it should be on its way toward Florida. Or maybe it'd just stay in the ocean and leave everyone alone. There was at least one model suggesting that option.

As long as it didn't continue on its westward path, we'd be fine. And we could continue our voyage and our dive trips.

I strode toward the marina offices. The quiet was unusual. No one was out and about. Strange. Lights glowed inside the building, though, so I should at least be able to see what the consensus on diving was when it came to this island. The harbor master had his—or her—finger on the pulse of things. They wielded enough authority that they often *set* the pulse.

I knocked on the door, then pushed it open. "Hello?"

It took a moment, then a dark-skinned woman about my age, her hair in tight braids that were all pulled back into a tail, appeared from the depths of the offices. She tipped her head to the side and grinned. "Sunshine? Long time, no see."

"Beverly. Wow. Harbor Master?"

She nodded. "For a month now. Just in time for hurricane season."

I laughed. "No one can handle it better."

She shrugged. "I hope you're right. You're in the yacht?"

"I am. Solo passenger. He's got a dive shop in the States and is looking for the best trips to offer his clients." It was better to keep the information as sparse as possible. Beverly was great. She was also a man hunter. If she had any suspicion that Wes was young, single, and hot? She'd be hanging around trying desperately to make him the next notch in her belt.

"Hmm." Beverly narrowed her eyes. "What you don't say is as loud as what you do. But, it doesn't matter. I've changed."

My eyes widened as Beverly held out her left hand to show off the ring encrusted with sparkling stones. "Wow. Congrats. Anyone I know?"

"Jeremiah."

I laughed. "No way."

Beverly's face reddened. "Do I have to admit out loud that you were right?"

"It never hurts."

Beverly shook her head. "Fine. I guess 'thank you' is also appropriate."

"When's the big day?"

"Three months ago."

"That was fast." I'd been down this way in January. That was when I'd pointed out that Jeremiah had a thing for her. Beverly had dismissed it and gone on to mention that she wasn't interested anyway. So much for that.

She shrugged. "When you know, you know."

I nodded. I'd felt the same way about Luca. Our courtship had also qualified as a whirlwind. I didn't necessarily recommend it, though it had worked for us. We'd also had some big fights our first year—or two—that probably could have been avoided if we'd dated longer. Although, on the same hand, if we'd fought like that while dating, we might never have ended up married. It was only because neither of us were willing to consider divorce that we'd plowed through.

"So. Diving?"

"Yeah." I studied Beverly's face. "Have you shut it down?"

"Not officially. I'm not sure you'll find anyone willing to take you out though, if you needed that."

I bit my lip. Technically, I didn't. I had all the qualifications. I knew the spots. But I also hadn't been here since January, and things could change. This was one of the islands I'd been hoping to bring a local along for. "You think they'd join if I did the driving?"

"Can't say. You should ask. Best bet will be Danny."

I wrinkled my nose. "I was afraid of that."

Beverly chuckled. "You could do worse."

"Could I?" Danny was okay. When diving. But he was self-assured to the point of being cocky. He was the opposite in every way of Luca. Maybe on some planet that would be what I should look for if I were planning to fall in love again. It would stave off comparison, wouldn't it?

"For diving, certainly. For the rest?" Beverly shrugged. "That's up to you."

"He still hanging out at the juice stand in the mornings?"

"You know his schedule pretty well for someone who's not interested."

"Self-defense." I grinned. "Is that a yes?"

"Yeah. You want a scooter?"

I debated. The juice stand was walkable. And walking was going to be safer for me if I was taking Wes along.

He could probably drive his own scooter. That was another option. But it would raise questions since I hadn't gone that route initially. Ugh. I couldn't say I regretted giving in to my curiosity about how it would feel to have Wes close. Except maybe I kind of did. Because now I couldn't get away from the desire to experience it again.

"We'll walk. Thanks."

"Sure. When will you head out?"

"Depends on the weather. I'm hoping the storm veers and we don't have to hunker down somewhere."

Beverly scoffed. "Good luck."

"Are you seeing something I'm not?" I frowned. I hadn't checked the models yet this morning—I wanted to touch base here first.

"Probably not, no. But you know storms do what they want. I have a feeling."

Hmm. Beverly often had feelings. Sometimes they were right. "I guess I'll keep playing it by ear. You have room if we need to stick here?"

"Of course. Even if we didn't, for you I'd figure it out."

"Thanks." I reached out and grasped her hand. "Guess I'll go get the client and head over to see Danny. Tell Jeremiah hi for me."

"I will. He'll probably come down to say hi in person once I let him know you're around. He keeps going on about how he owes you."

I laughed. "No, he doesn't. You two would've ended up together eventually."

"Maybe. Maybe not." Beverly made a shooing motion. "Go do your work."

With a chuckle, I headed out of the building. The sky had lightened while I was inside and it looked like it was going to be a beautiful day. A light breeze blew, making the trees dance and pushing away the humidity.

I hurried back to the boat and stepped aboard.

"Morning. Everything okay?" Wes looked up from his coffee and clicked to darken his phone screen.

"Yeah. Just checking in and seeing if we were on for diving today."

"And?"

I nodded and forced my gaze not to linger on his face. I definitely didn't need to notice how the scruffy stubble on his chin added a reckless air to his appearance. Of course, he looked just fine clean shaven, too. I swallowed. "We need to see if we can find Danny."

Wes's eyebrows lifted.

I gave a mental groan. Even I'd heard the distaste in my voice when I'd said Danny's name. "He's okay. Just one of those men who thinks he's God's gift. It can be exhausting."

"We don't have to dive if he's the only option. Or, if you know the spots, I trust you. We can do without a local."

I shook my head. "You need a contact. For all of his personality issues, Danny's a good dive master. Professional on and under the water."

"But not on land?"

I sighed and moved to the kitchen area to pour myself coffee. "I don't think he'll bother your female clients, if that's what you're asking. Not unless they seem amenable. He's always backed off, fast, when I've told him no."

"But he keeps asking?"

I frowned. In reality, yes, Danny was persistent. He claimed —and I'd seen it for myself—that some women liked that. Preferred it, even.

"I'll take the silence as a yes." Wes scowled into his mug. "He's really the best option?"

According to Beverly, with the storm brewing in the east, right now he was our only option. I would have tried one or two other people before resorting to Danny if everything was usual, but I probably would have gotten around to him eventually. "Yeah. He is."

"All right. We'll give him a shot. If I don't like the vibe, I can always just avoid this as a destination. I have plenty of other options thanks to you." His voice warmed and the smile he shot me sent liquid heat through my veins.

It ought to be illegal to smolder like that.

I cleared my throat and took a big gulp of scalding coffee. I set down my mug. "When you're ready, we'll walk over to Danny's usual hangout and see what we see. Did you eat?"

"I was waiting for you."

I glanced up and his gaze locked onto mine. I could get lost in his eyes if I wasn't careful. Boy, oh boy, did I need to be careful. "I'm not hungry."

A tiny frown tipped his lips down and lines formed on his forehead.

Before he could say anything, I skirted around the far side of the boat toward the stairs leading below. "I'll be in my cabin. Knock when you're ready."

I hurried down the stairs and into my room. I pressed the lock on the handle as quietly as I could before leaning against the door and closing my eyes.

What was wrong with me?

I wasn't a schoolgirl. I'd been around good-looking men

before. Tons of times. Wes wasn't even the most handsome man I'd ever met. So why? Why did he do this to me? I was tongue-tied and all fluttery inside. And I was old enough to be...well, not his mother. Thank goodness. But not really his sister, either. Not unless we'd had a lot of siblings in between.

I pounded my fist into my forehead.

We had a little over two weeks together still. Then he'd get on a plane and head back to the States and I'd go back to my cottage on the beach and wait for another job to pop up. The payment from this one would mean I could say no for a while, too. If I wanted.

The knock on my door startled me.

Wes's voice was muffled. "Ready when you are."

I cleared my throat. "Okay. One sec and I'll meet you up top."

I listened, praying for calm and clarity. Finally, his footsteps clumped up the stairs. I pressed a hand to my stomach and took a deep breath. I was stronger than this. I was not some ditzy teenager who lost her brain when someone hot looked at her.

I shot a glance over at Luca's photo and pressed my lips together.

I'd had my lifetime love. My soulmate.

Love like that didn't happen twice in a lifetime.

I gathered my wits and opened my door, then headed up.

Wes stood in the sunshine, hands in the pockets of his baggy shorts. His tight T-shirt hugged his shoulders in ways I knew better than to notice.

I snagged my sunglasses off the boat controls and fixed them in place. At least they would hide how much I ended up staring at him. It would be mortifying if he caught me. And I didn't need to make things awkward between us. We still had two weeks together and I was supposed to be a professional. A guide. A teacher.

None of those things left room for drooling infatuation.

"Let's go." My voice was gruffer than I intended.

If Wes noticed, he didn't say anything, just fell into step beside me. "How are the storms?"

"One already dissipated. The other is strengthening."

"Heading this way?"

I felt his eyes on me. "Right now? Yes."

"Should we plan to stay here? Find a place to shelter?"

I shook my head. "We have a day or two before we need to make that call. And the models are showing it heading north. I think it'll miss us."

Wes nodded. "Okay."

I glanced over. Just that? No argument? It was a good reminder that he trusted me to know what I was doing. He relied on that. Wes had put his life fully in my hands, and I didn't need to get distracted by whatever random hormones had decided to rear their heads, and end up making a mistake.

I gestured for him to turn left as we reached the end of the marina parking lot. "It's down this way a couple blocks."

"Okay." He looked around. "It's quieter here."

"It is. They don't get as much tourism. No cruise ships. No major airport." It was one of the reasons I liked it down this way. Fewer crowds. Better, quieter dives. And none of the open-air markets designed to sell trinkets at all costs. Oh, sure, they had a market, but it was for locals. And the trinkets that were there weren't peddled aggressively.

"I like it. It's a more relaxed vibe."

"Relaxed is a good word. Definitely applies to just about everything down here."

"That's good. It's one of the reasons I started my dive shop."

"Relaxation?"

"Yeah." He shot me a grin. "Having never owned a retail business before, I didn't really understand just how not-relaxing parts of it were going to be. But it's still better than dragging myself through traffic every day to a job that I didn't love to sit in a cube for eight or nine hours doing work that I knew the client would change the next day. Or a week later. Or whatever. It was never going to be right."

I chuckled. "Never had a job like that, but it sounds awful."

"It was okay when I didn't have options. But the money gave me options and suddenly, I couldn't take it anymore."

"If you didn't have the money, you'd still be working there?"

Wes was quiet for several moments. "Probably, yeah. They paid well. I could afford my mortgage. I could eat out with friends. Pursue hobbies. It wasn't a bad life. I was happy."

"And now? Are you happier?" I kept my gaze focused ahead. The juice stand was just visible in the distance.

"I'm probably the same happy. The General—my mom's husband—always says happiness is something you choose, and I tend to agree. But I'm more content now than I was."

"Which is also something you choose." I'd done a lot of wrestling with the idea of contentment after Luca died. Along with happiness and joy. Wes was right that happiness was a choice. So was contentment. And joy? That came from Jesus.

"You're right." He nodded. "So that's on me. But I feel like what I do matters a lot more now. Maybe a dive shop doesn't seem like a place where someone serves Jesus and makes a difference in the lives of others, but it does to me."

"I think you serve Jesus and make a difference for people no matter where and what you do. Because that's a choice, too." I slowed my steps as we approached the juice stand. I lifted my hand in greeting. "Hey, Danny."

Danny, short and stocky, with wavy black hair and tan skin, turned. His brown eyes lit and I felt his gaze drift over me from head to toe. "Chica. You came back."

My smile was tight. "I'd like you to meet Wes Allen. I'm showing him around the islands. All the good dive sites."

Danny's gaze flicked over to Wes then back to me. "You're here to dive? I'll take you. You know there's a storm."

It was a clear dismissal and I prayed Wes wouldn't be offended. "I do. I also know the storm's far enough away and projected to turn. Beverly said she wasn't shutting things down."

Danny's head tipped to the side as if he heard my unsaid "Yet."

He nodded. "Anything you're hoping to see?"

"Wes?" I turned to him.

"Just a good dive site for moderate skill levels. I don't think I'd bring beginners this far. We found enough easy spots farther north."

My lips twitched and I fought a smile at Wes's bland tone. He obviously saw through Danny.

I glanced at Danny. "I was thinking the blue hole. But I wasn't sure if it was still good. I know there was a late fall storm near there."

Danny shrugged. "The storm missed it. That's a good spot. You staying on island after?"

"I don't think so." I didn't want to give Danny any ammo to push for us to crash at his place. It was one of his favorite tactics.

"Then I'll meet you out there. Give me thirty before you start?"

"Okay. Thanks, Danny."

Danny lifted an eyebrow. "You're paying, right?"

"Of course." I reached into my pocket and pulled out my phone. I'd slid money into the case that morning. I tugged it free and held it out.

Danny plucked the bills from my hand, counted them, and nodded. "Thanks."

I turned and started back toward the boat.

Wes jogged a few steps and caught up. "Great guy."

"He's not...ugh. Yeah. But he's one of the best. I'll give you info on the other two people I like here and you can reach out. They're just not diving today."

"Because of the weather."

I glanced over. It hadn't been a question, but I nodded an affirmative anyway.

"Are you sure we're safe?"

"I am. But if you're worried, we'll wave off. We can either hunker down here or we can zip along to the next port and plan to hunker there." I paused and bit my lip. "I'm not sure we could get back to Puerto Rico in time for you to get a flight out, since that'd be heading in the direction of the storm. But we could also hightail it to Grenada. They should be out of any of the paths, and they have a good airport. Your call."

"Let's keep that as a backup, I guess."

"You're nervous."

He nodded. "A little, yeah. I'm not used to hurricanes."

I patted his arm.

He flashed a wry smile. "I don't want to be a chicken. I also don't think lost at sea is going to make my mom and The General happy."

"You mentioned the general. That's who again?"

"Stepdad. Sorry. He's great. But even Mom calls him that. He just kind of *is* his rank."

I'd known men like that. I wouldn't normally call them great, though. Sounded like Wes's mom had found the one who was the exception to the rule. "You get along with them?"

"Yeah. Mostly. They're not on board with my fervor for, as they call it, all the Jesus stuff. But they recognize I'm an adult. And they're better about it than my dad."

"Sorry."

Wes shrugged. "Thanks. I'm used to it. Mostly. Although lately Dad's been big on asking me for investment money."

"I see those air quotes." I smiled, trying to lighten the mood.

"Yeah. It gets old. I keep hoping he'll understand the word 'no.' Maybe on Sunday he got it. But I think he took it as a no to a relationship with him, too. Which wasn't what I was going for." Wes sighed. "Family is hard."

"They can be." I considered the difference between our families. "Mine isn't hard so much as distant. They never approved of my marriage or of me moving down here. So we talk now and then, but I think I just confuse them."

"Sorry."

"Thanks." We finished the walk to the boat in silence. The times I glanced over at him, Wes seemed lost in thought. I didn't want to intrude. I spent the time reminding myself of the reasons we weren't going to get involved. As well as the reasons I didn't spend a lot of time thinking about my family.

When we stepped aboard, I checked the time. "We've got about fifteen minutes before we should head out to the dive spot. If you want to double-check the air tanks, I want to go take a look at the latest weather."

"Sure. Sounds good."

I hurried below deck to my cabin and shut—and locked—the door. I got my laptop and settled on my bunk as I pulled up the weather.

Maybe making a beeline for Grenada was the better choice.

Hunkering down somewhere else with Wes? The thought caused a lot of feelings I wasn't ready to analyze.

Maybe it would be better all-around to get him on a plane and out of my life.

11

WES

I took a big step off the swim platform of the boat into the water. I probably didn't need the thin wetsuit I'd dragged on, but Sunshine was wearing hers over her suit, so I followed her lead.

Danny bobbed in the water a couple of yards away. His BCD covered his bare chest and I worried over what kind of trunks he had on. He seemed the type to dive in a Speedo that left nothing to the imagination.

I fought a shudder and moved out of the way so Sunny could join us.

"Ready?" Danny pulled his goggles down over his eyes.

I lifted my fingers in the hand signal for OK before adjusting my own goggles and fitting my regulator in my mouth.

Sunny tapped my shoulder and signaled for us to descend.

I loved the moment the water closed over my head. My ears filled with water and everything took on a sense of thickness. Sounds were muted. Bubbles slowly rose to the surface as I breathed and let some air out of my BCD, encouraging the weights inside to pull me down deeper.

Even near the surface, brightly colored fish darted curiously nearby.

I checked my gauges and looked around. There she was. The bright red slashes on Sunny's BCD made it easy to spot her. She grinned at me. Even with most of her face covered with equipment, I could tell it was a grin. We'd talked about it some—she got the same thrill from diving as I did.

She had just as much trouble explaining it as I did.

Maybe people who were good with words could do it. There were probably poems out there that painted the picture. I was content to drag people along and make them experience it for themselves rather than attempting to explain it.

Everyone had their own impressions, anyway.

Danny had already descended to our target depth. He must enjoy skirting the edge of responsible. Which just confirmed my initial impression of him as reckless.

I definitely wasn't bringing beginners down here. Not if he was going to be our local POC. I wanted people to learn to dive safely. Part of that meant not courting the bends, a painful, potentially deadly, and completely avoidable condition. And that meant descending and ascending slowly. Even if you were anxious to get to the "good parts."

I always tried to teach my students that all of the parts were good if they paid attention.

Sunshine and I leveled out, adjusting for neutral buoyancy. I signaled my readiness and glanced between Sunny and Danny.

Danny pointed ahead and then started swimming in that direction. I waited until there was a good separation between me and his fins, then kicked off. Sunny swam a little behind and to my left. I could see her, which was how it should be with a dive buddy, but we both had space.

There wasn't much current. At least, it wasn't noticeable to me as we swam. And while this wasn't as amazing as some of the reefs we'd seen farther north, I still appreciated the quantity of fish available to watch.

Sunny grabbed my hand.

I looked at her and she pointed. I let my gaze follow and froze as I spotted the enormous sea turtle sailing through the water up ahead.

She'd said turtles were the most likely animal we'd see at this time of year. There were whales, sometimes, in February.

I watched the turtle for several minutes before continuing along and working to close the distance between us and Danny. He'd paused above the front mast of a wooden ship. Oooh. Neither had mentioned there was a wreck, but this had to be why Sunny had considered the spot.

I descended a little and shone my flashlight along the front of the ship, looking for a name. But I didn't see anything.

We spent some time slowly circling the wrecked pieces. There was nothing left of the inside. Either the passage of time or the flow of water had done it on their own, or the island had in an attempt to find the balance between keeping divers safe but leaving something interesting to see. Wreck diving was a special certification for good reason. But a wreck this close to shore was bound to get attention. So it made sense, somewhat, to do what they could to make it safe.

Past the wreck, we descended another fifteen feet. I checked my gauges and made a mental note that divers would need their advanced certs to do this dive. We'd passed the typical depths for recreational diving and this would now be considered a deep dive. Honestly? That made me like it better. It gave this location something unique.

When we'd been under for half an hour, we turned and retraced our route back toward the boats. Danny surfaced much faster than Sunshine and I and he was sitting on his swim platform, arms crossed, when we finally surfaced.

"Well?"

I tugged my goggles down around my neck and smiled. "It's a good dive. Thanks. The turtles are cool."

He nodded once. "It's better December through March. Maybe April. You see more."

"That's when I'd be bringing groups. The wreck was a nice surprise."

Danny scoffed. "Everyone thinks so. I don't understand the draw of waterlogged wood, but I'm glad you liked it."

"Gosh, Danny. Your cheerful disposition is always so great." Sunshine's voice dripped sarcasm. "Thanks for the tour."

"Whatever. You're really leaving?"

"We are." Sunshine dipped her head back and rewet her hair. "The weather still looks stable. And we have other spots to evaluate. I'll make sure Wes has your number so he can coordinate when he's got a group ready."

"Yeah, okay. Thanks. Nice to meet you, man." Danny's voice finally thawed.

"Same. Appreciate it." I didn't. Not really. I would absolutely touch base with the other two contacts Sunny had here before reaching out to Danny, but I wasn't going to tell him that. No need to burn a bridge just yet.

I swam toward our boat and hauled myself up onto the step. I unhooked my BCD and shrugged one arm free, then the other. I laid it down carefully before removing my flippers and standing, grabbing my tank, and moving out of the way so Sunshine could climb aboard.

We made quick work of rinsing the equipment and setting it up to dry in a way that it wouldn't move around.

Within thirty minutes, we were underway.

"Are you all right?" I leaned against the side wall of the boat and watched Sunny as she studied the instruments.

She glanced up. "Yeah. Thinking."

I lifted my eyebrows as an invitation for her to continue. Maybe she would, maybe she wouldn't. But I found that I was more curious than I probably ought to be.

She sighed. "Another of the models shifted."

"Which means?"

"It means that maybe the storm is going to head this way. When it was just one prediction, it was easy enough to consider them an outlier. Now that there are two? There's something those services are picking up on. It just increases the possibility. I'm not sure what the right decision is." Her hands were in her lap, deceptively still, until I spotted one finger twisting the ring she wore on her right hand.

"If you're nervous, let's head for Grenada. We can skip the other planned stops. I have so many contacts and good dives, there's no reason to risk anything. I suspect most of my groups are going to want to stay in the northern islands anyway. They're more familiar."

Sunshine laughed. "They are. And therefore more crowded."

I shrugged. She was right. It was definitely a factor in my initial plan to have spots all the way down the chain of islands. "Not worth the risk of damaging the ship though."

"All right." She blew out a breath. "It's the right choice, but I don't like it. If the storm doesn't turn, we've wasted your time."

"No, we haven't." I reached out and rested my hand on her arm. The electricity zinging through me at the touch was expected. I just didn't know what to do about it. Nothing. Of course the answer was nothing. Chemistry was well and good, but practicality mattered, too. And nothing about being attracted to Sunshine was practical.

Her gaze locked with mine.

My mouth went dry. It was all I could do not to lean in and kiss her. Would she let me? Everything in me screamed to find out.

She looked away. Her voice was slightly unsteady as she said, "Okay."

I shoved my hands in my pockets. "I guess I'll go let the guys know the change of plans. You said Grenada has a good airport?"

"It does. You should be able to get a flight home on any number of carriers."

"I, uh, have a plane." My face burned.

She glanced up, eyes wide, then quickly schooled her expression. A smile hovered around the corners of her lips. "Of course you do."

"We share it. Me and the guys." I was defensive and there was no reason for it. It made sense. And we had the money. It wasn't as though we were skipping meals to look like we had this ridiculous lifestyle. We all lived more frugally than we had to.

"I'm not judging. Promise."

It had sounded like it, but fine. I nodded. "I'll let you do... whatever it is you have to do to change our plans."

I stepped away from the helm area and, after a brief hesitation, headed up the ladder to the top deck. It was still sunny and hot. There was a good breeze from our speed. Looking around, I would never have imagined a storm was on its way.

I plopped on the long, padded seat and opened the group text.

> Storm predictions are changing so we're calling it. The new plan is to make for Grenada and I'll fly home early.

TRISTAN

> Good. I'm glad. They just bumped it to a cat two.

> Wow.

NOAH

You didn't know?

No. I leave that to the experts. Isn't that what you all told me to do?

NOAH

I guess. Just seems like you might also peek at the weather on your own.

Just because you're named after a guy who built a boat doesn't mean you know more about sailing than me.

NOAH

Har har.

Hey. It's been a while since I could make a Noah joke. You gotta find fun where you can. Especially when your vacation is getting cut in half.

NOAH

I guess.

TRISTAN

Sorry, man. That stinks. Positive side? We miss your face.

Does that mean you've actually been showing up to things?

TRISTAN

I show up!

SCOTT

Tristan, my dude, we love you, but you absolutely do not.

TRISTAN

Whatever, Scott. Cause you never miss because Beckett is sick.

> Guys. Chill. I just wanted to keep you in the loop. Way things are going, I might be home in time to win at poker on Friday.

CODY

> Dream on.

Cody added six crying laughing faces after his text.

I chuckled and closed out of the text.

I opened another message to our pilots and tapped out a quick request for a pickup in Grenada. Then realized I didn't have any idea what our ETA was. I sighed, frowning at the unsent message.

I closed the app without sending. I'd go down and ask Sunny about that later. Much later. I'd gotten the distinct feeling that she'd prefer I not be there breathing her air right now. So, I'd stick to up here. So far on this trip, when I was up here and she decided she wanted me for something, she came to find me.

That would work just fine.

I checked the signal on my phone and once again thanked God for satellite technology, then called my mom.

"Oh, honey. I'm glad you called."

I chuckled. "Hi, Mom. You know the phone works both ways."

"I was trying not to be a worrywart."

I nodded. "Tell The General it's okay for you to check in on me."

"I heard that." The General hollered. He sounded closer when he continued speaking. "And while I appreciate the thought, I don't think you know what you're saying. At least not if you're going to be out sailing around in the Caribbean."

I winced. "Sorry, sir."

"Pffft." I imagined the General waving off my words. He

cleared his throat. "I'm just saying, it's harder for your mother when you're out of the country."

"And there's a hurricane." Mom chimed in.

I suspected that was the real problem. "Well, then, you'll be glad to know we're changing plans. We are, even as we speak, on our way to Grenada."

"Still in the Caribbean." Mom's tone was dry. "Not as helpful as you'd imagine."

I snickered. "But home to a good airport. And, also, out of the path of the hurricane even if it does manage to come this direction, which is open to interpretation at this point. Most of the models are showing it turning and heading north."

"Listen to you, all weather-wise." I heard the smile in Mom's voice. She let out a breath. "I'm glad you're being smart. Though I guess I'm sorry you're cutting your trip short."

"Thanks. All in all, I have what I came for. It's not like I can't come back down and do the southern islands separately another time. Maybe my initial plan was too optimistic."

"I'm sorry. I think I'm going deaf. Could you repeat that last part?" Mom was laughing.

"Yeah, yeah. You told me so. You were right. I acknowledge that my mother continues to know more than me. Happy?" I shook my head, grinning. I'd been hoping I could sneak that past her. I should've known better.

"Deliriously."

"Great. Just great. Thanks, son. Now she's going to be insufferable." The General's voice was gruff, but I heard the affection under it. He was good for Mom. I was glad they'd found each other.

"I guess I should get it out of the way and admit you were right about Dad calling looking for money, too. He tried to hit me up on Sunday."

"Oh, Wesley. I'm sorry." Mom's voice hardened. "That man."

"Mom. It's fine. I said no. He's currently never speaking to me again. Honestly, I'm okay with that." Mostly. I was mostly okay with it. In a perfect world, both Mom and Dad—and The General for that matter—would see how much they needed Jesus. Then we would have better common ground for improving our relationship. But for now? I'd just try to continue to show them all Jesus as consistently as I could. I wasn't perfect —probably being okay with Dad having his silent-treatment fit was a clear indicator of that—but I was working on it.

"I can try to talk to him." Mom's tone suggested she'd rather jump into a pit of snakes.

"No. Don't. There's no need for you to get sucked into the drama. He also respectfully declined the invitation to cruise with us over the holidays."

The General snorted. "Respectfully?"

I cleared my throat. "In his way."

Mom laughed. "Oh, Wes. I should've handled that, too."

"Why? I'm an adult and it was my idea. You don't have to run interference for me anymore. But I appreciate that you want to. I love you."

"I love you, too." Mom sniffed. "I'm glad you'll be home soon. You'll keep me up to date?"

"Of course. If you want to start looking at different cruise options, that would help. We can get together and book something as soon as I'm home." Giving Mom a project was the best way to keep her from worrying. This was something I'd learned pretty young. I didn't always use it for good reasons—she'd been easy to distract and it had kept her from noticing things like my underage drinking and how late I got home from parties—but now it didn't seem like a bad idea for her to have something to focus on.

"That's a good plan. Thanks, son." The General got it. He'd been known to use the same technique. It was why there was always something getting remodeled or redecorated at their house.

Whatever. It worked for them.

"Remember I'm paying, okay? I don't want you to choose something based on the prices."

"Oh, but—"

"Nuh-uh." I cut Mom off. "Ignore prices. Find what looks like fun."

She sighed. "All right. Thank you."

"I benefit too. Don't forget that." While I might not have been super excited about the idea when it first came up, after this short cruise? I was all in. Who knew I'd come to love boat travel so much? Of course, cruise ships were sure to be a different animal, but they wouldn't be worse, would they? "I'm going to let you go. I'll touch base when we get to Grenada."

"Be safe." The General cleared his throat. "We love you."

I blinked. The call ended before I could respond. I was used to Mom saying she loved me. But The General? He was more of a "show them how you feel by what you do" kind of guy.

I slid my phone back into my pocket and stared out at the horizon.

What I told Mom was accurate. I had what I needed for the dive trips. But I'd left out the part that I was hesitant to admit even to myself.

I didn't want to end the trip early.

I wasn't ready to walk away from Sunshine.

It was stupid.

But still true.

12

SUNSHINE

I bit my lip as I manned the controls.

The water was rough. It had been getting rougher through the night. Rough enough that the autopilot couldn't hold the course, so I'd been here, mostly awake, the whole time. I was either going to have to give Wes a crash course on driving so I could grab a nap or we were going to need to find a place to dock and hunker down.

I rubbed my burning eyes and tried to ignore the churning in my gut.

"Morning." Wes grinned as he came up the stairs from the cabins below. Then he took a second look and frowned. "Are you all right?"

"No. I've been up all night."

His eyebrows lifted. "What's wrong?"

"The models have basically all shifted now. It's heading this way and we're not going to be able to outrun it on our way south like I'd hoped." I held the wheel as the boat hit a wave.

Wes steadied himself. "Can we pull over? Or heave to or whatever it's called?"

I smiled in spite of myself as he struggled to find the right sailing jargon. "I need to figure that out. The short answer is that I took us east to give us a better route to Grenada, so now, if we wanted to get to one of the islands in between, we'd have to head toward the storm. I'm not sure how well that will work, if I'm honest."

"Can we just head east? Forget Grenada and work on avoiding the storm?"

I shook my head. "I don't think so. There's no guarantee we'd avoid the storm if it's really coming this way. Plus, the farther east we go, the less likely we are to find a place to land and hunker down."

He frowned. "What can I do?"

"Can we start with coffee? Then I guess I'll give you a crash course on keeping us heading the way we're trying to go so I can sleep a little and figure out our best next step." I hesitated to tell him the worst of the news. I needed to. Definitely. But I couldn't quite get the words out.

"I can do that." Wes looked nervous.

I imagined it wasn't the coffee making that was throwing him. "You'll do fine. You just have to keep us on the plotted course. Promise."

"Okay." He moved to the kitchen area and set about making coffee. "What do the people at the charter company suggest?"

I winced. "That's the bad news."

He whipped his head my direction. "What do you mean?"

"The storm is already interfering with our communications. Contact is spotty and only going to get worse." This was why I didn't always rely on technology—it was only as good as the infrastructure supporting it. I had charts in my cabin and would absolutely be consulting them when I worked out what we were going to do next. But I sure would love to get Zee on the line and see what she suggested.

Wes didn't respond. He turned back to the kitchen and opened the fridge. "Can I make you a sandwich?"

"Sure." I wasn't positive I'd be able to keep it down, but if it helped him feel useful, I'd go with it. If it came back up? Well, it wouldn't be the first time I'd been sick on board. Probably wouldn't be the last.

I checked my cell phone. Still no signal. Awesome.

"Here." Wes came up beside me with a steaming mug that he offered handle first and a plate holding a sandwich that would make every cartoon sandwich jealous.

"That's a big meal." I took the mug and gestured for him to set the plate down next to the controls.

He shrugged. "Figured it was better to try to use things up before they go bad."

I frowned. "Why would they go bad?"

"I'm not stupid, Sunshine. Chances are high that we're going to end up shipwrecked. That means no power. In turn, that means no refrigeration. At this point, I'm hoping we manage that shipwreck near some kind of land instead of just bobbing along at the mercy of the ocean in a hurricane." He turned and strode back to the kitchen area.

I sipped my coffee. "I don't think it's that dire."

Wes grunted.

"Seriously." I turned and watched as he carried an identical sandwich to the banquette and sat. The controls beeped urgently at me and I hurried to adjust our course back to the plotted line. "We're going to be okay."

Wes shot me a bland look.

And okay, fine. I didn't know we'd be all right. I couldn't promise it. But there was no reason to jump straight to the worst-case scenario. We *might* end up being just fine, and I was going to cling to that.

Even though it did seem entirely likely that an unplanned landing was in our future.

I preferred the sound of that to "shipwrecked."

I pinched the bridge of my nose. "Look. You might be right. But can we try to stay positive?"

"Sure." His voice was muffled by the food in his mouth.

I blew out a breath that was half-laugh, half-exasperation. Great. I did not have time or energy to carry his emotions right now. So if he wanted to be Mr. Negativity, I'd let him.

I reached for the sandwich and took a bite. It was surprisingly good. And the churning in my stomach had, apparently, been partially due to hunger, because it settled some after I swallowed.

We were going to be fine.

I was going to assert that to myself as many times as I had to.

Right, God? You've got this. I'm trusting You here. Because in all honesty, I'm not sure what else to do.

I guess that wasn't entirely true. I had a plan of sorts. Unfortunately, some of it was a lot like Wes's prediction: find an island, land one way or another, don't die.

As plans went, it was bare bones.

But I really liked the last part.

I blew out a breath and took another bite, then washed it down with a generous gulp of coffee.

"I'm sorry." Wes pushed his plate away from himself. He scrubbed his hands over his face. "I'm not always great in situations like this. Not initially, at least."

"Been shipwrecked before, have you?" I lifted an eyebrow and allowed one corner of my mouth to poke up in a smirk. "That would've been good information to include in your reservation."

Wes snorted. "No. First time. Sorry."

"Hey. Me, too." I laughed. "It's going to be fine."

"Promise?"

I shook my head. "No. I absolutely do not promise. But I'm praying. You should, too."

He nodded. "Right. Good idea."

He bowed his head right then and I turned back to focus on the controls and my food. I really needed to get to those charts and see what, if anything, was close enough to consider as a backup plan. And then I should fire up the radio and see if I could get it working, or if it was just as impeded by the storm as the satellite technology.

Theoretically, it should work better. There was a reason it was aboard as a backup. But I also knew the charter company owner and his love of saving money by playing the odds. Right now? I had a sinking feeling that he didn't always do the maintenance like he was supposed to.

But that was borrowing trouble.

I jolted when Wes put his hand on my shoulder.

"Sorry." He flashed a tight smile. "You said you needed me to know what to do."

Right. Okay. I took a deep breath and walked him through the bare-bones basics. Enough that he could avoid catastrophe while I nabbed...well, an hour was probably not the wisest choice, no matter how much I wanted a full night of sleep...so twenty minutes? Cat naps were good, too.

"I'm going below. I'm going to nap for twenty, maybe thirty minutes. But if something goes wrong, come get me. I'm serious." I pinned him with a stern look. "I can sleep later if I need to."

He nodded.

"If I'm not back up here in half an hour, come get me." I waited for him to nod again. "All right."

I hurried down the stairs.

In my cabin, I stretched out on the bed and closed my eyes.

Exhaustion pulsed through every muscle of my body, but my brain wouldn't quiet. I tried to turn the thoughts to prayers, but they came back to a series of steps and "what ifs." I tried counting backwards from a hundred.

Nothing.

With a groan, I sat up and dug out the charts and my laptop. I carried them back up to the main deck.

"That wasn't even ten minutes." Wes tore his eyes away from the controls for a moment to frown at me.

"I know. Too much adrenaline, I guess. But you keep doing that. I'm going to work on a new course." At least I hoped that was what I could do. A new course would mean there was an island nearby that we could shelter on. It'd be small. Probably private. But hopefully the owner would understand. Given the time of year, many of the privately owned islands would be deserted.

I couldn't decide if that was better or worse.

Probably a mix of both.

"Tell me our current coordinates?" I glanced up at Wes.

He rattled off the numbers.

"Okay. We're going to make for this island." I tapped the tiny dot. "It's private. I don't know who owns it. Hopefully, they're hospitable. Or not home."

Wes nodded.

Good. At least he didn't push for some other course of action. I could make an argument for staying the course and just running for Grenada. But there was no guarantee. And what I really didn't want to do was end up in the lifeboat hoping for rescue. At least on an island there ought to be shelter and some sort of food.

I switched places with Wes and reprogrammed our course, turning the boat until we were underway. "It's still going to be a couple of hours."

A lot could go wrong in those hours. I bit my tongue to keep the words from coming out. He didn't need to know that. Or, more realistically, he knew. He just didn't need to hear it from me. I was the positive, reassuring one on the boat, apparently.

I handed the controls back to Wes and did what I could to get the radio working. It seemed like it was functional—but I wasn't getting any response. There were plenty of reasons for that, some good. Others less so. I went ahead and sent an email with the details as well, in the hopes that once the satellites were cleared of the storm, it would send, and at least then someone would know where we were and reach out.

If all went well, the boat would be fine and we could wait out the storm, hop back aboard, and head for Grenada as planned.

"I think now I'm going to try for that nap. You all right?"

Wes shrugged. "I guess?"

"Wake me up if you need me." A yawn cracked my jaw. "Or when we're about twenty minutes from the island. You remember how to tell?"

His nod was hesitant.

I shot him what I hoped was a bolstering smile before descending to my cabin. This time, when I stretched out, sleep claimed me as soon as I closed my eyes.

"Um."

I bolted awake. "What?"

"I don't—you should come."

I rubbed my eyes and the details of our situation came rushing back. "Are we close?"

"I think so. I see land, at least." Wes started out of my cabin. "But it's beeping and I don't know why."

Beeping wasn't good.

I threw my legs over the side of the bed and stood. I took a moment to steady before hurrying after Wes. I kept a hand on the wall. The boat was pitching and rocking on the waves. How had I slept through that? The water had been rough when I went down, but not like this.

I flipped on the emergency weather radio, hoping we were close enough to get broadcasts from somewhere. Surely, with land in sight, we were?

Static.

The boat angled dangerously to the left and I clutched for the rail. "Whoa."

Wes, looking a little green, nodded. "Yeah."

I frowned at the instruments and silenced the alarms. "This doesn't look right. The depth readings are off. You followed the course?"

"I did what you showed me." A hint of defensiveness crept into Wes's tone.

"Sorry." I offered a tight smile. Of course it wasn't his fault. It was mine. I was the one who was supposed to be driving. If we'd gone off course, that was on me. I took a closer look at the coordinates and fought to keep my expression neutral.

There was no if.

We were decidedly off course.

Which meant the island in front of us wasn't the one I'd planned for us to find. It wasn't the one I'd told people we'd be on.

A loud, crunching, rending sound accompanied the jolt that threw me backward from the controls.

"Well, crap." I stopped the boat and closed my eyes.

"What was that?" Wes gripped my arm.

I looked over at him. "That was us running aground."

He stared at me.

I blew out a breath. The positive, if I could call it that, was that we were wedged onto the rocks enough that the ocean wasn't as able to throw us around as it had been. The negatives —and oh boy, were there negatives—started with how we were still a good ways from shore. I didn't want to try to swim it. Not with the water as choppy as it was right now. Which meant the lifeboat.

"We need to get the inflatable up and head to shore. Grab what you can fit in a duffel bag. We don't have room for the diving equipment. Think about survival necessities." I'd already switched into emergency mode, and my tone was brisk.

Thankfully, that seemed to snap Wes out of his daze. He closed his eyes for a moment before heading down to his cabin.

I dug out the emergency supplies from where they were stowed, sent off the new coordinates—or tried to, since that was all still dependent on things clearing enough for a signal—and then hurried below for my go-bag.

When I returned to the main deck, I wrestled the deflated emergency boat out of its storage, then hooked it up and got the pump running. Thankfully, the boss wasn't so cheap he expected us to use a handpump in emergencies.

By the time Wes arrived with two duffel bags, the boat was inflated.

I hooked a line to it then maneuvered it into the water by the swim step. "Let's load up and get out. The water's only getting rougher at this point."

Wes hurried to help heft the supplies into the craft, then stepped in. He held out a hand for me and I had to stifle a chuckle. Now wasn't the time for chivalry. Although, in some ways, I still appreciated it.

"Let's hope the motor is strong enough to handle the waves." I wasn't sure it would be, and I really didn't want to end up unable to make landfall because of how angry the water was. There were oars, but I didn't trust our ability to paddle any more than I did the engine.

It took three tries to get the motor started. I tensed my jaw as

I navigated toward the land. A hard, stinging rain began to fall as the wind whipped up the waves.

We had definitely found the hurricane.

"Hold on!" I had to yell over the noise of the boat and the storm as a wave crashed over the top of the boat. A tiny part of my brain wondered how waterproof the bags were, but that was definitely a problem for future me.

If current me lived long enough to have to deal with it, I was going to be elated.

It felt like hours before we finally reached the shore. I jumped out into the waist-high water, nearly getting sucked completely under by the waves as I did. I snagged the boat and started dragging it the rest of the way up.

Wes hopped out the other side and helped.

With a final heave, we got the boat out of the water. I watched as Wes stumbled, then crashed onto the beach.

"Not the time for drama!" I yelled over the storm. We needed shelter. Dry clothes. We might be on land, but we were nowhere near safe just yet. "Come on, Wes. Get up."

I rounded the boat and froze.

Blood flowed from a gash in Wes's head and he lay unmoving beside a jagged rock that jutted out of the beach, his leg twisted in a dangling rope that was caught on something under the boat.

For one, horrifying moment, Luca's body replaced Wes's in my vision. I nearly crumpled under the weight of grief and whispered, "I can't do this."

13

WES

My head was killing me.

I groaned and shifted, sending lances of pain shooting out from my head and other spots on my body.

What. On. Earth?

"Do you want some water?"

I pried open my eyes. Sunshine's face filled my vision. She smiled and some of the pain in my head dimmed. "Water is good."

"Can you sit up?"

"Think so." I shifted again, ignoring the twinge in my ribs, and after a little struggle, managed to achieve a sitting position. I accepted the plastic cup from Sunny and looked around. "Are we in a house?"

"Such as it is, yeah. It's in rough shape."

"But it has walls. And a roof." That had to be a good thing, right?

"True. In this room, at least. All the windows are broken. I'm pretty sure the birds are annoyed that we've moved into their home." Sunny shrugged. "But I was grateful that I didn't have to try and build something out of tree branches."

"How...?" I wasn't sure how to finish the question. I sipped the water. It was cool and soothing.

"Well, being full of grace and poise, you tripped while helping drag the boat out of the water and managed to crack your head on a rock. You probably need stitches, but I don't happen to have that ability on me, so I did the best I could with the emergency glue for the inflatable boat."

I reached up to where pain radiated from my head.

"Don't touch it."

I stopped and lowered my hand. "So I knocked myself out?"

Sunshine chuckled. "You did. Which meant I then got the joy of rolling your deadweight into the boat so I could drag you to shelter. Super fun times, let me tell you."

I couldn't help but laugh. "I'm sorry. If I could go back and do it again, I promise I wouldn't trip and knock myself unconscious."

"You say that. But I'll point out, it got you out of the heavy lifting." Sunny grinned. "I figure you would've done the same for me. But I'm pretty sure the boat's toast now. It isn't meant to be dragged over sand and rocks. And I used the repair glue on your head. So we're going to need to pray that whoever comes to find us has their own way to get to shore."

"How long was I useless?"

"That's a loaded question." Her eyes danced with laughter.

I shook my head and immediately regretted it. "You know what I mean."

"I do. But you really should take more care with how you phrase things." She shrugged. "I'm not sure. Couple hours, I guess. Once I got you inside, I took a nap. I've only been awake a little while myself. All the electronics got soaked between the rain and the waves, so they're no good. And since this place has clearly been deserted for a while, it doesn't run to functioning clocks. Toss in the hurricane making everything dark and your guess is as good as mine."

I winced at her tone. Gone was the teasing from a moment ago. Now? She was angry. Rightfully so. I was kind of ticked myself. But I also didn't see the point in taking it out on the person I was stuck with for however long we were going to be stranded here. "What can I do now?"

"Nothing. There's nothing to do. I collected some of the rain, so we have water. We have granola bars and freeze-dried food. If we need a fire, the living room has a fireplace that looks like it should be okay to use. But it was also floor-to-ceiling glass on both of the long walls, so it's wet and windy in there. Not sure the fire is worth it."

I wasn't cold. For all that there was a hurricane, it was warm and humid still. "Is it okay if I change clothes?"

"Yeah. Of course. I thought about trying to strip off your wet things, but I wasn't sure you'd appreciate that."

I had about twelve inappropriate responses zip through my brain at her words. Thankfully, I was able to keep them from popping out. My head injury must not be too serious. "I'm mostly dry at this point. But the sand."

"I get it. I changed, too." She nudged my duffels toward me then stood. "I'll go wander the house again and see if I can find anything else useful. There's a toilet, so we can fill a bucket for flushing."

"I guess if you're going to get shipwrecked, it's nice to do it on an island that has indoor plumbing."

Sunshine chuckled. "Be nicer if the house was weather proof, but yeah. Small bonuses."

I watched her stride from the room. With a groan that I did my best to manfully muffle, I pushed to my feet. I wavered for a moment before finding my balance. My ankle and leg were sore but didn't seem to be out of commission. That was good. I'd already been a burden.

My face flamed at the thought of Sunny having to drag me to shelter. So masculine to need rescue.

I blew out a breath. I couldn't change it now. But I could do everything in my power to make sure I carried my weight from here on out.

The problem, of course, was that I had no idea how to survive on an island. I'd never been a scout. My dad was not a camper or outdoor survival kind of guy. I'd had to be shown how to change a tire by my girlfriend in high school.

The General had tried, but by that point, I was over it.

I tugged my shirt over my head, grunting when my ribs protested. Sand showered down and I leaned forward to brush it from my hair as best as I could. I twisted, eyeing my side. An abrasion ran down from just below my armpit to my waist. Little droplets of blood seeped out here and there.

I looked around but didn't see anything that would work for a bandage. Or even a wipe. I glanced at the shirt in my hand and shrugged before pressing it to the area gently. Even still, I winced. What was it from? Rolling me into the boat, maybe? Or when I fell?

There was no way to know.

Sunshine probably had a first aid kit in one of the emergency bags. I peeled the shirt away and sighed at the speckled dots of blood on it. My side looked better though. So maybe it didn't need any sort of dressing.

I squatted and unzipped one of my duffels. After digging around, I found a black T-shirt and another pair of shorts. They were damp. Ish. But still better than my current clothes. I pulled on the shirt, then crossed to the doorway Sunny had disappeared through and looked into the next room.

She wasn't there.

Okay. I shucked off my shorts and, after a moment of thought dug into the duffel for a clean pair of underwear as well. I used the old clothes to brush away sand, then dressed quickly in the clean clothes.

I would've killed for a hot shower.

We had water purely because of the storm raging outside, so that was off the table. Maybe—and it was a big maybe—there was a possibility of a hot bath. But just the thought of collecting enough water and figuring out how to heat it up was exhausting.

"Sunshine?" I picked my way across the floor of the room that had probably been a closet when someone lived in this place. A good-sized walk-in closet, but still a closet. I stepped through the door and the next room confirmed my suspicion. This was definitely a bedroom. One whole wall was missing, and shards of glass were sprinkled on the floor near the opening.

My jaw dropped as I looked out at the rain hammering down at a sharp angle and the wind lashing the trees so they bent at angles that surely should have cracked the trunks in two.

The sound was incredible. No wonder she hadn't heard when I called.

There was a door to the left. That had to lead to a hallway, didn't it? I crossed the room, noting that the condition of the wood floors wasn't as bad as it might have been. A good sanding and sealing and they'd probably be fine. Maybe one or two planks would need replacing.

Lots of glass, obviously, would have to be put back in.

In the hall, I couldn't stop a smile as I looked around. The architecture leaned heavily midcentury. Glass had once formed the other side of the extra-wide hallway. Some had survived, but not all. These openings faced the incoming rain, so the floor was pooling with water as the storm raged outside.

"Sunshine?" I pitched my voice louder.

"Over here." Her head poked out down the hall.

I hugged the drier side of the hallway as I made my way to her, pausing to peek in rooms as I passed them. Then I stepped down into the sunken living room and tried not to gasp.

"Wow."

Sunshine glanced around, her eyebrows drawn together. "That's one word for it."

I frowned. "You don't see how amazing this is?"

"Was. Not is. And I mean, okay. But who can afford a private island?" Her cheeks reddened as she said the words. "Right. Never mind."

"I'm just saying, if you're going to own your own island, a midcentury glass and steel is the way to go."

Sunshine scoffed. "Maybe if you get hurricane-proof glass."

I nodded, conceding the point. "Or storm shutters."

She glanced at me and pointed a finger at my chest. "Smart."

I wasn't sure what she meant, so I just stood, watching, while she marched toward the far wall that was once glass.

She looked in the sides, then up, not seeming to notice the soaking she was getting. Then she motioned to me. "Come here."

"I just got dry."

"Don't be a baby."

I groaned, but crossed the floor to where she stood. She pointed up. "Does that look like a shutter that would roll down?"

I squinted. There was something up there, definitely. "Could be."

"I wonder where the mechanism is."

"The one that is surely powered by electricity? Which we don't have? That mechanism?"

Sunny scowled at me. "Don't be a spoilsport. If we could close off this room to the rain, we could use the fireplace. Then we could cook. Some of the meals in the emergency bag are pretty decent if you have hot water to mix in them. They're a lot less good when you have to use cold."

That was a compelling argument.

I turned and scanned the room. Off to the side, propped in a corner, was a long metal pole. I crossed to it, then brought it back to where the window would have been. "Do you think this does anything?"

Sunshine grinned and took the pole from me. "Yep. Watch and learn."

She squinted into the rain and, after two false starts, got the pole attached into a slot designed for it. From there, she was able to get the shutter unlocked and lowered enough that I could reach up and pull it the rest of the way.

"I wonder why they didn't close all the shutters when they left." I certainly would, if it was my island. It didn't make sense to tempt nature like that.

"Same reason they didn't lock the doors, probably." Sunshine shrugged. "I'm glad for that last one. Though I agree on the first. Let's try the other side."

The pole worked for that storm shutter as well.

The downside was that it also closed off what little light we'd been getting from outside. Granted, that hadn't been a ton, but with the shutters closed, the room was black as tar.

"Now what?" I was hesitant to move. I didn't want to ram into Sunny. I also didn't want to trip on anything. Neither of us needed to get injured worse than we already were. Or I was. Wait. Was she injured? "Did you get hurt at all?"

"Me?" Her voice was closer now. "When? Oh, with the boat? Not really."

"What does 'not really' mean?"

She chuckled and her fingertips—well, I assumed they were her fingertips—brushed my arm. "Means you're heavy. Especially when you're deadweight."

Her fingers trailed down my arm then laced through mine. I fought a shudder of delight at the sensation that was so close to a caress. "Sorry."

Was that my voice? I cleared my throat. Must be the mustiness in the air from the house being vacant that caused it to rasp. Right?

"If I thought you'd done it on purpose, I would accept your apology. I'm just glad it doesn't seem like you have a concussion. That's lucky. Or God. Probably God." She chuckled. "Now. Let's try to shuffle our way back to the hallway where there's possibly more light since I notice you left the lantern in the closet."

Lantern. Of course that was why there was light in the closet. Duh. "Sorry again. I didn't think."

"You did hit your head." She tugged my arm as she shuffled forward, her feet making scuffing noises on the floor. "Ow. Found the step up."

My toes bumped the step, too, and we turned the corner into the hallway. It was some lighter here, but still dark. The rain continued to sluice onto the floor in sheets, as wind wreaked havoc on the trees outside.

"Should we see if there are shutters here?" I frowned at the floors. They were going to be ruined. I shouldn't care. Why did I care? Maybe because the architecture spoke to me in some deep, soothing way. Or maybe because I'd hit my head and I was grateful for any sort of safety from the storm that raged outside.

"If you want. But let's get the lantern and bags and move into the living room. It's a better space for hunkering down." Sunny marched down the hall toward the bedroom that held the closet we'd been in when I woke up.

With a shrug, I followed. She didn't need to lift all the bags by herself. Although, she'd had to do that when she found this place. And me.

I frowned.

When I entered the closet, she already had three of the bags slung over her shoulders.

"Let me get the rest." I reached for one of the emergency supply bags. My ribs protested, but I ignored it. "How did you get all this, and me, into the house?"

She picked up the lantern. "A little at a time. You were the hardest, but you came to enough to help some. You don't remember?"

I shook my head.

"Hm. Maybe you lost a teeny bit of time with the knock you gave yourself." She didn't elaborate and I could only stare as she left the room, taking all the light—physically and metaphorically—along with her.

I hurried to follow, my muscles protesting as the bags banged against me.

Back in the living room, Sunshine had arranged everything near the fireplace. It was centered on a wall and far enough from what had been the glass walls that the floor looked dry. Ish.

I tripped on the step down and took a couple of jogging steps to avoid falling.

"Careful!" Sunny lurched to her feet, arms outstretched. "Maybe you should sit down."

"I'm fine." My face was hot. "Just clumsy."

"Sit anyway, okay?" She took the bags off my shoulders and finished her arranging. "Use this as a backrest."

"I can help. Honestly. I'm fine." I crossed my arms.

Sunny tipped her head to the side and lifted her eyebrows. "Really?"

I nodded.

"Okay." She drilled a finger into my ribs.

I sucked a breath in through my teeth as pain radiated out from her touch.

"Sit." She pointed to the clever arrangement of bags that

would probably end up being comfortable. Because apparently Sunshine knew everything there was to know about making the best of a shipwreck situation.

"Fine." I scowled at her and stomped over to sit where she'd indicated. I crossed my arms. "Now what?"

"Now, maybe you need some aspirin and a nap." She squatted beside one of the emergency bags and dug through until she pulled out a first aid kit. She unzipped it and rifled through the pockets until she found a sealed packet of pain reliever. "Here."

I eyed the packet. I really wanted to refuse, just on principle. But my ribs had gone from aching to actively hurting, and my head was throbbing. As was my ankle. With a sigh, I took the packet and ripped it open. I shook the pills into my hand then tossed them into my mouth. It took a moment to work up enough saliva to swallow them, but they went down.

Most of the way, at least.

"Let me get you some water." Sunshine dug around in the bag again until she tugged out a bottle. She stood and jogged back to the hall.

She was back before I could wonder where she was getting water.

"It's rain." She shrugged as she offered me the bottle. "But I figure at this point, it's clean enough and better than nothing."

I took the bottle and drank deeply. Honestly, at this point I wasn't worried about the quality of the rain water. It was a relief to get the pills unstuck and quench the thirst that had been building without me realizing it. "Thanks."

"You're welcome." She smiled slightly. "I'm serious about the nap. Do you want a blanket?"

"I don't want to nap." I sighed. I heard the petulant whine for what it was. "But I guess. Yeah."

Wordlessly, Sunshine reached into the emergency bag again

and pulled out a small square of shiny foil. She opened the packaging and shook out the space blanket, then draped it over my legs and torso.

I shifted to a more reclined and slightly comfier position. "What will you do?"

Sunshine settled on the floor a couple of armlengths away. She pulled a paperback out of the pocket of the duffel she leaned against. "I have a book."

I wanted to caution her about reading in the dim light. But then I actually noticed the lantern light and what it did to her face and I lost my train of thought. "You're beautiful."

Sunshine shook her head. "You hit your head. Go to sleep."

I wanted to protest, but the look she gave me left no room for argument. She opened her book and I could feel the purposeful way she didn't look at me. Fine.

I turned my head and studied the tilework around the as-yet-unlit fireplace. Between the dim light, the sound of the storm raging outside, the warmth of the blanket, and my injuries, my eyes drifted shut.

14

SUNSHINE

I'd been staring at the same page in my book for the last ten minutes and I wouldn't have been able to tell someone what it was about if they'd offered me a billion dollars.

I looked up through my eyelashes and silently let out a breath. Wes had closed his eyes. His chest moved evenly as he breathed. Slept.

I closed the book and set it aside, his words ping-ponging in my head. I was not beautiful. I knew this about myself. I could accept "cute," maybe even "pretty" on a good-hair day. But not beautiful. I wasn't ugly. I didn't have horrible self-esteem or anything, either. I just believed in being realistic.

Luca hadn't even said I was beautiful. And he'd loved me with everything in him. The same way I'd loved him.

Look where that had gotten us.

Nowhere.

He was gone. We'd never gotten around to starting a family. All I had were memories of him, and they were all tied to these islands. It was one of the reasons I stayed. If I left—pushing aside the whole "where would I go" question—would Luca fade away into nothing? Besides, my life was here.

Well, not *here* here. This island—name unknown from what I could tell without electronic input—held neither my life nor memories of Luca.

And so it was going to hold memories of Wes.

I wasn't sure what to do with that.

When the storm was over and it was safe for rescue missions to get underway, we'd get off the island and he'd go home to Virginia and his friend group. I'd go back to my beach cottage and a life of driving boats with the occasional afternoon hangout with Zee.

It was fine. Good, even.

I'd be all right.

I always was.

I closed my eyes. I might insist on being realistic when it came to my looks, but I recognized delusion when I heard it. Of course I wasn't all right. I hadn't been all right since Luca. And that was long enough that I was ready to declare that whatever this current state of being I was in was the new definition of all right.

Nothing else seemed reasonable.

But I was going to miss Wes.

And that was stupid.

I pushed to my feet and glanced at his sleeping form. I pressed my lips together and fought the urge to stretch out next to him, pillow my head on his shoulder, and drift off to sleep myself.

Instead, I picked up the lantern and continued my exploration of the abandoned house. It had been gorgeous once. From the state of things, no one had lived here for at least a year. Maybe two. I headed away from the bedrooms to explore the rooms on the other side of the one where we were now set up. The first appeared to be a dining room, if the built-in console that ran the length of a short wall was any indication. I could picture it loaded down with dishes and platters and bowls for easy serving during a party. The chandelier hanging in the center of the ceiling was another clue.

I continued on, past another bathroom and the kitchen, to the garage. I blinked as I studied the ATV and golf cart parked inside. It made sense. Whoever had lived here certainly hadn't needed a typical car. From what I'd seen as I'd dragged everything to the house, there weren't paved roads—although there was a spot on the horizon, near the far edge of the island, that might have been. But it also could have been a trick of the light during the storm.

Why hadn't these been taken, too?

To move onto an island like this, the owner would have had to get furniture delivered. And, before that, building supplies. The furniture had been taken when they left, so why not the vehicles?

Strange.

I looked away from the vehicles. The shelves that lined one wall of the garage were empty. But there, under the bottom rack, was a stack of firewood.

I smiled and stepped fully into the space.

Wes hadn't asked about how we were going to light the fire. I considered that part of his head injury, honestly. So far on this trip, he'd been pretty quick to identify problems and help find solutions. But with the storm raging outside, it wasn't as if cutting down a tree was an option. And any deadfall would be soaked.

I'd had backups in mind. There were dry floorboards we could pry up. Cabinets in the kitchen. But I hadn't wanted to start destroying the house if we could avoid it.

Now it looked like we could.

I gathered four of the split logs into my arms, ignoring the twinge of my back. I'd pay for all the heavy lifting I'd been doing, but hopefully not until Wes was back to one hundred percent. Or, better, not until we'd been rescued.

I lugged the wood and lantern back to the living room, careful to step around Wes and be as quiet as I could. The only major benefit of hurricanes was that they moved fast. We shouldn't be facing landfall, either, so we'd just get hit by the arms. Not that that was minor.

If I had to guess, I would put this storm at a category three. Maybe even a four. When it did hit land? It was going to do some serious damage.

Even still, I was holding out hope that the boat would somehow escape the brunt of it and we'd be able to swim out, climb aboard, and rescue ourselves.

In my heart, I knew it wasn't likely. But it was still absolutely my prayer.

It took a few minutes to figure out how to open the flue. I didn't understand the previous owners at all. Why close the fire-place flue but leave the storm shutters open? Whatever. When I finally figured that out, I got a small fire going with one log. Enough to add light and allow us to heat water once Wes woke. Not enough to add much to the heat.

I settled back against the bags and finally gave in to the temptation to let my gaze rove over Wes as he slept. For the first time since Luca died, it didn't feel dishonest to notice a man. I wanted to be grateful.

Instead? I was conflicted.

I scooted closer. Not close enough that we were touching, but it wouldn't hurt to lie nearby. Would it?

I NOTICED three things when I woke: the slow, steady heartbeat that thumped under my cheek, the quiet outside, and the weight of an arm locking me in place. For those first few, sleepy moments, I thought it was Luca. I breathed in, expecting the warm, familiar scent of my husband. But while it was a pleasing mix of man, rain, sea, and sweat that met my senses, it wasn't Luca.

Wes.

My eyes flew open. I shifted, gently. His eyes remained closed. His breathing was deep and steady.

I swallowed.

I needed to move. I *definitely* didn't need to lie here reveling in the sensation of being held. And I needed to figure out a way to erase this memory from my consciousness.

I reached down and slowly eased his arm off me and onto his abdomen. I got a brief mental flash of him standing shirtless on the deck of the yacht. My mouth watered and my gaze flicked up to his mouth.

No.

Bad idea all-around for more reasons than I could count.

I scooted away, careful to keep my movements slow and quiet. When I'd created space between us, I crawled across the room to where I'd initially set up a resting spot for myself and stood.

What had I been thinking?

I gave myself a mental tongue lashing as I used one of the extra logs I'd brought in from the garage to prod the fire in the hearth back to life. Then I dug out the small camping pot, took the lantern, and headed into the hallway. I blinked in the light when I turned the corner, then spun and set the lantern back on the floor in the living room. If Wes woke while I was gone, he'd probably piece together that I'd gone this way.

I looked out through the trees to the water. I could see the yacht, still stuck on the rocks, tipped slightly to the left. I frowned. That was probably bad.

I needed to swim out and check. If I hadn't used the inflatable as a gurney to lug Wes into the house, it wouldn't have huge rips in it and I could get back out there much easier. I sighed. I'd make the same decision again.

But first, food.

I strode down the hall to the end where a door led outside. Rainwater buckets lined the outside wall of the house and I blessed the previous owner for their forethought as I dipped into the pot.

I took a moment to breathe in the clean, fresh post-storm air. The sky was clear. The water was calm.

Other than the water dripping off the trees, and the branches littering the ground, it would be easy to doubt there'd ever been a storm.

I carried the pot back into the house and to the living room. Wes still slept.

Good.

I wasn't ready to interact with him yet. I needed to get myself back under control. Find the professional footing I was so proud of. Because I had taken plenty of good-looking single men on boat trips. Granted, not usually as a solo passenger, but that shouldn't matter.

I opened the bag that held our emergency food and found a freeze-dried breakfast scramble. My stomach rumbled as I read the description. It wouldn't taste as good as it sounded—I'd been camping enough to know that—but it was better than a granola bar.

I put the pot on the hearth near the flames. There was no rack. No way to put the thing *on* the fire. So we'd just have to hope that proximity would get it boiling.

My gaze flicked over to Wes. Proximity to some things could certainly make heat.

Ugh.

I looked away. He was my *client*. I was responsible for getting him safely home. At which point, I would never see him again.

I should have gone and slept in the closet by myself. I certainly shouldn't have moved closer like I had. Thankfully, right now I was the only one of us who knew what had happened. So. Good. I would pretend I hadn't woken up in his arms. I would ignore the blissful delight it had caused from my head to my toes. We would figure out how to get out of this mess we were in. And we would go our separate ways.

I moved closer to the fire and stared into the pot.

"Pretty sure that's how you keep it from ever boiling." Wes's voice, low and husky with sleep, did crazy things to my insides.

I forced my lips into a smile before I turned. "I've heard something like that. But I'm hungry. You?"

"I could eat." He pushed himself up and twisted from one side to the other before rolling his head in circles. "I'm too old to sleep on the floor."

I laughed. "I'm older than you."

"You're too old to sleep on the floor then, too." He flashed a grin and wobbled to his feet. "Did the storm stop?"

I nodded. "We should open the shutters again, let some light in."

"Any idea what time it is?"

"Not really. Judging by the sky, I'd say midafternoon. But I could be completely off." I shrugged.

Wes walked over to the shutters and squatted down. He grabbed the bottom and yanked as he stood. The shutters opened with intermittent squeaks of metal as they rolled back into their storage location.

Sunlight poured into the room.

"Wow. Look at that view." Wes hooked his hands behind his back and stared outside.

It was gorgeous. The clear, blue sky met the ocean on the

horizon. Waves lapped at the beach. Birds chirped. But what truly drew my gaze was the man looking out. If we hadn't just sheltered from a hurricane, I would consider this a stand-in for Eden.

Hissing from the hearth drew my gaze away from the view. I grinned. "Guess you're right."

"About?"

I gestured to the pot. "I looked at the view and the water boiled. Eggs?"

"You have eggs?" Wes crossed the room to where I sat.

I held up the pouches. "Don't get too excited."

He chuckled. "Still better than starving. Eggs it is. Any chance you have hot sauce?"

"Maybe? Check that duffel." I indicated the correct one with a nod. "Grab forks while you're at it?"

"Sure."

I picked up the pot and splashed some water into each of the pouches. It would be better if I could measure it, but that was out. So I tried to keep the liquid to a minimum. I put the pot back down on the hearth and shook the bags carefully to mix the water around.

"Here." Wes offered me a fork.

I set one of the bags down and used the fork to stir the first. Then repeated the process. "Now we wait."

"Wait? I'm hungry." His stomach growled, emphasizing his point.

I laughed. "Trust me."

"Fine." He gave a mock sigh, then smiled. "Maybe I'll go visit the facilities."

"Sure. Probably be ready when you get back."

Wes nodded and I forced myself not to watch him walk away.

Oh boy. I had it bad.

15

WES

"Are you sure about this?" I stood on the beach with Sunshine and stared out at the yacht. "It doesn't seem like the best idea."

"I'm sure. We need to see if the boat is usable. And maybe, now that the sky is clear again, the satellites will connect and I can get in touch with Zee." She turned and crossed her arms. "That boat's the only way we're getting you home on any kind of reasonable timeline."

I frowned. "Let me go. Or I'll come with you."

She shook her head. "You're still injured. You have an open wound on your head."

"It's glued closed. That's about as not open as it gets." I set my jaw. "I don't like you going out there by yourself."

"I'm in charge here. What I say goes."

"What you say is stupid. I'm coming too."

"Look, buster." She jabbed her finger into my chest and my eyebrows raised. "You're staying here. I'm going out there." She jabbed in the direction of the boat. "End of conversation."

I held up my hands. What had gotten into her? She'd been

off—just a little—since I woke up. Maybe it was the situation. I could understand that, sort of. But it didn't feel like that was the issue. "All right. Fine. You're the boss. Do you think you could have Zee touch base with my emergency contact and just let them know I'm okay?"

"Of course." Her face softened a little. "I shouldn't be long."

I fought the urge to roll my eyes. The swim alone would take her some time. I could see the boat from the shore, sure, but there was a reason we'd used the inflatable to get to the island in the first place. I sighed and lowered myself to the beach. She might not be letting me come along, but I wasn't going back in the house. I was sitting right there and doing what I could to make sure she was all right.

Which, admittedly, was very little. But whatever.

Sunshine kicked off her shoes and walked out into the water. There was a decent stretch of wadable beach out there. She was able to walk, the water just up to her waist, maybe a quarter of the way to the boat. Then, with a brief wiggle of her fingers over her shoulder at me, she dove into an oncoming wave and began to swim.

She had great form.

She had *a* great form, but I wasn't concentrating on that. At all.

Her strong strokes pushed her through the water. It was mesmerizing to watch.

The guys would give me no end of grief about this. All of it. I probably wouldn't mind as much if it was just the hurricane. Who would have predicted it? Other than, of course, having come down here during hurricane season, so yeah. There was that. It was early enough in the year that most of the time nothing should have gone wrong.

But this...*thing*...I'd developed for Sunshine? They were

going to tease me mercilessly. If I protested or dismissed them, they'd do the whole bit about objecting too much. Maybe it'd go away once I was back home and she was here.

That was more likely than anything. Sunshine just happened to be the only woman I'd been around, and we'd been together twenty-four seven. Which meant we'd either drive each other crazy or we'd end up like this.

Whatever this was.

And pushing aside that she didn't seem to be feeling any of the same things I was.

Major bummer.

I'd had the best dream, too. It had been so real. I'd felt her snuggled up against me. Talk about delusional. If that had happened, surely she would have had something to say about it this morning. But she didn't. So it had to have been a dream. I definitely wasn't going to bring it up. How would I even do that?

Oh, hey, Sunny, did you happen to snuggle me last night?

I snickered. She'd give me that look that she had and mention my head injury the same way she did when I'd told her she was beautiful.

I cringed.

Talk about an idiotic move. Of course, most women I'd met in my life—scratch that, *every* woman I'd ever met in my life—tended to like knowing someone found them beautiful. But not Sunshine.

Of course not Sunshine.

Why did I like that about her?

I sighed and watched as she finished the swim to the boat. The sun heated my arms and legs, but the breeze off the water kept it from getting hot.

She swam around to the back. Probably using the swim step to get aboard, which was smart. But I didn't like losing sight of her. A couple of minutes ticked by and I was about to go after her, despite what she'd said, when I saw her waving broadly from the deck.

I waved back and relaxed. She was there. Safe. And despite her saying it wouldn't take long, there was plenty for her to do. Which meant sitting here on the beach watching was bordering on stupid. I couldn't help her if she needed it. Not now.

Fine.

I stood, brushed the sand off my pants, and looked around. My gaze landed on a well-worn path. A walk sounded like just the thing. Maybe I'd find something useful and be able to contribute to the situation instead of having to be the one making problems worse for Sunny.

The path went along the front of the house. I paused and admired the clean, long lines of the building, picturing what it might look like with the glass in place. Was the diving here any good? Would we be here long enough that I could convince Sunshine to let me find out?

The seed of an idea rooted in my mind as I continued to walk.

I passed a section of yard near the house where raised planting beds were laid out in three rows of three. I smiled and moved closer. Even without someone tending them, some of the plants had grown and produced vegetables. The storm had bent or broken everything, but that didn't mean we couldn't gather what was there. I'd rather have fresh veggies than another of the weird rehydrated egg scrambles.

I could honestly go the rest of my life without eating rehydrated eggs again.

I snagged a fat, red tomato before continuing along the path. There were slight ruts on either side that suggested some kind of small vehicle traversed this way frequently. There was a little overgrowth, but not much. Clearly this place hadn't been deserted for too long. A year? Maybe two?

The path led under the canopy of trees and I hesitated. It wasn't likely to be a wild, untamed jungle. There was a house here, after all. But I also didn't know what kinds of animals I might encounter. Could snakes end up on an island? Any sort of big cat? I honestly had no idea.

I bit my lip and glanced back the way I'd come.

"Don't be a chicken, Wes." I muttered.

Fine. Ugh. I kept walking, my pace increasing as the jungle thickened. Jungle? It certainly wasn't the type of forest I was used to, so the word would work. But locals—not that there were any specifically to this island...probably—more than likely had a different word for it.

I was almost at a jog when the path brought me out from under the trees. I slowed to a walk, then stopped. A grin slowly spread over my face. There was pavement ahead. And not just any kind of pavement. That was definitely a runway. There was even a bright orange windsock, slightly tattered, fluttering on a pole at the near end.

I hurried to the edge of the pavement and propped my hands on my hips. Oh, yeah. If the satellite connection was working again, I could get in touch with the pilots, give them our coordinates, and we'd be home in no time.

Even more than that, this island was incredible. I turned to look back toward the house. I could make out bits and pieces through the trees, and there was a good view of the beach, too. I continued to turn, but the far side of the island was a mystery. There had to be a way to explore. I could walk, if nothing else, but I wished again that the inflatable was still a viable boat. Wouldn't it be amazing to go around the whole thing and see what was what?

Maybe there was a better marina. Surely private islands with airstrips also had boat access. Obviously, we'd chosen the wrong beach. Not that we'd chosen, really. I'd managed to run into rocks because Sunny had been busy working out a plan.

And that wasn't on her.

She was a great teacher.

Driving a boat wasn't anything I'd wanted to learn. Certainly not in the middle of dire circumstances. But she'd been clear and calm and made it seem easy. I wouldn't be ready to go on my own, but it was nice to know I could handle things in a pinch.

Or sort of.

There was the whole rock situation, after all.

The only other big question I had? What was the diving like here?

Well, that, and was the island for sale? Or just abandoned.

I turned back to the airstrip and walked onto the pavement. It was in decent shape, even after the hurricane. Not crazy long, but enough for the kind of plane I owned with the guys. And that was a large enough craft to take a small dive group.

I'd still want to do more commercial trips. They'd be cheaper, probably, for one. Plus, I could arrange it so people who wanted to do other things in the island could set up a few days of diving and then go off and do the rest of their vacation on their own. Some of the dive operators I'd talked to had been happy to suggest tour operators who handled hikes and zip lines and all those sorts of experiences.

I nodded once, then started back down the path to the beach.

Sunshine was going to be excited.

Well, unless the equipment was damaged and we didn't actually have a way to get in touch with anyone. That would put a kink in the plans. But I was going to choose to believe we were on our way home.

A sharp pang speared through my chest.

Home.

Away from Sunshine. And the islands.

That was the down side. And it was a big one.

But it wasn't as if she and I had any kind of future. Honestly, she would probably be glad to get rid of me. That dream of her snuggling against me might have felt real, but it was definitely wishful thinking.

I could be honest and admit I was interested in her, here under the canopy of dripping trees where no one but the birds could see me. But I was old enough to know that nothing could come from my infatuation. There were too many obstacles.

Number one? She didn't see me that way.

"Get a grip, man." I sighed and continued trudging toward the beach. I wasn't going to let those thoughts derail the happy news that there was an airstrip. That was important. More important than anything else.

I passed the house, pausing again to look up and imagine what it would look like fixed up. I might need to add some guest cottages. The main house would work for eating and hanging out in the evenings though. I'd have to see how horrible it would be to hire some help, too. We'd need a caretaker to keep things clean. Probably not full time, although I wouldn't mind if someone wanted to live on the island yearround. Then, when groups were here, I'd need a chef. Probably housekeeping, too.

There were a lot of details to consider.

I rubbed my hands together in anticipation. I couldn't wait to get started figuring it out.

I crossed the beach to the spot where I'd watched Sunshine swim out to the boat. I could see her sitting on the main deck, head bent.

I frowned.

What was she doing? Praying? Crying? Talking to someone? Reading?

I groaned, frustrated. She was too far away to tell. And she was too far away for yelling to do any good, either. So I'd stand here, watching, willing her to look up and see me. Maybe she'd be able to give some kind of indication which way things were going.

I stood long enough that my legs started to get tired. She'd moved around some—I took that as a good sign—but she never looked back toward the shore. Maybe she'd given up on that after I disappeared to explore? But why wouldn't she check occasionally?

I sank to the sand, my gaze still locked on the boat.

Gradually, the light began to change. I looked up at the sky. Where was the sun? She couldn't be planning to swim back after dark, could she? I'd swim out to her before I'd let that happen.

Finally, she looked up and out. I waved my arms over my head.

She waved back.

I pointed to my wrist. Hopefully she'd get the point.

Sunshine leaned out and looked up at the sky, then pulled her head back in. I watched as she moved around, unable to determine exactly what she was doing, but I let myself believe she was tidying up and getting ready to swim back.

She moved toward the aft, and disappeared. I held my breath, waiting for her to appear in the water on her way back to shore. Then she did and I breathed out. Good.

I had to admire her strong strokes. She was clearly at home in the water. And that was just one more reason nothing could ever happen between us. I lived near the Potomac River, sure. But no one swam there. The ocean—and any decent beaches—were hours away. Throw in the hustle and bustle of the area, the complete opposite of island time, and it would be like expecting a bird to live underwater.

Could I relocate here permanently?

I frowned, then shook my head. Not really. I might be willing to try, if she asked, but I had the shop. I'd put so much time and energy, and money, into it. I wanted to make it succeed. I wanted to be personally involved every step of the way.

And there was the gang.

Not that I thought any of them would object if I had to leave because I'd fallen in love. Not that I had. But I'd miss them. I wanted to be cool Uncle Wes to their kids. I wanted to clean their clocks at poker. And I needed their steady encouragement to continue to walk with Jesus even when it was hard.

They were my brothers in every way but blood, and I couldn't just walk away from that.

What was I doing even thinking that way? Sunshine might be everything I ever imagined finding in a woman, but that didn't mean we belonged together.

And if we did? God was going to have to figure that out. Because I certainly didn't have the answers.

"It works!" Sunshine reached the shallower water and began jogging to the shore. "I was able to get in touch with Zee. Boy was she glad to hear from me. I gave her the coordinates and she's going to work on a plan to get us. But it could take upwards of a week. She said the storm did a ton of damage to the islands nearest us. They're without power and probably will be for a while."

I stood and brushed off the sand. "Puerto Rico has power though?"

"Yeah, the storm is still heading west. They're now saying it'll make landfall in Mexico in a day or two. It's already back up to a category five, so it's liable to do a lot of damage there, too."

"Yikes." I made a mental note to pray for the people in the

path of the storm. I'd been entirely too focused on my own situation, especially since I wasn't in dire straits. "What would you say if I told you we don't have to wait a week?"

Sunshine stopped a few feet from me and tipped her head to the side. "The boat needs an overhaul. I was able to patch it enough that it stopped taking on water, but it's not seaworthy."

"There's an airstrip." I pointed in the direction of my discovery and grinned. "I can get in touch with my plane and they can come get us."

She blinked.

My smile faltered. "Is that a bad idea?"

"No. It's great. I just—wow." She shook her head. "I didn't even think—"

"Neither did I. But I went for a walk and there it was. You have our coordinates, right? So it should be doable." I tucked my hands in my pockets to keep from reaching out to...I wasn't sure what I wanted to do. Shake her? Hug her? Well, obviously hug her. I worked to keep my voice casual. "We won't even need to hunt around for a volleyball to name."

Sunshine laughed.

The tension between us eased.

"I don't think swimming back out now is a good idea. Not with the sun starting to set. But first thing tomorrow, we can head out to the boat and you can make those arrangements. And I'll let Zee know." She closed the distance between us and patted my shoulder. "What do you say about dinner?"

"I say, 'let's eat.' And also wonder if you're up for adding some fresh produce to that meal. I found a garden bed. The plants are broken and knocked over, but the tomato I ate was still delicious." If she wanted things to be light, I would keep them light. I was probably—no, definitely—imagining the hint of disappointment in her face when I'd mentioned a faster rescue.

"I can go for fresh veggies. Lead on." Sunshine cast a quick glance over her shoulder toward the boat. "The water off this beach would be great for snorkeling."

I started down the path that led in front of the house and, ultimately, to the garden patch. Sunshine fell into step beside me. "Yeah? Think the diving is good, too?"

"Maybe we can find out tomorrow. After the arrangements are made. Tanks are plenty full for something short. It'd be a good way to pass the time."

I nodded slowly. "Provided we'll have enough non-diving time before the plane gets here. I'd like that."

"They'd be coming from the States, right?"

"Yeah. They were going to head back to Virginia in case the other guys needed or wanted to go somewhere."

"So we should be fine, but we can do the math tonight and make sure we keep things safe." She brushed my side as we turned the corner on the path.

I gestured to the little garden and grinned at her expression. We gathered up everything that looked good, using my shirt as a makeshift basket. Then we headed back the way we came and up to the entrance of the house.

I wanted to grab her and pull her close. I didn't care that she was still dripping from her swim. Now that a plan was in place, it was like there was a giant, ticking countdown timer booming over our heads.

I swallowed the words I wanted to say. There was no future here. I needed to get past that idea. No matter how much I might want to talk with her and see if there was any sort of chance, it wasn't fair to do that.

I shouldn't—couldn't—put her on the spot like that. Especially not right now when we were still trapped in this space. Sure, there were other rooms where she could sleep. But it wasn't as if she could truly get away and be alone.

So I would keep quiet and we'd continue being friendly. And if that hurt? Well, I was man enough to take it.

We made our way down the hall to the living room.

Sunshine dug into the emergency rations and pulled out some packages. "Our dinner options are beef stroganoff or cowboy stew."

"Yum."

She laughed. "The stroganoff is pretty good. The stew isn't awful."

"I'll take good over not awful. Wait. How did you classify the eggs this morning?" I went to the fireplace and studied the logs. Once upon a time, I'd been able to do this. Maybe I'd remember the tricks.

"Not awful." Her voice was full of laughter. "Stick with the stroganoff. I'll have the stew, that way there's still another of each for tomorrow."

I lit a match and held it under the bottom log. "And we have granola bars."

"True. You can do that instead of eggs tomorrow morning."

"I accept." I dropped the match and blew on my fingers. It burned for a moment, then went out. "Do we have anything that would pass as kindling?"

"I can do it." Sunshine came over to the fireplace. She nudged the pot toward me with her foot. "Why don't you go fill this from the rain barrels?"

"All right. I'll be Gunga Din."

She shook her head. "You have weird cultural references."

"I like movies." I shrugged and picked up the pot. "Old ones. New ones. Doesn't matter. At least I haven't mentioned having a brain cloud."

"Except you just did. Thankfully, we have no volcano here, so I'm not going to call you Joe. So we should be good. Get the water. Dinner awaits."

I headed back down the hall to the rain barrels outside. She was entirely too close to perfect. Definitely not a flibbertigibbet, if I was going to keep the movie reference intact.

I sighed.

Too bad sailing off into the sunset was off the table.

16

SUNSHINE

I ran my hand over the leather that covered the plane's seat and had to force myself to keep my jaw locked so it didn't drop. This plane was...beyond.

I looked over at Wes. He was tipped back in his seat, eyes closed. Like this was no big deal. I guess, to him, it wasn't.

Talk about being from two different planets.

This was *his plane*. Even if he was quick to qualify that he shared ownership with his friends, all of them were billionaires in their own right. Sharing the plane didn't make it better. He still owned it.

And if I understood what he was muttering about yesterday after we did our short dive? He was considering buying that island.

Who bought an island?

Even more, who talked about doing so as if it was no big deal? Obviously, for Wes, it wasn't a big deal. But he talked about it like I'd talk about buying new flip flops. Honestly, I think I probably put more thought into new beach shoes than he was putting into the island. Especially since he'd have to sink even more into the place to make it habitable.

Would he live there?

My heart raced at the thought of Wes being near enough that I could reach him on a boat.

Dumb.

I couldn't say he hadn't given any indication that he was interested. I'd caught a few looks. A few touches that he probably could have avoided, if he'd wanted to. But he wasn't making a move.

It was for the best. We were on our way back to Puerto Rico. Just a two-hour flight, since we didn't have to deal with commercial airlines and all the hassles thereof. Just one more nice aspect of private air travel: flights were always direct, unless you didn't want them to be for some reason.

"Do you want something to drink?" Wes didn't open his eyes.

"I thought you were asleep."

"Just resting my eyes."

I snickered. "Okay, old man."

He opened one eye and glared at me. "Careful."

"Oooh. Or what?" Why was I flirting? Hadn't I just had this conversation with myself? Ugh. No willpower. At. All.

"I'll call you old lady." He smiled and unfastened his seatbelt. "I'm getting a soda. Want one?"

"If you're up, sure. Although, I'd rather have cold, bubbly water. I don't imagine that's available?"

"Let me see. We usually keep it pretty well stocked in here. I know for a fact that Whitney and Kayla both like that stuff." He moved into the little galley area toward the back of the plane.

I listened as bottles clinked. It wasn't long before Wes came back with a tray holding a can of Coke, a bottle of Perrier, a tall glass filled with ice, and a little bowl of lime wedges.

He paused in front of me with the tray. "I wasn't sure if you wanted a glass, but you mentioned cold specifically."

"This is perfect. Thank you." I looked up and met his gaze. I swallowed and had to look away. He couldn't see how much I wished things were different. It wasn't fair to him. Or to me. But I wasn't worried about myself. He was young. His life was still ahead of him. And fine, it wasn't as though I was dying tomorrow, but I also wouldn't be having kids.

Wes could.

And he should.

He'd be good at it.

I took a lime wedge from the bowl and squeezed it over the ice, then accepted the glass and bottle without meeting his gaze again. "Thanks."

"No problem." His voice was neutral.

I kept my gaze on my glass as I poured water into it, careful to keep it from fizzing over.

"There's a cup holder in the arm."

"Thanks. Again." I looked up with a brief smile before setting the bottle into the cup holder. I took a long drink of the water and sighed. "This hits the spot."

"I'm glad." Wes popped the tab on his Coke. "So. What's next for you? Another charter? Or do you get some time off?"

"Um. I'll probably take some time. I don't work a set schedule, really. Just take the jobs as they come. As I need them." I flashed a grin. "Pretty sure I'll get some kind of hazard bonus for surviving a hurricane."

He chuckled. "If you don't, let me know and I'll make it right. I appreciate you saving my hide. And hey, you found me an island."

"All part of the service." I took another sip of water. "You're really buying the island?"

"I'm really going to look into it. If not that one, then I'll poke around and see what's available. My mom suggested it initially, but I thought it was ridiculous." He shrugged and drank. "It might be. But now that I've gotten a taste for what it could be, I have to look into it."

I nodded. That made sense. Once I got past the whole "had the money to purchase a literal island" thing. I'd been thrilled when I had enough money to make a downpayment on my one-bedroom beach cottage.

"I might see about going on the salvage mission. I like that yacht. It'd be a shame if they weren't careful when they went to fetch it." I sighed. Of course, it would depend on the insurance, but I hoped they'd fix it up and get it back into service. There should be so many more voyages on the horizon for it.

"She's a good boat." He set his Coke in the cupholder. "You call them she, right? Boats are feminine?"

"For the people who truly care, yes. But I seem to recall mentioning that I wasn't hardnosed about seafaring language." I sipped my water. "And I don't like parrots, for the record."

He laughed. "I'll keep that in mind. There goes my thank-you gift idea."

I shuddered. "Don't you know you never give someone a live animal as a gift?"

"I think I heard that. I don't even give plants, so you're safe." Wes played with the tab on his soda can. When he looked up at me, his face was serious. "Thank you, Sunshine. For everything."

"You're welcome." I blinked my burning eyes and looked away. "If you ever need another charter, I hope you'll request me."

"Count on it."

It was a hollow promise. I knew it. He probably did, too. He was going to buy an island and fly in and out. He didn't need another charter. And the idea of taking anyone else out made my breath hitch.

Dumb.

This was my livelihood. I couldn't afford to start thinking it wouldn't be the same without Wes. It wouldn't. Of course it wouldn't. But that didn't matter. I swallowed.

"The two of you should buckle up. We're starting our approach to San Juan." The pilot's voice was actually understandable through the speakers. Chalk up another good point of private air travel.

I tugged on the loose end of my lap belt and took another drink of water. Maybe taking a break was a bad idea.

I could tell Zee I wanted the next available charter. That was probably a better option than salvage and recovery. I didn't need to do anything that was going to remind me of Wes. I'd be better off—so much better off—jumping into new experiences that would minimize memories of this trip.

The plane bounced gently on the tarmac, then slowed.

"This is my stop." I drained the water in my glass and looked around for where to put it.

"I can take it." Wes reached out. His fingers brushed mine. "Can I do anything to help? Grab your bags and walk you out? Anything?"

"Nah. I've got it. And you should get back in the air and on your way home. I imagine your friends are pretty excited to see you and make sure you're okay."

He nodded. "Yours, too. Right?"

There wasn't really anyone who fit that bill. Zee, maybe. But she'd been fine once she knew I was all right. In the interest of keeping things professional—or more accurately, putting them back into that professional space—I just nodded. "Absolutely. Thanks for the lift."

His eyebrows shot up.

The plane stopped.

I unhooked my seatbelt and stood. "Stay safe, Wesley."

He looked like he was going to say more. Something in his

eyes told me it was better that I not hear it. Not if I wanted to keep my heart safe.

It wasn't too late for that. No matter what it felt like.

Losing Luca had shattered me and I'd really only just put myself back together. I couldn't go there again.

I hurried to the front of the plane. The pilot had just finished opening the door and I bolted down the stairs with a mumbled, "Thanks."

He followed me down and went to collect my bags from the luggage hold. Because of course I couldn't just run off. Put that in the "con" column for private air travel.

I didn't look back toward the door. If that made me a chicken, so be it. I didn't want to know if Wes had followed me. If he was watching, waiting until I looked to say whatever words he had that were sure to devastate me.

And if he wasn't?

That was almost worse.

Better not to know.

I took my two duffels from the pilot. "Thanks. Have a safe flight back to Virginia."

I strode toward the airport. It took everything I had not to peek over my shoulder. But I knew if I did I wasn't going to stay strong. I lifted my hand. It was a casual goodbye. Almost a brush off. But it had to be done.

I felt the crack in my heart as I pulled open the door into the little private air terminal. My eyes burned. I hurried around a corner, then leaned against the wall and stared up at the ceiling. My breath came fast and I knew I was going to break down if I couldn't get it under control.

I swallowed and squeezed my eyes shut.

"Miss? Are you all right?"

I felt the cool touch of fingers on my arm and opened my eyes.

The concerned face of a flight attendant looked back at me.

"Yes. Thanks. Just...been a day. You know?" I was proud that my voice didn't break. And talking, trying to keep things steady, seemed to help push my emotions back into the box where I preferred to keep them locked.

The woman—a quick glance down revealed her name was Angela, if her nametag could be trusted—chuckled. "I do. Are you catching a connecting flight?"

"No. This is home." It wasn't. But it was the home base for the charter company, and I needed to check in with them first. Then, maybe, I could take my personal boat and get back to my little beach cottage. Or, I could find a laundromat and jump into the next available charter. I still wasn't sure which was the right choice.

"Lucky you." Angela patted my arm. "I'll let you get home. I hope you know it'll be all right."

I wanted to make her promise, but instead I just nodded. "God's got this. I know."

Her smile broadened and she nodded.

I pushed off the wall and started in the direction of the bigger main terminal, following signs until I got to the transportation options.

Zee had offered to come pick me up, but she was needed there. My charter wasn't the only one that had been affected by the storm. Wes and I had gotten the worst of it, for sure, but several other boats had been forced to stay in port while waiting to see what was going to happen. Not surprisingly, customers were unhappy with having their plans curtailed.

Like we could control the weather.

I stepped out into the bright sunshine and made my way to the first taxi in the line that was parked and waiting. "Fairytale Charters, please."

The driver nodded. "Sure, I know it."

Maybe he did, maybe he didn't. He had a phone mounted on his dash and was using the GPS so we'd get there either way. I settled into the back seat and closed my eyes. It was the easiest way I could think to avoid conversation.

Before I was mentally ready to face Zee and all her knowing questions, the cab slowed to a stop.

"Fairytale Charters."

I opened my eyes, checked the readout on the meter, and dug out my wallet. I had cash to cover the fare plus a tip. It cleaned me out, but I could get more. "Thanks."

I grabbed my duffels, exited the cab, and strode up the sidewalk to the main entrance.

Zee manned the phones behind the counter inside. "Yes. Of course. Yes. Bye now."

She ripped off her headset and hurried from behind the counter, arms outstretched. "There you are."

I dropped my bags and let Zee engulf me in her tight hug. It was a little like being swallowed up by the Michelin Man, but it was more comforting than anything I could imagine.

A sob hitched in my throat. Then another. And then the dam broke.

"Shh, child." Zee rubbed circles on my back as I sobbed into her shoulder.

The storm raged longer than it should have. Long enough that as my tears dried and I hiccuped back the sobs, mortification set in.

"I'm sorry."

"No. You don't say that. Not to me." Zee leaned back and held my gaze. "After what you've been through, who wouldn't be upset?"

Upset was an understatement, and I loved her for it. I sighed. "Thanks, Zee.

"Always." She jerked her head toward the back office. "Let's get you some of that fancy water you love and you can tell me all about it."

"I'll take the water, but...can the rest wait?"

Zee tipped her head to the side and studied me. Finally, she nodded once. "All right. If that's what you want."

"It is." I didn't want to think about Wes right now. Or talk about him. Especially not to Zee, who was going to see more than I wanted her to. She already had her ideas about the two of us, since she was always on the lookout for someone for me. As if I needed a new husband to be whole.

Before Wes, I had brushed off the thought as ridiculous. Now? I could see where she was coming from.

Which was why it was impossible. Because it couldn't be just any man. It had to be Wes. And the reasons why that wouldn't work didn't change simply because I wished they would.

I followed Zee into the break room and sat in the chair that she pointed at. She opened the fridge and selected a bottle of Perrier.

"You brought that in just for me."

"Of course I did. Once I knew you were on your way back. Consider it my welcome home." Zee set the bottle on the table in front of me and took the seat across the way. "You don't want to talk about it."

"I don't. I'll write it up. I don't think we did anything wrong. And honestly, I don't see the client trying to come after us for negligence." Not when I'd inadvertently found him an island to buy. "We watched the weather. Took precautions. The majority of the models showed it heading north."

Zee nodded, but she watched me.

I shifted uncomfortably in my seat.

"Hmm."

I took a long drink of water from the bottle. "There's no hmm."

A slow grin spread across her face. "Mmmhmm."

"Zee."

"Sunny." She shook her head. "I won't push. Or say I told you so. But I want to."

"You're wrong." I drummed my fingers on the table. "Anyway, it wouldn't work. Whole bunch of reasons."

"Maybe. Maybe not. Doesn't mean you don't try."

I sighed. Hadn't that been the kind of thing I'd said about Luca? And that had worked beautifully. "Nobody gets a second chance at perfection, Zee."

"I don't believe that. But it doesn't matter what I believe. It matters what you believe. If that's your stance. You're right. I'll leave it alone." Zee took a deep breath and let it out. "What are your plans?"

"What do we have available?" Work was probably the right choice. If I was busy, I wouldn't mope.

"There's recovery, obviously. Did you want to be part of that?"

I bit my lip. I did. But I didn't. "I can be, if I'm needed."

Zee shook her head. "I don't think you are. Though you'd be welcome."

"Any clients?"

"We have a family coming to town tomorrow who want the sailboat. Just little trips between here, St. Thomas, and St. Croix. You could do it in your sleep."

I nodded. "That sounds like the perfect thing. Live aboard?"

"No. They have resorts lined up. I guess the wife isn't a great sailor."

I wrinkled my nose. That was less appealing. But it wouldn't be too bad, hopefully, if she stayed where she could see the horizon. "No one else is slated for it?"

"They just called. I haven't had a chance to look at the roster."

"I don't want to butt in line."

"You aren't. We don't work that way, you know that."

"All right." I took another long drink. "Sign me up. I guess I'll find a place to do laundry and crash. What time tomorrow?"

"After two. I'll email you all the details." Zee studied my face. "You're sure you don't want to go home?"

I wanted to go home. Desperately. But I'd wallow. Nothing good came from wallowing. "Work is better."

"Okay. You can crash at my place, you know."

I shook my head. "Appreciate the offer though."

I couldn't stay at Zee's. She might let me off the hook here at the office, but if I was at her place after hours? She'd drag every thought and feeling out of me. Even the ones I hadn't realized I had.

I wasn't ready for that.

I probably never would be.

I just needed time and space to stuff my feelings for Wes into a box where I could forget they existed.

Or at least pretend that I had.

17

WES

"Nice tan." Scott grinned as I opened the door of my townhouse. He held out a bag of chips. "I brought provisions. I wasn't sure if you were really up for hosting."

"I volunteered." I stepped out of the way and gestured for him to come in. "I set up the table in the back den."

"Kinda figured you volunteered before you got voluntold." Scott walked down the skinny hall that led from the front living room, through the dining and kitchen area and into the smaller room that had probably been an enclosed porch originally.

Sometimes I thought about taking it back to porch status, but the place was small enough that having more room on the main floor was always better. "Maybe. Doesn't mean I don't know how to get groceries delivered."

Scott set his chips next to the food I'd laid out on the buffet that ran along the far wall under the windows. "So I see. You even got subs?"

"I'm hungry. Figured we might as well have options." I paused, listening. "I think that was the door. Be right back."

I didn't wait for Scott to respond. It wasn't as if he was likely to have something important to say. He'd make a joke about the food—probably to do with my sub topping choices—I'd respond. I shrugged as I strode back to the front door. It was the kind of banter I enjoyed with my friends. And had missed, somewhat, while I was away.

I tugged open the door and laughed. "Did you all carpool or something?"

"Basically." Cody stepped into the house. "It was Tristan's idea. We're in the back?"

"Yeah." I stepped out of the way as the rest of the guys filed in and followed Cody. When they were all in, I closed the door and flipped the lock, then headed back myself.

Tristan already had a plate in his hand and was in the process of piling food onto it when I joined them.

"Nice spread. You should host more often." Tristan scooped a handful of chips onto his plate. "I'm starving."

"Been busy?" Austin took a plate off the top of the stack and began to fill it with food.

"I'm always busy." Tristan shrugged. "Seems like more now than usual though."

"You work for yourself. Can't you just tell people no?" Cody dug through the bucket of ice and drinks until he found a bottle of root beer. "Seems like that's one of the major perks of being your own boss."

Tristan sighed. "It's not always that easy."

Cody frowned. "It's one word, man. How is that hard?"

I chuckled. Tristan had a big heart. It didn't always seem to mesh well with his decision to be a lawyer, but once you got to know him it made perfect sense. "For someone like Tristan? It's pretty hard. You know that."

"I guess." Cody shook his head and took a seat at the round table covered with green felt. He reached for the cards and began to shuffle.

Austin brought his plate over and sat beside Cody. "Do we need to start sending food to you at dinner time, Tristan?"

Noah snickered. "That's a great idea. I can get the ladies at church on it."

"Don't you dare." Tristan scowled as he took a seat. "I eat. Just ends up being later than I'd like most days. Anyway, I think I'm finally at the end of this nasty divorce case that I got coerced into taking on. That'll make life a lot nicer."

"I thought you weren't doing divorces." Scott sat on the other side of Cody. "You hate them."

"I know. It was a whole thing. I can't get into it." Tristan scowled. "But I also couldn't get out of it. And the guy I'm representing is a real piece of work. He leaves a thick coating of slime all over everything anytime I have to talk to him."

I frowned. I knew that type. We got them in the dive classes now and then. Apparently, scuba was a manly sport and they wanted to show off how amazing they were. Then they realized they had to do some basic math and learn a little science to get certified and suddenly they were a lot less interested. "Sorry, man. Glad it's almost over though."

"Thanks." Tristan took a big bite from his sub. He chewed for a moment, swallowed, and continued. "It took a lot of finagling to get him to agree to a settlement in mediation. He really wanted to go to court and make a big spectacle. I won't be surprised if he decides to try to sue his ex when it's all over. But he'll need a new lawyer if he does."

"You going to be able to say no?" Scott popped the tab on his can of soda.

"Yeah." Tristan didn't elaborate.

I waited a moment to see if anyone else was going to speak, then nodded to Cody. "Why don't you deal and we'll get the game going?"

"Sure. And you can fill us in on the whole shipwreck thing."

Cody tossed cards into neat piles around the table. "Was there or was there not giant fish involvement."

"Har." I slapped my knee under the table. "I don't know why I missed you guys at all."

"That would imply he was running from God's will." Austin snagged his pile of cards.

"Exactly." I picked up my cards and fought to keep my face blank. I definitely wasn't winning this hand unless everyone else also got trash. "Which I was not. I also didn't get bit by a snake when lighting a fire, thankfully."

"Paul. Nice." Scott chuckled. "Any other biblical shipwrecks we need to discuss or can we get back to the whole two weeks on a yacht, alone with, from what I gather, a gorgeous older woman?"

Noah wiggled his eyebrows. "Ooooh. I'd forgotten that. Wes has always had a thing for the older ladies."

"I have not." My face heated. I set my cards face down on the table. "You guys are jerks."

"Classic redirection." Tristan shook his head. "Aus, we're waiting on you, man."

"Right. Sorry. I was distracted by all the over-the-top protesting going on over there by Wes." Austin tossed some chips into the center of the table.

"I'm not protesting! I'm simply setting the record straight." I crossed my arms. Why had I thought I missed these guys again?

"Uh-huh. What was that? Oh, right. More protesting." Austin grinned at me.

Noah tossed some chips in. "Maybe we should come at this from another direction. Are you protesting that you like older women or that the one in question was good looking?"

I pressed my lips together. I could spot a trap when I saw one. I shook my head. "I take the fifth."

"Counselor?" Noah glanced at Tristan.

Tristan shrugged. "I don't generally recommend that. It's basically an admission of guilt. It never saves you."

I blew out a breath as play came to me. My cards were trash, but at this point, I wasn't going to fold. I could at least see what we ended up getting to work with. I tossed in chips. "Fine. Yes, Sunshine is lovely. And older. And also very professional."

"Were you walking on su—"

"Don't." I cut Cody off. I absolutely wasn't in the mood to go down the rabbit hole of all the sun or sunshine related references they could come up with.

"Ooh. Testy." Cody dealt a card into the center of the table.

"Defending her honor." Noah nodded. "Always a good look."

I closed my eyes. Maybe it was better to just address it head-on. Then they could all quit ragging on me about it. I couldn't even think that seriously. They were never going to quit ragging on me. But...they were the guys. So maybe addressing it was the right way to go anyway.

"Look. She's hot. And older, and sure, okay, maybe I like more mature women. But she's a full ten years older, and that seems like a little too much." I studied my cards, but they didn't really register. "For all of that though? There are a ton of reasons things could never work between us, and not really any reasons why they would."

"How does that make you feel?" Scott used his best Freud-inspired voice.

I snickered. "We definitely don't want to get into talking about my mother, if that's where you're going. Although, Mom's okay. Dad though? He hit me up for money again while I was down there."

"No way, man." Cody's voice was full of sympathy. "Why can't the guy take a hint?"

I shrugged. "And Mom and The General want to do this Christmas cruise. I invited him along, because it beat trying to split the difference and not deal with his guilt trips. He's a big no on the cruise though, and probably isn't speaking to me anymore."

"Mixed blessing." Cody shot an understanding glance my way. "My dad's currently in the same boat. All because I don't want to meet the woman he cheated on Mom with."

I winced. "Sorry, man."

"So there really isn't a chance for something between you and this woman?" Austin tossed his cards into the center. "I'm out."

I shook my head. She hadn't even looked back, not once, when she got off the plane in Puerto Rico. She'd practically run off the plane in the first place. Now, a week later, I'd had two emails and one phone call from Zee to close out my dealings with the charter company and when I'd worked up the courage to ask about Sunshine, I'd gotten the brushoff. A professional one. But still a brushoff.

I tossed my cards in. "I'm out. Cody can't shuffle for beans."

"Hey. It's not like I know what I'm dealing to anyone. You get what you get."

Scott pointed at Cody, then me. "And you don't have a fit."

I laughed. "How's that work on Beckett?"

Scott waggled his hand from side to side. "Depends on how much he wanted whatever he didn't end up with."

"Exactly." I blew out a breath and pushed away from the table. "On the positive side, I think I might buy that island."

"Whoa. Back up." Noah set his cards down on the table. "You want to buy an island?"

"Yeah. I think I do." I lifted a shoulder. "I get how it sounds. I mean, come on. Who owns a whole island, right? But it'd be great for hosting dive trips. Totally unique compared to what other operations are able to offer. And I'd be happy to vacation there."

"What about the Caymans?" Scott frowned. "We have a house there. I guess I thought you'd all either hang there or get your own place nearby. It's kind of our thing, you know?"

"I know. It's not like I can't do both." I stood and went to the food table. Maybe it was dumb, but I couldn't get the island out of my mind. I'd done a little online digging and was pretty sure I'd found the real estate listing for it. The coordinates were close —not exact—and the photos of the house were spot on.

If I pictured Sunny in all of them? Well, that was my own problem to deal with.

"Anyway. I'm going to reach out to the listing agent on Monday. Then we'll see what we see." I dropped another half-sub on my plate and returned to the table.

"What's it listed for?" Tristan added more of his chips to the pot.

"Twenty-five." I left off the million. It felt odd to tack on. And the guys would figure it out.

"For an island? That's cheap." Tristan rested his cards on the table. "What's wrong with it?"

I laughed. Only Tristan. "The house needs some work. Hopefully not a complete demo and start over. It's a little over two hundred acres, which appears to be in the midsize range for private islands in the Caribbean."

"Who knew?" Austin shook his head.

"Yeah." I took a bite of my sandwich. "It's only got the one house. There's a dock of sorts on the other side of the island from where we landed, but the pictures suggest it'll need a ton of work, too. I think that factors into the price."

"So how much are you going to have to put into it to make it livable? Or functional for your dive stuff?" Scott tossed his cards in. "I'm out."

"Dunno. That'll be part of negotiating, I guess. The current owners got into some tax issues, so when they left, they didn't care if stuff got ruined. It's not a short sale, but they're also pretty motivated."

"Tax issues?" Tristan frowned. "That could be bad news."

"Not really. I guess the owners didn't realize that just because it was a private island it wasn't also a sovereign nation. So they weren't paying property tax." I pulled out my phone and made a note to ask the agent what that was likely to run. I could afford the purchase. I could afford to rehab the house and build up the dock. But if it was going to be a big outlay every year for taxes, I might have to rethink if it would be worth it in the end. "It's part of the decision-making though, for sure."

"Shoot me the info when you get it. I'll do some research and see if there's more you should know before you dive in. International real estate isn't my field though." Tristan shook his head. "You and Scott, man."

"What did I do?" Scott held his hands out, insult obvious on his face.

"You bought that place in the Caymans?" Tristan didn't add a "duh" but it was clearly implied.

"Was it really that bad to handle the paperwork for us? Because I recall offering to find someone who did specialize in international real estate and being told not to be dumb." Scott pinned Tristan with a glare.

"True. And yet. I thought it'd be a one-time thing." Tristan offered a tight smile and looked around the table. "Or are you all going to go buy stuff offshore? Should I go back to school?"

"Maybe take on a partner who already specialized?" Noah grinned.

Tristan let out an exasperated grunt.

"I liked it better when we were teasing Wes about his older lady friend." Tristan glanced at Cody and Noah, the only two currently still in. "Would the two of you hurry up and figure it out so we can start a new game?"

"Oh, fine." Noah pushed all his chips into the center of the table. "Let's do it, Cody."

Cody shook his head. "Nah, man. I'm out. You got it."

"Excellent." Noah put his cards down and pulled the chips to himself.

"Aren't you going to show us your hand?" Cody nodded toward the cards in front of Noah.

"Nope." He snagged the other discarded cards and quickly mixed them in with his.

"Seriously?" Cody scowled. "You were bluffing, weren't you?"

"You'll never know." Noah looked at Austin. "Your deal, man."

I breathed out a tiny woosh of relief when Tristan's attempt to restart the conversation about Sunny seemed to fizzle. As much as I loved these guys, I needed some time. Space. Something.

Whatever it took to get back to the place where I wasn't picturing her as part of all the pieces of my life.

She'd only been in my life for two weeks. It didn't seem right or fair that everything without her was a little less vibrant.

But telling the guys that? Talk about opening the door to endless ribbing.

Hard pass.

I could get over her. Move on.

I had to.

18

SUNSHINE

I dropped into the chair on my porch and propped my feet on the rail with a sigh. It was good to be home.

I stared out over my little stretch of sandy beach to the water that lapped at the shore, then let my gaze drift farther out across the blue. Birds called to one another. The waves whispered. My windchimes tinkled cheerily in the light breeze.

I'd spent the last week and a half working as many charters as I could. Finally, Zee and the owner ganged up on me and sent me home. There were other captains. I should share. All the usual objections to me using work as my coping mechanism for grief.

So. Fine.

I was home.

And maybe, in some small way, they were right.

I could breathe a little easier here.

But I could also think. And that was really the hard part. Because here, in the cottage Luca and I had built, where we planned to spend our lives, I couldn't escape memories of him. And I couldn't keep from picturing Wes here, either.

It was ridiculous. We'd known each other two weeks. Maybe

we'd spent more time together in that brief acquaintance than many people did if they dated once a week for months, but that didn't mean I was in love with him.

It wasn't possible to fall in love with someone you'd never hugged. Or kissed. Or walked with on the beach, hand-in-hand.

Was it?

"Doesn't matter." I murmured.

That was the other down side of being at home. On a boat, with clients around, I could keep my thoughts to myself. People generally didn't want to hear their captain muttering to herself as she went about her day. Or at least, that was what I'd noticed.

Here at home? There was only me to care. And I didn't.

Sometimes I liked the company.

"I should get a TV." Then at least I'd have conversations going on that weren't between me, myself, and I. Or I would when I had power, which wasn't all the time. That was a joy of small island living that many people didn't know.

Lots of residents had generators. Luca and I hadn't bothered. We weren't here all the time, for one. And neither of us really minded being cut off from civilization for a few hours. We could always bike into town if we wanted company and power.

My phone rang. I lifted my eyebrows as I saw Zee's name. "Yeah?"

"You made it home all right?"

"I did. I meant to text you. Sorry." I winced. I shouldn't allow myself to get so wrapped up in myself, in my thoughts, that I forgot that I had Zee. She cared about me. Even if I didn't always like the way she went about it.

"It's okay." She paused. I could almost hear her picking through words, trying to choose them.

"Just spit it out. Am I fired?"

"What? No. Goodness, girl, this place couldn't survive without you for long. You know that."

"No, I don't. Remember the whole 'we have other captains who need work' conversation the boss gave? You were right there, nodding along with him." Bitterness laced my voice. I could understand where he was coming from, but Zee's agreement had been a betrayal. She'd known why I needed the work.

"Pfft." Zee's little breath of air dismissed my hurt.

I scowled. "Is that all? I was enjoying watching my waves."

"No. It's not all. But now I'm not sure you deserve to know."

"And you're in charge of making that decision, I guess?" Even as I bristled, I wasn't sure why I was picking a fight with Zee. It wasn't the right move. And she didn't deserve it. But I couldn't stop the hurt and anger that oozed through me now that she was on the phone.

"I guess I am, since I have the information and you don't." Her tone was brisk, no-nonsense. "And your childish behavior just confirms that we were right to send you home. You don't have to like it."

I closed my eyes. I didn't like it. I hated it. But... "I'm sorry, Zee. Just tell me. Then you can hang up and leave me to my foul mood. I'll get over it."

"This'll either help or make it worse. I wish I knew which." Zee sighed. "Wes called looking for you. Couple of times now. You didn't give him your number?"

"He didn't need it."

Zee's silence said more than a five-minute lecture.

"Fine. I didn't want him to have it. Happy?"

"No. Not really." She paused again. "Are you?"

I stared out at the ocean. I could picture Wes walking up out of the surf with his flippers in one hand, his wetsuit unzipped and hanging around his waist. Chest bare and glistening with water droplets.

Of course, that had been after our last dive. The one at the island before his plane came and took us home. Even knowing our time together was ending, I almost hadn't been able to keep from crossing the line and telling him how he made me feel. Asking him if there was some way, *any* way, that we could try to be together.

"I'll be all right."

"All right isn't happy, which is what I asked."

"Ugh. You're annoying, do you know that? No. I'm not happy. But I also know that happiness isn't the ultimate goal in life, okay?" I swallowed and took a deep breath to steady my heartrate. "It can't work."

"That's certainly true if you never try." Zee's voice was full of frustration. "Why are you closing yourself off from living?"

"Because I'm tired of hurting. Don't you understand that?"

"I do. You know that we aren't promised a life free from pain though. So I have to ask if this stance of yours—the one where you hole yourself up in your secluded beach cottage or behind the thick walls of professionalism—is one that you've prayed about."

I winced. "Sort of."

"Hmm."

"What?"

"I just wondered how you sort of pray about something."

"Zee."

"No. I'm serious. I suspect I have things I could sort of pray about and be lots happier with the outcomes. It's a good idea."

I groaned.

"What was that?"

"You're saying I'm praying wrong?"

"You tell me. Are you praying and listening to see what God tells you? Or are you praying and telling God what you want Him to rubberstamp?"

Ouch. I didn't know how to respond to that. It was definitely closer to how I was handling things. Weren't we supposed to use our heads, too? If I knew something was better for me...I couldn't even really finish the thought. Because no. I didn't know better than God, no matter how much I might like to believe that was the case.

"You're quiet."

"I'm putting on a bandage."

Zee laughed. "Girl, you know I love you."

"I do. Love you back."

"Good. Stop being stupid."

"Should I smack myself in the back of the head, too?"

"Only if you think you need it. I get the feeling maybe you've figured it out."

I sighed. "Zee, I don't want to hurt again."

"I understand that. It's reasonable to feel that way. But isn't the chance at love worth the risk of hurt?"

I wasn't sure I could answer that. Before Luca, I would have said yes. Absolutely. Which was why I jumped in with both feet when he came on the scene. Would I have chosen differently if I'd known how it would end?

I tried to picture my life if I hadn't known Luca. Without all of the memories we'd made together. But I couldn't.

"Should I send you his contact information?" Zee's voice was quiet, like she knew the turmoil in my brain.

"Yeah. Go ahead." I wasn't promising to call him. If she asked, I would make that clear. But maybe...maybe I'd pray about it. Really pray, without a pre-determined outcome I was planning on. And then see what God had to say about it.

"Good girl. I'm praying for you."

"Thanks, Zee." I ended the call and set my phone aside.

A few minutes later, I heard the incoming email chime. Zee was nothing if not efficient. But I didn't reach for my phone. I wasn't in a hurry to open the email. To see his contact details. To be forced to make a decision about what to do.

There was time.

I STOOD on the shore and let the waves lap up over my ankles. The power had gone out yesterday afternoon, and it didn't seem like it was coming back on this morning. The battery on my phone and laptop were nearing zero. One of these days, I ought to go ahead and invest in solar chargers for my devices, at least. But the enforced disconnections were actually kind of nice. Sometimes.

Today, I should probably go into town and charge them up again. See if I could get information on when things might come back on.

Maybe go ahead and respond to one of the many emails Zee had sent asking if I'd gotten in touch with Wes yet. Although, "No. Stop bugging me" was probably not the verbiage I ought to use when I did that.

It had only been two weeks since she sent me the info.

And okay, fine, that was two weeks after Wes and I went our separate ways.

A month that felt simultaneously like five minutes and three years.

I had no idea what, if anything, that meant. Zee would probably tell me it meant I was a big chicken and I needed to just call the man already. Part of me wished I'd told her to send him my info. Then, if he wanted to reach out, he could. Then again, knowing Wes? He wouldn't. He'd want it to be my choice. My decision.

It was both charming and infuriating.

Why couldn't God just send me an email with clear, step-by-step instructions?

I sighed and headed back up the beach to my cottage. I knew

what I needed to do. Had known for at least a week. But I'd wanted that extra week to be sure, because I wasn't convinced God had the right idea here. I didn't want to get in touch with Wes. I wanted to bury whatever feelings I had for him until they got tired of being ignored and went away completely.

On the porch, I used the towel hanging on the rail to dry my feet and get off as much of the sand as I could, then I went inside, the screen door slapping against the frame as it closed behind me.

I crossed the open space that served as living, dining, and kitchen area and went into the bedroom. I hadn't made the bed today. Normally, that was the first thing I did when I got up. I paused and flipped the blankets back up and smoothed them. My gaze landed on my nightstand—on the photo of Luca and me, wrapped in an embrace on the beach under a full moon. I traced a finger over his face, my heart aching.

He wasn't coming back.

And no matter how much I might try to convince myself otherwise, Luca would've liked Wes. I could see the two of them being friends. More than that, Luca wouldn't want me to languish in grief, alone forever. Maybe it wasn't something we'd talked about—because who did that? Not two young people in love, that was for sure. But as I'd prayed about reaching out to Wes, my certainty had grown.

I just didn't want to acknowledge it.

But today felt like a good day to be brave.

I got canvas sneakers out of my closet and slipped them on, then hooked a finger through the loop on the top of a woven backpack that hung on one of the hooks on the door. I went back out and gathered my laptop, its power cord, the charging cord for my phone, and my cell. I dumped them into the backpack and slung the straps over my shoulders as I headed back out the front door.

I skipped down the two steps of the porch and reached for the handlebars of my bike. I straddled the seat and pushed off, wobbling slightly as I made my way over the sand to the road that would take me into town.

I loved the feel of the wind on my face and in my hair as I biked. Every time I did this, I wondered why I didn't do it more often. Although, I also knew that answer. I liked being home, alone, too. I didn't need people around me every day. I could probably ride to town and back without stopping to see people.

Hmm. That would serve as exercise, too. Not that I suffered from a lot of sitting idle. I walked on the beach. I swam. Still, mixing it up was never wrong.

After the first two miles, I started to see more houses. Most of the residents on our side of the island liked being closer to shops. I could understand that, to a degree. But they also missed out on the solitude.

I waved to familiar faces as I passed them. Then, closer to town, I had to pay more attention to scooters and the occasional car. Plus increased foot traffic. Finally, I reached the main square and stopped. I parked my bike in the rack to the side of the little fountain that gurgled cheerily.

"Sunny! You're coming out of your cave?"

"Marcus. Hi. Power's out."

He nodded. "Heard that. You should be back up this afternoon, I imagine. George was working on the lines."

"You hear what happened?" It didn't matter, but sometimes it amused me to know what it was this time.

Marcus shook his head.

"All right. If you do hear, you know I'm always curious."

He chuckled. "Sure. I'll let you know. You going to the café?"

"Yep. Gotta charge my phone."

"Have a good one." He waved and went on with his day.

I crossed the square, stopping to have a brief conversation

with two other townies as I made my way to the café. A little bell over the door rang as I pulled it open, and a blast of cold air hit my face. Goosebumps covered my arms. I should've thought to bring a sweater.

"I wondered if we'd see you, Sunny." Clara grinned from behind the counter as she wiped it with a cloth. "Here for a recharge?"

I laughed. "In more ways than one, yeah. Can I get a caramel latte and one of your Cuban sandwiches?"

"Absolutely. There should be a spot in the corner near the plugs." Clara nodded toward the far side of the café. "If not, make Bennie move. He's been here too much anyway."

"I heard that." Bennie looked up from his laptop. "You know how to get me to leave."

"You're not serious." Clara propped her hands on her hips.

"Aren't I?" Bennie's busy gray eyebrows lifted, blending into the generous mop of gray hair that covered his head.

Bennie and Clara were both probably in their late sixties. They'd been friends for as long as I'd lived on the island. First, with their spouses, but it had continued without interruption when both had lost their mate.

I tipped my head to the side. "What did I miss?"

"Nothing." Clara scowled at Bennie. "I'll start on your order."

I looked at Bennie.

"I asked her to marry me. Not going home until she says yes."

I grinned. "Really? That's great."

"No, it isn't!" Clara called from the kitchen.

"Yes, it is. Don't be stubborn, Clara." I looked after her then back at Bennie and shot him a thumbs up.

Bennie reached up and patted my arm. "Thanks. Good to have you on my side."

"Stubborn?" Clara stomped out of the kitchen and pointed her spatula at me. "I'm stubborn? Are you seeing someone?"

I bit my lip.

Clara straightened. "When did this happen?"

I hunched my shoulders. "It hasn't yet. But...I'm getting there. It's one of the reasons I need to charge my laptop. I need to send an email."

"See? It's not an affront to nature to remarry after all." Bennie sent a longing, puppy-dog worthy look at Clara.

Clara sniffed, then spun on her heel and marched back into the kitchen.

"Sorry. Hope I didn't get your sandwich burned." Bennie looked sheepish.

"Worth it if it means she reconsiders." I shot him a conspiratorial wink before heading to the table tucked in the corner. There were indeed plugs underneath. I set up my laptop and phone, plugged in both, and looked out over the café tables. Bennie sat, submersed in his laptop again. A smattering of other tables were full with locals as well.

I smiled slightly. Here in town, everyone knew everyone else's business. I didn't mind being part of it for a little while, but I'd be just as glad to get back to my cottage. Of course, now that I'd told Clara about Wes—publicly, at that—the news would make the rounds. More than likely, I'd have a few of the folks I knew better than most swing by to see if it was true.

Well, so be it.

I flipped open my laptop and started it booting.

"Here." Clara set my latte and sandwich down, then she pulled out the chair across from me. "You really think I should marry that old man?"

I reached for my coffee and took a sip. "I think there are a lot of things that would be worse."

She laughed. "That's not an answer."

"I guess I'd want to know if you love him." I looked down at my latte. It was a question I wasn't sure I could answer myself. Not right now. Then again, Wes wasn't asking me to marry him yet.

"Of course I do. I've loved him for years. My husband loved him, too. Just like I loved his wife. But that's not the same thing as loving him the way I loved my husband."

I nodded. "No. Although, I guess I'm starting to realize that love shifts and grows and steadies into different forms over time."

Clara sent me a long look before nodding slowly. "It does."

I sipped the latte Clara brought me and the corners of my lips curved. She had a way with them. Nothing I managed at home ever tasted as good. "My mother, for all her dubious other qualities, asked me a good question when I was deliriously in love with Luca and rushing headlong into everything. She asked me to picture two futures—one with him in it, one without. At the time, being in that rush of young love, the one I imagined with Luca practically had cartoon hearts floating in the sky, but I figure you're smart enough to understand the real point."

Clara laughed. "How can I imagine a future without Bennie when he's in my café constantly? He's not going anywhere."

"Maybe you should try to picture it anyway." I glanced over at Bennie. He was working intently on his computer. He ran a property management company on the island—short-term rentals, longer term rentals, vacation properties. I'd also glimpsed his screen and seen some sort of video game happening. Definitely not what I would have imagined for him. But people could surprise you.

"I don't like it. It's hard to even get there, but if I do?" Clara rubbed a hand over her heart. "It's like my husband has died all over again. The ache here."

"So maybe that's something to think about." I lifted an eyebrow and held her gaze.

Clara sighed and pushed to her feet. "Not sure when you got so smart."

I laughed. "It's a gift. Invite me to the wedding."

She pointed a finger at me. "We'll see. I still have some thinking to do on it."

"Praying, too?"

Clara nodded once then turned and went back to the kitchen.

I blew out a breath and stared at my laptop. I had Wes's phone number as well as his email. Calling would be faster. And I'd get to hear his voice.

Was that a positive or a negative?

No. Email was smarter. I could go over what I wanted to say. Make sure it had just the right tone. I still didn't know—not one hundred percent—what I was hoping would come from this. If I pictured my future without Wes in it, it looked a lot like the last few years without Luca. And I was okay with that. I'd found a reasonable facsimile of contentment.

I had my cottage. A job I enjoyed that let me work when I wanted—or needed. Time to myself. Town was right here when I needed other people. And I had memories of Luca to keep me company, too.

I didn't need Wes. Or any new man. I'd had such a wonderful marriage, it seemed greedy to expect another chance.

Was that the same sort of thought Clara was having?

I pushed the laptop away and slid the plate with my sand-wich close. I picked up half and took a bite, enjoying the sting of spicy mustard as it mixed with creamy melted cheese.

What would life with Wes look like?

I chewed and tried to imagine it. All I could come up with were memories from our boat trip. Diving with him. I smiled slightly, remembering the visible joy that he exuded when we were underwater. He'd been a quick study, too, when I'd shown him different ways to do things—tips that I'd learned diving down here that varied from the skills needed in a pool or freshwater. Even though he'd been diving in the Caymans, he'd been using mostly tourist operations. They did things a certain way— and it made sense for what they were doing—but he'd seemed to appreciate learning from me.

I frowned and took another bite. I didn't want him to see me as his teacher, though. That implied a power imbalance that made me uncomfortable. And our age difference already caused me plenty of hesitation.

Would a future with Wes be more mother-son than anything else? Not that I was old enough to be his mother, but still. I had more experience if only because of the years I had on him. I didn't want to always have to be in charge because of that.

I took a sip of latte and moved the sandwich aside. All of this rumination was pointless. I didn't have enough information to make this kind of decision. The only thing I needed to choose right now, was whether or not I wanted to get back in touch and see where it led.

I wasn't going to let fear make the decision for me.

19

WES

I flipped the lock on the shop doors and groaned. What a day. My employees—all two of them—had both called out, leaving me to do everything. Which, of course, meant that I didn't get as much of my work done as I would have liked.

I could run the place on my own. No question. But I liked the freedom that having someone to mind the store provided. Basic sales and fielding phone calls were easy enough to manage, but they also took up time that I could spend doing other things.

Of course, in recent days, the only "other things" I'd managed had been obsessing about Sunshine.

"This has to stop." I shook my head as I walked through the storefront to the hall that would lead me to the office. I had a little time before I was supposed to meet the guys for poker. At least I wasn't hosting this week.

They gave me a lot of grief for not hosting often, but my townhouse was small and they were messy. I didn't consider myself fussy or fastidious—two words that the guys liked to throw my way—but I would accept "particular."

I sat at my desk and booted the computer for the first time

today. I could at least check the shop email and make sure I hadn't missed an important inquiry. Then I'd head out. And since we were meeting at Tristan's, I'd swing over to pick up some wings on the way. He was almost a worse host than me.

Of course, with Tristan, it was because he was just busy. Constantly.

I shook my head. He had to love it. Otherwise, why would he keep at it, now that he was a billionaire? I sure wouldn't.

I opened a browser and logged in to our email. There were vendor contacts—I'd need to check inventory and see what reorders needed to be made. An offer to trial a new wetsuit brand. Hmm. I was pretty happy with the choices I offered, but this company was looking to hit the lower end on the price point. If they could do that and still offer quality, it'd be nice to have that option.

I hit reply and typed out a quick response. I'd get some different sizes and see if the gang would all come give me their opinions. The women were all also divers, even if some of them didn't love it. I hesitated before sending, then deleted one of the women's sizes. Kayla was expecting. When I'd seen her at church, she was sporting a bump. I didn't know a ton about pregnant women, but I didn't imagine she'd want to try to haul a wetsuit on. Plus, she'd probably only be safe to swim, not to strap on the rest of the gear. I didn't actually know. I'd never had a pregnant woman show an interest in diving.

I opened a new tab and did a quick search.

Okay, that was a big no. Hmm.

I pulled up our standard waiver that we used for classes and skimmed through the list of medical conditions we asked about. Oh, nice. Pregnancy was already there. Score one for Tristan. Or, probably, whatever service he used for boilerplate legal forms. Still, I was glad that I hadn't been remiss in asking about an important condition.

I went back to the email, read it through again, and hit send. Then I filed it under vendors and moved on.

Three class enquiries followed and I replied with the standard response and attachments of schedules, costs, and forms. I grinned. I was going to have a great initial certification class starting in August if everyone from these emails signed up. More certifications meant more equipment sales. Or rentals. And more people who might go on trips. Because experience was showing that, around here at least, people were happy to settle on my place as "their dive shop."

We were building a little community.

Which was just what I wanted.

I checked the time. I should probably get going. I skimmed the rest of my inbox and froze when I got down another six messages.

Sunshine?

I bit my lip and clicked it.

Wes,

Hey. Zee let me know you'd been calling and asking about me. I'm taking some time off—the hurricane survival bonus I got from your charter means I don't need to fight for some of the trips right now. Plus, I missed my cottage and watching the sunrise from the porch.

Anyway. This is my email. So you can reach out directly instead of tagging Zee. If you want, of course. Maybe you're satisfied to know that I'm doing fine. Hopefully the same is true of you.

Yours,

Sunny

I read it again. And then once more.

Feeling foolish, I hit print before closing out of the email program. I waited for the printer to spit out the sheet of paper before shutting down the computer. I took Sunshine's email and folded it into a tiny rectangle, then shoved it into my pocket as I headed out of the office, pausing to flip the lights off. I did one more check of the conference room and changing area on my way through the shop. Then I set the alarm and left through the main doors, pausing to check that the locks were set, before heading across the parking lot to my car.

When I was behind the wheel, I dug out the email and opened it. Zee had gotten in touch with Sunshine. Was that because I'd been obnoxious? I'd been going for persistent, but maybe I'd crossed the line. Of course, I'd also hoped I could just get Sunshine while she was there and have a minute to hear her voice.

Which was also why I'd suggested maybe Zee could give Sunshine my number.

Did Sunshine choosing to email instead mean something? And she'd emailed my work. Was that a brush-off? Her words could certainly be interpreted that way. They were a breezy, "Hey, I'm fine. Why're you bugging Zee?" That was definitely the vibe.

But then at the bottom, she'd signed it "Yours." Not "sincerely", which was usually what I went with on professional emails. Or, I guess, the old standby of "thanks."

Maybe "yours" was Sunshine's default?

Ugh. I was overthinking. Massively.

I folded the email back up and dropped it into one of the cupholders in the console. Then I started the car and headed toward the best wings in the area.

It took longer than I'd expected, between a long wait for a takeout order—note to self: call ahead next time—and excessive summertime Friday night traffic. But finally, I was able to squeeze into a parallel parking spot near Tristan's building. I grabbed the takeout bag and then, after a quick internal debate, Sunshine's email, and got out of the car.

"Hey, Wes. You're running late too." Scott jogged a few steps to catch up with me. "I was worried I'd be the last one."

"I stopped for wings." I held up the bag. "I imagine Tristan is going to suggest pizza."

"He always does. Wings go good with pizza." Scott paused and grunted. "Wings go *well* with pizza."

I shot him a glance with eyebrows raised. "Do I need to worry about holding out my pinky when I drink my soda now?"

Scott glared as he reached for the door into Tristan's building. "Whitney's on a bit of a tear. I guess Beckett's grammar isn't as wonderful as she wants it to be when he goes to kindergarten."

"Kindergarten?" I glanced over as we crossed the lobby to the elevators. "He can't be ready for kindergarten."

"That is almost exactly what I said when Whitney started on about making sure we were modeling correct language usage. Then she pointed out that we have, in fact, celebrated his fifth birthday."

"And that means kindergarten." I shook my head as the elevator doors opened. I walked in, holding them as Scott followed, then punched the button for Tristan's floor. "Are you going public?"

"That's the next question. The schools here are..."

I nodded. Scott didn't have to finish the sentence. This area was a bizarre mix of professionals who could afford the historic homes and riverfront views and families who barely made ends meet with considerable government assistance. The families who could afford it, usually sent their kids to private schools. Meaning that the public schools were left to struggle.

And they did.

"Have you talked to Austin and Kayla?" If anyone could give Scott good advice about making a smart choice for school, it would be the two former public school teachers. They believed in the school system, and in doing what they could to help the students—all of them—succeed.

"Not yet. I thought I might mention it tonight and see if Austin had a gut reaction. Maybe he and Kayla are even talking about it, since they'll have one of their own before too long." Scott shrugged.

"What's Whitney thinking?" The elevator stopped and the doors opened. I stepped into the hall and started toward Tristan's door.

"She's all over the place. She's even looking into homeschooling. I don't know." Scott knocked on Tristan's door, then twisted the handle and pushed it open. "It's us."

"You're late!" That was Cody.

I snickered and followed Scott in. "Like you're never late, Cody."

"Never. Ever. Not even one time." Cody grinned, then his gaze zeroed in on the bag I carried. "But you brought wings, so you're forgiven."

"Well, that's a relief." I made a show of dragging my hand across my forehead.

"I walked in with the wings, does that excuse me?" Scott plopped onto the couch beside Cody.

"No. You didn't even carry a watermelon." Cody shook his head. "Sorry man. You're on the list."

Austin rose from his seat and ambled over to the island where I was setting out the wings. "Aren't you the king of that list, Cody? He's in good company."

"Hey. I'm not late that much. If anyone is the king of late, it's Tristan." Cody nodded to where Tristan sat, staring intently at his phone. "We're at his place and he's basically late since he can't put his work away."

"Sorry." Tristan clicked the button on the side of his phone and set it on the table. "Better?"

Cody waggled a hand from side to side.

"Are we getting pizza, too?" Noah glanced over to the island. "Knowing Wes, he got atomic wings and I'm not actually in the mood to spend all of tomorrow in pain."

"Har har." I stuck my tongue out at Noah. "I actually thought about your delicate princess constitution and got the medium."

"I still want pizza." Noah stood and made his way to the island. He peered at the wings before leaning over and sniffing carefully. "I'm not convinced I trust you not to lie just to screw with me."

"Wow." I clasped a hand over my chest. "You wound me, sir."

Austin snorted. He picked up a wing and bit into it. After a moment of chewing he looked at Noah. "Definitely medium. Maybe even mild. You should be fine."

I loaded some wings onto a plate before looking at Tristan. "I'm actually surprised there isn't pizza here already."

Before he could speak, there was a knock.

Tristan stood and hurried toward the door. "I'll get it."

Cody laughed as Tristan came back with two large pizzas.

"I guess I'm predictable." Tristan set the pizzas down beside the wings on the island.

"There's nothing wrong with predictable." I flipped open the top box and breathed in the mixture of smells emanating from the loaded pie. "At least you get the good stuff."

"Ugh. I have explained more than once that Beckett will only eat pepperoni. It doesn't make sense to get something that no one but me will eat when there are leftovers." Scott flicked his fingers at me. "Deal with it."

"Whit doesn't eat supreme?" Cody carried a heavily laden plate back to Tristan's couch. "I thought she was all in on vegetables. Shouldn't she love it?"

"Apparently pizza is the exception. She claims to be a purist." Scott shrugged and loaded his plate.

"While this little foray into the ins and outs of married life is fascinating, maybe we could all get food and get down to the business at hand?" Tristan put two wings on his plate and a single slice of pizza.

I shot him a pointed look. "You on a diet?"

"No. I just happen to acknowledge that at some point in the near future, my metabolism is going to stop acting like I'm twelve. I don't want that occasion to come with an extra thirty pounds." Tristan sat in his chair. "I'd think someone whose livelihood now involves wearing a wetsuit would consider that wise."

I laughed. "Scuba burns calories."

"Can we rewind to the business at hand comment? I thought we were playing poker, not convening a meeting." Cody took a huge bite of pizza. "Pretty sure the girls are just hanging out and having fun. So if we're working, I'm gonna leave and go join them."

"You're such a newlywed." Noah muttered.

"Guilty as charged. You should try it." Cody waggled his eyebrows. "Have you even set a date yet?"

Noah checked his phone. "We've literally been engaged two months."

"Plenty of time to choose a date." Cody pointed a chicken bone in Noah's direction. "Unless you're going to do that whole engaged for five years thing."

"No. We're definitely not doing that. I don't want to live in my apartment that long when I own a house."

I laughed. "Glad you've got your priorities straight there, Noah. Does Jenna know it's all about the house?"

"Shut up. You're such an idiot." Noah balled up a paper towel and threw it at me. "We're talking about New Year's Eve. I have reservations."

"Reservations as in you've secured a spot or reservations as in you aren't positive about the choice?" Tristan wiped his fingers on a paper towel.

"The second one." Noah frowned down at his plate. "Isn't that kind of...weird? I mean, that's a big party holiday for almost everyone. Would people want to give up their plans to come to a wedding?"

"Will there be food?" I mopped up the wing sauce with my pizza crust. "Dancing? Celebratory things that might also be party-like in nature?"

"And that's basically Jenna's point. She wants to get married at the house. Reception in the yard." Noah set his plate aside, cleaned his hands, and reached for the cards. "Don't ask about the weather. She's got it figured out with tents and heaters. It'd have to be small. I don't have a problem with that. I guess I'm just wondering if this signs us up for a lifetime of hosting New Year's Eve."

Tristan laughed. "Now we get down to the real problem."

I chuckled. Tristan was right. That was absolutely what Noah wanted to avoid.

"I don't think so. I won't hold you to it, at least." Scott picked up Noah's plate and tucked it under his own before standing and carrying them to the kitchen. "Most of us go somewhere anyway. So I really don't think it's an issue."

"Also what Jenna says."

I tilted my head to the side. "You getting cold feet?"

"What? No." Noah shot me an appalled look. "Why would you ask that?"

"I dunno. Doesn't sound like you're rushing to the altar. You're sitting here saying all your objections have been countered with reasonable explanations by Jenna. So if not cold feet, what's the issue?" I stood and took my plate to the kitchen. I left it on the counter. I might want another slice of pizza, even though Tristan's snarky comment about metabolism was echoing in my head. I opened the fridge to grab a drink. I pulled out a can and held it up. "Seriously, Tristan? Diet?"

Tristan shrugged. "If you don't like it, there is also water."

"Maybe you ought to be the one getting married if you're only going to stock girl drinks." I popped the tab on the Diet Coke and took a drink, then shuddered. "Bleh."

"No one's forcing you to drink it." Tristan scowled.

"You're right." I took another drink. I'd live. "You okay?"

Tristan took a deep breath and closed his eyes. After a moment, he nodded. "Just a little stressed. Not really in the mood to be dragged for making healthier choices."

"Sorry." I resumed my seat, set the soda on the table, and reached for the cards Noah had dealt. "I vote you get married on New Year's Eve, Noah. We all leave Tristan alone because he's going through some stuff. And you all tell me what it means when someone signs an email 'yours.'"

"Sounds good—wait." Austin put his cards down in front of him. "Nice try sneaking that last one in. Sunshine?"

I nodded.

"Hmm." Lips pursed; Austin tapped his fingers on his knee. "I'm not sure I've ever signed an email that way."

"I know I haven't." Cody turned to look at me. "What's the rest of the email like?"

I sighed. I should have known they'd ask. Maybe I had known and that was why I'd brought it in. I dug it out of my pocket and tossed it to Cody.

Cody scanned the paper, then handed it to Austin. "Huh."

"Right?" I took another drink of soda. "I don't even know if I should write back."

"You definitely need to write back. You can at least be

friends." Austin handed the paper to Noah. "Friends is a good place to start."

It figured that Austin would say that. He and Kayla had been BFFs for a lot of years before their relationship shifted. Not that he was alone in giving that advice. Mom always said how she thought a lot of her trouble with Dad was that they hadn't had a solid underpinning of friendship before they got married.

I looked around the room at my friends. Everyone in a relationship had been friends first. "Yeah, okay."

"So you write her back, mirror the tone. Casual, cheerful. Go ahead and use 'sincerely' if you have to at the end." Austin tossed the email on the table. "Though I'd choose something a little friendlier myself. See what happens."

I reached for the email but wasn't fast enough. Tristan snagged it first. I could practically watch the gears turn as he read it. He smirked at the end before handing it over. "She's trying not to be interested. But she is."

I looked at the email again. "I don't see it."

"Trust me. I'm a lawyer."

I snickered and folded the email. "Not sure what that has to do with anything here."

"I get subtext. I'm the king of subtext." Tristan paused. "Maybe more like a prime minister? Something that shares the rule with others of their ilk. Because all lawyers—at least the good ones—are up on subtext."

"Ookay. And the email has subtext?" I almost unfolded it to read again. I sure didn't see any subtext.

"Yeah. It does. She's interested, but not sure she should be. Or even if she wants to be. But someone convinced her she's missing something in her life and you might just be the answer, so she's exploring it cautiously." Tristan picked up his cards.

Now I really wanted to look at the email again, because I

definitely hadn't seen any of that. I glanced at the other guys. "You buying that?"

Noah shrugged. "He's a lawyer. He's trained to see what people don't say."

And that totally wasn't an answer. I stuffed the email in my pocket. I could obsess over it later. "Are we playing cards, or what?"

20

SUNSHINE

I tugged on the line around my waist that attached to the buoy floating on the water above me. The wind and waves up top were causing it to drag behind me as I swam along the reef off the shore of my beach.

Technically, solo diving wasn't a smart decision. I knew this. I also didn't let it stop me. I'd let a couple of neighbors know my plan. I had the buoy. And generally, nothing went wrong. Most of the time, I'd talk one of those neighbors into coming along, but today I'd wanted the peace and solitude I could only find underwater and I hadn't even wanted the silent company of another person.

I checked my gauges. I'd been down about twenty minutes. It was probably time to turn around and swim back toward my entry point. I didn't want to end up walking home on the beach carrying my tank. It was a lot heavier out of the water than in.

I paused and watched colorful fish dart in and out. Were they playing with one another? Fighting? Chasing food?

I'd never given a lot of thought to the why of fish behavior. Maybe there wasn't much more motivation behind it than survival. I was pretty sure no one thought fish might be sentient.

Of course, this was yet another topic I'd never bothered to investigate.

I turned, checked my compass, and adjusted my position slightly before swimming toward home. The buoy was a persistent tug around my waist. I couldn't wait to surface and get rid of it. Especially since my dive hadn't really brought the peace I was looking for.

Wes had responded to my email on Saturday. He'd matched the light, breezy tone of the email I sent. He was looking into buying the island where we'd wrecked. He'd dropped that into the message like it was a normal thing people did. Then again, maybe it was a normal thing billionaires did.

I needed to remember that he wasn't like me.

In so many different ways, he was practically from an alien planet. What was I thinking, pursuing any sort of relationship with a billionaire? Even a friendship would be hard. Just look at his email. Buying islands. Planning dive trips for the winter. No mention of work in there, although the dive trips qualified as that. Maybe the island, too.

But it was no kind of work I was used to.

We'd been emailing back and forth—always light—for the last two weeks.

I reached the underwater landmarks that indicated I was at my beach and began to surface slowly. No need to rush. Nothing waited for me on shore except another day of figuring out what I was going to do with my life.

I needed to work.

The thought solidified in my mind as I ascended and my head broke through the surface of the water. I turned, orienting myself toward the shore, and began to swim. Before long, I'd reached shallower water. I paused to remove my flippers, then stood, and walked ashore. When I was clear of the water, I dropped my flippers in the sand and unhooked my

BCD so I could shrug out of it and gently lower it to the ground.

I tugged off my mask and tipped my face back to the sun, letting the heat soak into my skin. I hadn't bothered with a wetsuit. The water was warm enough to dive in just a bathing suit. On shore, however, the breeze brought out goosebumps.

I glanced around until I spotted my towel a few yards off. I hurried to it and bundled it around me. Better. My cell phone, which rested on top of my flip flops, lit up and began to ring. I dried my hand and picked it up. "Hello?"

"There you are. Where have you been?" Zee was nearly frantic.

"I went for a dive. What's up?" Given that I'd just been hoping for work, maybe Zee's call was exactly what I needed.

"A dive? Who with?"

"Zee. You called me?" I wasn't going to get into it with Zee about my occasional solo dives. She didn't approve, and I didn't feel like a lecture.

"That means solo. You know how I feel about that. Girl—" Zee broke off and huffed out a breath. "Well, you know, so I won't say it again. But you shouldn't have a death wish."

"I don't. Now tell me what's going on?"

"How soon can you get over here? You'll have to sail, obviously, since you were just diving. Javier showed for a two-week on the forty-foot sailboat. And he was trashed. Not just drunk, this time, if I know what I'm looking at."

I sighed. "You do. I wondered when he'd start branching out."

"I'm not sure it's the first time, honestly. He's trying to insist he's fine. The boss came in, took one whiff, and fired him on the spot. So not only is Javier not taking the two-week sail, he was scheduled for another right afterward. We need you."

"I need about thirty minutes to get everything here squared

away, then I'll hop into my boat and head over. If the two-week wants to leave today, it'll have to be after dinner. Tomorrow would be better." I started a mental list of chores as I slid my feet into my sandals and hurried across the sand to my dive gear.

"I can postpone till tomorrow. Pretty sure. It's a girls' trip. They were here when Javier showed up. They'll understand."

I winced. "That sounds like it was unpleasant."

"You have a way with understatement." Zee sighed. "I wanted you to have more of a break."

"I was going to call and ask to get on the schedule anyway, Zee. It's been long enough. I need to work. Too much down time and I'm in my head. You know that."

"Did you get in touch with him?"

I wanted to play dumb and ask who. But Zee was already having a bad day. "I emailed. He emailed back. We've been talking back and forth that way for a while."

"Email. Pfft." Zee grunted. "Why haven't you called him?"

"I have my reasons, okay?" I prayed Zee wouldn't ask what they were. I wouldn't be able to explain them thoroughly. And if I fell back on the age gap thing, she'd dismiss that without blinking. "I should run. I'll let you know as soon as I'm on the way."

"Okay. Don't think we're done talking about this though."

I laughed and ended the call. I hurried through rinsing my dive gear and hanging it to dry over the bathtub. Normally, I'd dry it outside, but I didn't want to leave it exposed to the elements that long. I shot a quick text to my neighbors letting them know I was up from the dive and that I was heading out to work. They'd keep an eye on my place.

I threw some clothes in a duffel bag, added my laptop, various chargers, and my Kindle, then paused in my living room and looked around. Was I forgetting anything? If I was, I didn't know what it would be.

I slung my duffel over my shoulder, took the boat keys off the hook beside the door, and hurried out to my bicycle. I pedaled quickly into town, tossing a quick wave to the neighbors I saw. They knew what it meant when I rode by with a duffel, so between everyone I'd told and those who had seen me go by? The whole community would know by dinnertime. Good enough.

As I approached the marina, I tossed my leg over the side and rode on one pedal to the bike rack, then hopped off. I chained my bike, waved to the harbor master, and jogged down the dock to my little boat.

There were checks to make and the homey tasks of getting ready to get underway, but I moved through them quickly and within ninety minutes of Zee's call, I'd let her know I was headed in her direction.

The weather was good—clear skies, easy seas. All the things I loved about living in the Caribbean. I wouldn't say I got over to the charter marina fast, but I made it in the expected amount of time. The sun was just sinking below the horizon when I pulled alongside the dock and tied up. I double-checked that everything was secure and would be fine for an extended stay parked here, then got my duffel and hopped out. I walked briskly to the charter offices, knocked once, and pulled open the door.

"How can I—oh, thank goodness." Zee jumped up from her seat behind the desk and crossed the room to pull me into a tight hug. "You're a sight for sore eyes."

I chuckled and patted her back. "I told you I was coming."

"I know, I know. It's still good you made it. I worry now."

"Oh, Zee. That hurricane was a freak accident. You have to know that." I had to keep reminding myself of it. But Zee didn't need to know that. These things happened and storms could blow up out of nowhere and cause problems. It was one of the reasons everyone didn't live in the islands. Living down here wasn't all only good things.

"I do."

I tilted my head to the side. "Is it the clients? Are they going to be problematic?"

"Oh, no. Nothing like that. In fact, I think you're going to like them a lot." She shook her head. "I guess the thing with Javier threw me off kilter this morning."

"They're still good with heading out tomorrow morning?"

"They are. I got them set up in a hotel tonight with some suggestions for dinner. They'll be here bright and early at seven."

I nodded. "Sounds like a plan."

"You'll come home with me."

It wasn't a question, but still I shook my head. "Thanks, Zee. Really. But no. I'm fine for a night on my boat. There's no need for you to be here that early and you and I both know it."

She sighed. "I had to try. You'll at least come have dinner with me?"

"Depends." I held up a finger. "Are you going to grill me about Wes?"

Zee wouldn't meet my gaze.

"That's what I thought. I'm going to pass. I know you mean well, but right now? Email is working for me. I still don't know what I want. Or even what's possible. Maybe we just develop a good friendship out of this and call it a day. I'll be okay with that."

"Will you?" Zee searched my face, then nodded slowly. "I guess you will. All right. But I can't promise I'm going to leave it alone."

"I wouldn't expect any differently." I smiled. "I'm going to go look over the paperwork for this charter in the office, grab a bite, and call it a night. It's been a long day."

"All right." Zee checked the time on the clock that ticked

quietly on the wall. "I guess I'll lock up and get on home. Check in with me while you're out."

"I will." I patted Zee's shoulder and moved through the lobby to the little office area. Zee had left out a folder with information for my charter and I sat down with it, one leg tucked under me, and read.

The next morning, I was up at five and on board the sailboat that I'd be in charge of for the next two weeks. I brewed coffee in the galley and checked that the sleeping berths below were ready for guests. Zee had stocked the fridge and pantry, and had done a thorough job of it. The girls who made the booking said they were happy to make their own meals, so at least I didn't have to do that. I could be invisible on this trip and stick to getting them from point A to B.

It was just what I needed.

The girls wanted to stay in the Puerto Rico and Virgin Islands area, which made it even easier. They could get hotel rooms ashore if they wanted. There wasn't a requirement to sleep on board, none of the trips between islands were long enough for that. Given that they'd scheduled several days on each island, I didn't understand why they wanted a charter. Whatever. Not my business.

At ten until seven, I made my way up to the charter offices and waited just outside the door. No reason to unlock it and let them in. But it was where Zee had told them to come. I guessed they weren't comfortable meeting at the boat.

A taxi pulled up and four women exited. The driver got out of the van and opened the back to unload their luggage. Each woman took the handle of a rolling bag, chattering with each other and the driver. I couldn't quite catch what they said, but their tone and cadence were friendly. That was a good start.

With a wave down the sidewalk to me, the taxi driver closed the trunk and made his way back around to the driver's seat. The women all looked my direction at once. I straightened and shifted my smile into professional and welcoming.

Their chatter quieted as they neared. The tallest one, and wow, she was tall, studied me to the point that I wanted to squirm. Finally, she spoke. "You're Sunshine?"

My eyebrows lifted. Zee usually told everyone I was Sunny. "I am. You ladies ready to sail?"

They exchanged looks. The tall one cleared her throat. "Before we go, we decided we ought to put our cards on the table."

"Not we. You." The blonde smiled apologetically, but crossed her arms. "I still think it's the wrong move."

"Noted." The tall woman rolled her eyes. "I'm Jenna. That's Whitney. This is Kayla. And in the back is Megan."

I shook hands with each woman as they were introduced. Something about the group of names was familiar, but I couldn't put my finger on it. Probably just the paperwork I'd read over last night. "Nice to meet you all. I hope you have a great time on your island vacation. The boat's down this way."

"Wait." Jenna reached out and put her hand on my arm. "We're all friends with Wes."

I froze. Then blinked. That was why the names were familiar. Wes had mentioned the wives and girlfriends of his pals. "I see. Well. I'm glad he gave a good recommendation even after the storm. We shouldn't have any weather problems this trip."

"Oh. He doesn't know we're here." One of the brunettes, Kayla I thought, interjected. She bit her lip. "I had to do a lot of tap dancing with Austin to get him to agree to keep this quiet."

"Me, too. Well, with Scott." Whitney nodded and uncrossed her arms. "And I kind of think we should have waited until we were sailing so you couldn't run screaming."

I laughed, although I was confused. "I don't plan to run screaming. I guess I'm not sure what's going on though."

"Wes has mentioned you about six hundred—"

"Million. Six hundred million." Kayla cut Jenna off with an elbow jab.

Jenna shrugged. "A lot. But then he clams up. It's not like Wes. He's usually the guy who can't stop talking about the woman he's seeing. So we got curious. I had some vacation I needed to use or lose. Megan was able to get coverage for the bookstore. The guys have a plane."

I nodded slowly. "We're just friends."

"See?" Megan pointed at me and shook her head. "He says that, too. In that same tone of voice. We don't buy it."

What tone? I hadn't used a tone. I'd simply said we were friends. And it was true. Ish. I certainly didn't know what else to call the relationship I had with him. "I don't know how to respond to that. Did you not actually want to sail? And I wasn't scheduled for this anyway. You could have all ended up down here and stuck with Javier for two weeks."

Whitney and Jenna exchanged a guilty look.

I frowned. "Or you roped Zee into your subterfuge."

"It didn't actually take convincing." Kayla bit her lip. "She was really glad when we called to set this up."

I bet she was. I wanted to go to her house, drag her out of bed, and shake some sense into her. That wouldn't be professional or polite. Especially since it'd mean leaving the women standing here in front of the office. "Well. I'm here. The boat's ready. It's up to you."

"Out of curiosity, on a scale of one to ten, how angry are you?" Whitney gripped the handle of her rolling bag.

Angry wasn't one of the emotions I was feeling. Maybe I was miffed at Zee, although I also couldn't blame her. The opportunity had fallen into her lap and she'd gone along with it. "How angry is Wes going to be?"

"Wes is pretty even keeled." Megan shrugged. "I imagine he's going to be upset on your behalf but not beyond that."

I nodded. That sounded like Wes. "I'm good. You've got a nice itinerary planned and I love taking out the sailboat. So if you're game, let's get on board and we can get going. Then you can start whatever third degree you have planned."

Jenna laughed. "I think I like you."

"Good to know." I started toward the boat without checking to see if they followed. I glanced over my shoulder and added with a wink, "I'll let you know when I figure out if it's recip-rocated."

Laughter followed me to the boat. I stepped aboard and turned, waiting for the women. As they approached, I reached over and hauled the suitcases onto the deck, then helped each of them to climb in.

"Are you going to stay on the boat at night, or will you want to get hotel rooms on shore?" Before I lugged their bags down into the staterooms, I figured I'd see if it would be necessary.

"What do you recommend?" Kayla was already looking a little green around the gills from the slight bobbing of the boat.

I gestured to the seats along the side. "You should sit. I think, looking at you, hotels are a better plan."

"Sorry." Kayla laid her hand on her stomach.

I noted the small bump, and two-and-two added quickly into four. "You're expecting."

She nodded.

"Then definitely a hotel. The beds below are fine, but they're not always kind to the back. Especially if you're not used to it. Plus, more consistent air conditioning and a lack of motion are going to be better if you're dealing with nausea."

"All right. I'll find us reservations." Jenna crossed to the desk and plopped onto the bench beside Kayla, then rubbed Kayla's leg. "You're a sport for coming."

"I wasn't going to miss it. You know that." Kayla smiled.

"I'll leave you all to get settled. I'm going to just stow your bags out of the way though, so you can get them later this evening. Make yourself at home. There's food and coffee in the galley below." I got busy stowing the bags and making preparations for us to cast off.

Before long, the sails were hoisted and full, and we were on our way. I stayed at the helm. I didn't know what to think. These women clearly cared about Wes. That was good. None were single. Jenna didn't have a wedding band, but the rock on her left hand definitely indicated she was taken. So it wasn't as if I worried that they were...guarding their territory. That was kind of the vibe, even though it didn't make sense.

Thing was, Wes wasn't *my* territory, either.

Oh, sure. Zee wanted him to be. She had this whole thing imagined out where we'd fallen in love on the island. I definitely had feelings for him. I wasn't ready to call them love. Maybe that was stubbornness. Maybe it was realism.

Maybe both.

Maybe it was just a leftover sense of responsibility for having gotten him shipwrecked and injured.

I wasn't analyzing it. That was the big thing. Because there was no point. I lived here. He lived there.

It sounded hollow now. It wasn't as though there was anything holding me here. I could move. I could probably even learn to love living away from the beach with the right incentive. I glanced back at the women who were part of Wes's life and sighed.

Maybe I needed to get to know them and see if they really thought I had the chance of a future with him. It wasn't as if I could tell from his emails.

And then what?

I shook my head. One thing at a time.

Step one? Admit I wanted to find out.

21

WES

Scowling, I banged a fist on Tristan's door. I tapped my foot and considered knocking again.

Locks clicked and the door opened. "What's up, Wes?"

"Did you know about this?"

Tristan's eyebrows lifted. "Know about what? Come in and have a drink."

I squinted at him. Tristan was a lawyer, which meant he'd be good at lying. But I didn't see it. I nodded and went in. I kept going down into the kitchen while Tristan closed and relocked his door.

I opened the fridge and scowled at the soda. Still only diet. Probably forever, now, given what he'd said last week. I'd deal. I grabbed a can and popped the top. "You want?"

"Sure, why not. Who needs to sleep, right?" Tristan took the can I offered and opened it. "What's going on?"

"The girls all went to Puerto Rico."

Tristan frowned for a moment, then his lips formed an O. "Wow. Gutsy."

"That's not the word I'd choose." I moved to the couch and

sat. "I don't get this. I have never meddled in any of their love lives."

"Hm. I think you participated in reminding Austin that he was stupid not to ask Kayla out."

I looked up and stared at Tristan. "Whose side are you on here?"

"Why are there sides?"

"What do you mean? Of course there are sides." I scowled at the soda and took another long swig.

"You aren't interested in this woman? What's her name again?"

"Sunshine." It came out as a mutter and I wanted to pull the word back and say it again without the petulance. I sighed. "And I didn't say that."

"Okay. So you're not *not* interested?"

"That sounds so high school." I leaned back and rested my head on the cushion. "I'm interested. On the island? I wanted to kiss her so bad—"

"Why didn't you?" Tristan watched me over the top of his soda as he sipped.

"Didn't think she'd be okay with it, honestly." I spun the can in my hands. "She's hard to read."

Tristan nodded. "Let's look at the facts of the case."

I groaned. "Why did I come to you?"

Tristan grinned. "Because I don't have a girlfriend, so I'm the closest to a neutral party as you've got in this little group of ours."

"Right. There's that, isn't there." I sipped. "All right, lay the facts of the case on me."

Tristan ticked things off on his fingers as he spoke. "You like her. You haven't shared many details about her with any of us, which makes it even clearer that you're pretty invested."

"Hold on. What does that mean?"

"It means when you have a casual thing going, you don't shut up about it. The two other times that I know about you having a serious relationship with someone? This is exactly how you've acted." Tristan leaned forward and set his soda on the coffee table. "Am I wrong?"

I thought through my behavior in the past because I really wanted to point out all the ways Tristan got it wrong. But he didn't. I gave a grudging nod.

"Now, when you factor in that the majority of our group is married or engaged, and that those women like to know all the things that are going on in everyone's life, does it surprise you that they took matters into their own hands?"

I laughed in spite of myself. "Not when you put it that way, no."

"What's the worst that could happen?"

"Oh, let's see, they could convince her to run screaming in the opposite direction. Or make it look like I'm too immature to just approach a relationship with her point blank, so I sent my friends to do it. Like passing a note in study hall." I groaned. She was already hung up on how much younger I was. And okay, sure, I'd struggled some with that, too. I was over it. Mostly.

"Come on. You know the girls as well as I do. Do you really think that's what they're going to do?"

I thought about it and tried to stay neutral. Finally I shook my head. "Probably not."

"Okay. So worst case? Sunshine finds out that you're more serious about her than she knew. Is that bad?" Tristan leaned forward and rested his elbows on his knees. "At some point, the two of you need to talk about that. This just accelerates it some."

"I guess." I rubbed the middle of my forehead. "I wish they'd talked to me about it before going off like this."

"What would you have done?"

I opened my mouth, then closed it. What would I have done? Probably told them not to go. "Dunno."

"Fair enough." Tristan sighed and leaned back. "I think this could be a good thing. Let it play out."

"You think?"

"What's the alternative? You're not going to get the girls to come home before they're ready."

I chuckled. That was true. The guys had all found strong, independent women. It was one of the characteristics I'd admired in Sunshine.

"Feeling better?"

I shrugged. "Feeling less like going to find the other guys and knocking some sense into them."

"It's a start." Tristan cleared his throat. "Since you're here, I should let you know your father has retained an attorney and they're making noises about suing you."

A tight, hot ball knotted in my stomach. "What?"

"They won't get anywhere with it. It's a nuisance at best. I've got it under control. But I figured you should know. I'd recommend you record any interactions you have with him. We're a single party consent state, so you don't have to inform him or get his okay." Tristan's expression was sympathetic. "I'm not sure he'll try contacting you. I made it clear to his attorney that it would be a bad idea."

"Why does money turn people evil?"

Tristan was quiet for a few moments. "I don't think it necessarily turns them that way. It just reveals what's already there, lurking."

I considered that, then nodded. That made sense. No one in the gang had gone rotten when we got our billions. The reality was, of all six of us, I was the one who did more billionaire type things than anyone else. I was the first to quit my job. Start a leisure business. All the cars. And sure, I did good things with those cars—I just didn't like to let on. Part of me enjoyed being seen as the frivolous one.

What did that say about my character?

"Should I call him? Tell him to stop?" I didn't really want to. I was mystified that my refusal to invest in his latest scheme would send him straight to suing me. What kind of father sued their son?

"I wouldn't waste my breath."

My shoulders slumped. Tristan's words were harsh, but true. Because it would be a waste of breath. Once Dad got on a train, he didn't usually get off voluntarily. "Thanks for handling it for me."

"It's what I do. And now that the divorce case is finally settled, I have more time to do the work I want."

"Yeah? It's done?"

Tristan nodded.

"Congrats. Don't promise people favors anymore. Except us. We won't do that to you."

Tristan laughed. "Believe me. I have already made that decision and it's nonnegotiable."

"So are you doing better now? You've been stressed and distant."

"That's what you all say. I think so, yeah. But you remember I'm not nor have I ever been the life of the party."

"Whatever." I drained the last of my soda. "You round out the group. It'd be different—wrong—without you."

"Thanks, man. Appreciate that."

I could tell he was trying to resist checking the time. I stood. "I guess I'll let you get back to work. You'd just leave this situation with the girls alone? Really?"

"I would. If you honestly have to do anything? Call Sunshine. Just talk to her."

Call Sunshine.

I'd been avoiding that since pretty much the minute she ran off the plane. But she'd reached out to me first. I'd kept responding in kind, trying to keep the ball in her court rather than taking a chance.

Maybe Tristan was right.

I waved and strode down the hall then let myself out of his condo.

If I called, I'd get to hear her voice. I wanted that more than I was willing to admit, even to myself.

I took the elevator down and marched through the lobby and out to my car. When I was inside, behind the wheel, I sat, mulling the options. I did a quick search to see the time difference. Then, before I could talk myself out of it, I scrolled to the contact I'd made for Sunshine and tapped the phone icon.

It rang three times. I was getting ready to hang up when it stopped ringing and I heard wind and laughter.

"Hello?"

Everything in me relaxed at the sound of her voice. I hadn't realized just how much I missed it. "Sunshine? It's Wes."

"Hi." I could hear the smile in that one word. "How are you?"

"Better, now."

"Oh?"

"Yeah. I spent the bulk of today pretty ticked at my friends. Tristan talked me down and convinced me to just call you."

She laughed. "I think I'm going to like Tristan. I like the women."

"Do you?" I wasn't surprised. They were likable ladies. But they weren't her generation, really. So there had definitely been a little concern that this would become yet another obstacle. "Most of the time I do, too."

"They love you. Did you know that?"

My eyebrows lifted. "Uh."

"Not in a way that's going to make their husbands jealous.

Don't be dumb. You know what I mean. I could hear it when you talked about your crew—you love them. It's definitely reciprocated."

"Okay. That makes sense, although being a man, I'll point out that it's weird to talk about loving my friends."

Sunshine snickered. "Get over it. It won't hurt you to get in touch with your softer side."

"It might." I grinned. "Tell me about the boat they hired."

"They chose the larger sailboat. They're sticking close to PR. Not even sleeping aboard."

"That sounds more like them. Let me guess, Jenna found resorts."

"Got it in one. I have a slip at one of the schmancy all-inclusives. They're trying to get me to hang out with them instead of staying aboard."

"You should do it. I can cover it for you." I bit my lip. Was that too much? It wasn't like I was trying to throw my money around to impress her. But at this point, I wanted her to get to know the gang. Maybe that would help win her over.

"I wasn't fishing for that."

"I know."

"You sure?"

Which did she mean? Was I sure I could cover it or was I sure I knew she wasn't hinting around for money? Actually? It didn't matter. I was sure of both. "Yes."

She sighed. "I could go for some girl time. If you really don't mind footing the bill, I'll take you up on it. Because your ladies have expensive taste."

"The guys spoil them." Which was as it should be, as far as I was concerned. "They're not always like that, though."

"Oh, I can tell. Like I said, I like them. I don't think I'd like spoiled and rich." There was a long pause, then she spoke again. "Can I ask you something?"

"Shoot."

"Why were you mad that they came down here?"

Something about the way she asked it clued me in that the answer mattered. I rubbed sweaty palms on my legs. "I guess it boils down to me not wanting anyone to pressure you to feel something you don't."

"You think I don't feel anything for you?"

My heart hammered in my chest. "I think you don't want to."

She scoffed. "You might be right on that. Or, I guess I should make that past tense. I like you, Wes. You're a good guy. I like being around you. I'm just not sure that you should settle—"

"Whoa. Stop there. No one is settling. Why would you think that? The age difference? Because I don't care about that."

"Are you sure? I'm pretty sure kids aren't in my future at this point. You could still have a big family."

I nodded. I'd gotten stuck on that for a little bit. "We'll be the cool aunt and uncle who take our friends' kids to do all the fun things their parents won't. And I just don't think this is one of those things we have to figure out immediately. We can worry about it on island time."

"There's no worrying on island time." She chuckled. "But I take your point. I didn't think, from your emails, that you were interested."

I blinked. Seriously? "Yeah, well, back atcha."

"All right. That's fair. Although you did sign yours 'sincerely.'"

I groaned. "What was I supposed to do? Put 'all my love'?"

"Maybe?" She cleared her throat. "If that isn't out of the realm of possibility."

"It isn't. But you go ahead and ask the girls if I take risks when I'm not reasonably sure of the outcome."

"Ah." She blew out a breath. "Okay, if you need a tutorial

here, when a woman signs her email with 'yours,' she means it. I'm yours, Wes. Unless you say no."

My whole body warmed. "I'm not saying no. I—"

The call dropped.

I stared at my phone. "I love you."

I sighed and set the phone on its cradle. I wasn't going to call back right away—if they'd lost signal, who knew how long it would take to come back. But I would text Megan and make sure they picked up Sunshine's tab on everything. I could settle up with them later.

In fact...I reached for my phone and sent the text right away. No point in opening the door for it to get weird.

I put the phone back on its cradle and started the engine. I'd go home. Fix some supper. And then maybe send Sunshine an email and sign it "With love."

22

SUNSHINE

I tiptoed out of my room and into the suite's spacious living area. Just this part of the room was bigger than my entire cottage, and that didn't take into account the three other bedrooms, all with their own bath. Just like mine.

The girls had been thrilled to have me join them at the resort. It grated some to call them that instead of women, but it was how they referred to themselves, so it probably wasn't anything I'd be able to change; and in fact, it would probably qualify me as unnecessarily stubborn. They were so excited about the idea, they'd called Zee up and said they were just going to base themselves here and if they needed the boat back to feel free to come get it.

I wasn't privy to how that conversation went from Zee's end, but I'd gotten a text message with about sixty question marks for the entirety of the text, so I could guess. I'd responded with a shrugging emoji. Client is king? Zee was usually on board with that. At the end of the day, the boat was still in its slip—I could just make it out through the wall of glass that looked out over the private beach to the water—and I was under orders to have a good time.

I wasn't sure what that would translate to in terms of getting paid, but maybe it didn't matter. I wasn't racking up expenses here, thanks to Wes, and I was doing okay financially otherwise.

Thanks, again, to Wes.

I owed him a lot, it seemed.

I watched other early risers leave their rooms, snag chairs, and drag them down into the sunshine. It was mostly couples, although I saw one other group made of older women—older even than me. I smiled. What would it be like to have a group of friends who you traveled with every year, regardless of your age?

"You're up early. Want coffee?"

I turned and spotted Jenna pulling the door to her room closed. She and Kayla had both ended up solo. Megan and Whitney had said they were happy to share.

"I do. I wasn't sure if the noise of making it would wake anyone."

Jenna's gaze flitted to the kitchenette and she bit her lip. "It's a good question. Darn it."

I chuckled and nodded toward the beach. "The tiki bar looks like it's doing a brisk business. I bet they have coffee. Maybe even some eats."

"That works for me." Jenna glanced down at herself. "Is this okay, do you think? Or should I change?"

"I'm guessing you're fine. Shorts and T-shirts are the unofficial uniform of the island."

"Yeah? What's the official uniform?" Jenna slid her feet into flip flops.

"Swimsuits." I grinned and unlocked the sliding portion of the glass I'd been looking out. The breeze that came in brought the scent of the ocean with it. I breathed deeply. "Ready?"

"Yep. It's weird not needing a wallet."

I nodded. "All-inclusive isn't usually in my budget, either."

"The guys aren't crazy spenders, but they do like to treat

their wives." Jenna shrugged. "I'm caught between getting used to it and feeling like I shouldn't do that. I don't want to take it for granted."

How was I supposed to respond to that? I couldn't imagine having access to money like that. And, despite the conversation with Wes last night, I still didn't think I was in danger of being a billionaire's wife any time soon. So I settled on a noncommittal "Hmm."

Jenna snickered as we crossed the sand. "You say that now. I think maybe you don't realize how gone Wes is over you."

"I...gone over me?" I shook my head. "I don't think you're reading him right."

"I guess we'll see." Jenna slipped into line at the tiki bar.

I stood beside her. "Looks like they have a breakfast buffet set up over on the right. Do you see it?"

Jenna turned her head. "Now I do. Yum. Fancy coffee, then breakfast buffet. Sound good?"

"Sure." We inched forward in line. The group in front of us ordered mimosas with giggles that suggested, at least to me, that this wasn't going to be the first round for them.

"Kinda early." Jenna whispered.

"Right?"

The woman at the rear of the group scowled over her shoulder at us. "It's five o'clock somewhere. Besides, we're on vacation."

"No offense." Jenna held up her hands. "Just an observation."

"Well, keep your observations to yourself." The woman huffed, reached for her drink, and stormed off behind her group of friends. She clearly filled them in, since the group all turned and shot glares in our direction.

"If looks could kill." The bartender chuckled and shook his head. "What can I get you ladies?"

"Can I get the biggest iced caramel latte you can make? With coconut milk?" Jenna tucked her hands in her pockets.

"That sounds good, actually. Make it two?"

"Coming right up." He moved to the giant coffee machine and got to work.

"Should we have left a note?" I wasn't sure what the group dynamics were. Was it okay to simply disappear? Would they worry? Would they even notice?

"I'll text Whitney when we sit down to eat. Of all of them, she's the one most likely to wake next. Although, having a chance to sleep in and not deal with her early-rising son, she might not. But I'm pretty sure she turns her phone off at night."

"Good enough." I took one of the tall cups of creamy brown liquid that the bartender set down and started toward the buffet area. "What did you all want to do today? Are you sunbathers? Or swimmers? Or...I don't know, go-into-town-and-shoppers?"

Jenna scanned the tables, then pointed. "Let's snag that one over by the omelet station. We'll figure out the day's plan eventually."

Since she'd taken off without waiting for a response, and because I didn't actually care where we sat, I followed. I put my coffee down in front of one of the chairs, then strolled to the start of the buffet line. I picked up a plate and moved to the first dish.

"Can we return to the conversation about Wes?"

I glanced at Jenna as she stood beside me, frowning at the chafing dish holding grilled fish. "Were we having one?"

"Ugh. You're perfect for him. He likes to deflect, too."

I laughed and snagged two sausage links from the dish. "I don't know what you're expecting, honestly. You've seen the movie *Speed*, right?"

"Uh. Maybe?"

My eyebrows lifted. "The age difference is an issue. Sandra

Bullock? Speeding bus? Relationships formed during adrenaline fueled experiences don't last?"

"Oh. I do know that one. I like it. But that last part is wrong. They're still together in the second movie, right?"

I shook my head. Much to my disappointment as a twenty-something at the time, Keanu Reeves turned down the second film. Of course, after watching it, I could see why. It wasn't fabulous.

"Oh." Jenna frowned and stopped in front of the omelet maker. "Can I get just cheese?"

"Sure." The man dipped eggs from the cylinder beside him and swirled them into a hot pan. "For you?"

I met his questioning look. I hadn't planned on an omelet, but why not. "Tomato, onion, and spinach?"

He nodded.

"That actually sounds good. No. I'm sticking with cheese."

We watched as he flipped the eggs, added the ingredients, then folded over half into a perfect semi-circle. He slid Jenna's onto her plate, first, and then mine.

We thanked him and moved to our table.

"Can I pray?" Jenna folded her hands in her lap and watched me.

"Sure." I finished spreading my napkin in my lap and closed my eyes. Jenna's prayer was short and to the point, but not perfunctory. It made me think of Wes. Maybe that was one of the reasons their group had been drawn to one another.

"Okay." Jenna picked up her fork and cut off a corner of her omelet. She poked it and held it aloft, cheese stringing from the bite to her plate. "Back to Wes."

"You're like a dog with a bone." I cut off a piece of sausage, then a corner of omelet, and stuck both in my mouth.

"I don't consider it a bad thing." Jenna grinned and took her bite. "He's been mopey since he got back. After a lot of prodding and nudging—because the guy can be a vault, apparently—Noah says Wes finally admitted that he really liked you. Like really, really liked you. But you ran off the plane and never looked back. So he's pretty convinced you aren't into him. And that's a bummer. True or false?"

I took another bite and chewed thoughtfully before taking a sip of the iced latte to wash everything down. "I wouldn't say I *ran* off the plane. We were parked and it was time to go. So I did."

"Seriously?" Jenna's eyebrows lifted. "That's the part you want to talk about?"

I crossed my arms. "I don't like being misrepresented."

"Okay. So you did look back? Say goodbye? Chit-chat and joke around a little, like people do?"

"Well, no." I sighed. "It's complicated."

"Bzzt. Nope. Wrong answer." Jenna stabbed the air with her fork as if to make a point. "That's what people say when they either don't want to explain or they don't want to think about things."

"You're tough." I picked up my fork and speared a sausage link. "It's awkward to talk about this with someone I barely know."

"All right, that's fair." Jenna considered me while she took a long drink of coffee. "Can you at least say if you like Wes even a little?"

I hesitated. There was probably no harm in it. Other than it being basically the first time I'd said it out loud. "I do."

Jenna grinned. "Yay! So what's the plan?"

I blinked. "Plan? I don't have a plan."

"Oh, come on. You like him. He likes you. There are some obstacles, obviously. How are we getting over them?"

"We?" I tipped my head to the side. "Are you part of this now?"

Jenna laughed. "Might as well be. That's how this group works. Believe me, I get it. I had never had a group of friends like this before and when Noah and I were figuring things out, Megan was relentless. All of them were, honestly, but Megan in particular. It took some getting used to, but now I kinda like it. It's good to have people who know me and who are going to make sure I get help when I need it."

"Whether or not you want it?" I heard the hint of snark in my tone and winced. "Sorry."

"No. You're right. And yeah, probably. Because that's what friends do."

I nodded and reached for my latte. That did sound like what friends were supposed to do. Maybe I was a bit more like Jenna though. I'd had Luca. And he was basically all I had. He was all I wanted—and needed—though too. And then he was gone because another boat full of people mixed too much alcohol with their fun on the waves.

So maybe now the right choice was to broaden my horizons when it came to friendships.

"I heard he's buying the island where we wrecked. Is that true?"

"He is. The guys are a little grumpy—well, Scott is—because they figured everyone would settle on the Caymans. Now, though, Wes is talking about everyone building for themselves on the island instead. I can't wait to get down and see it."

"Do you know if he has a trip planned?"

Jenna tipped her head to the side, the start of a smile tugging at the corners of her lips. "I don't. But I can find out. Are you being sneaky? It seems like you might be, and I have to say, I love it."

My face heated. I wasn't sure I'd call it sneaky so much as strategic. My life was in the islands. And while I wasn't opposed to relocating to the States, there was something appealing about seeing Wes again down here where it all began.

"What if it's not for a while?" Jenna's expression clouded. "You're not going to wait a long time, are you?"

"We're emailing. And he called yesterday." Finally. I didn't want to be the one doing all the chasing. I was old enough that it didn't feel...seemly, I guess would be the word. And sure, people Wes's age might not care about that. But it mattered just enough to me that I couldn't bring myself to be the first one reaching out that way. Sending the first email had been hard enough. Even though he'd been in touch with Zee and asked about me.

"That's enough for you?" Jenna frowned.

"For now. Yeah. I'm a big believer in being friends. Above, under, over, through everything else, there has to be a friendship. That's what gets you through the tough times."

"That sounds like experience speaking."

I nodded. "It is. I've been married. I know how important it is to have a foundation that lasts when the romance goes on vacation."

"What happened?" Jenna winced. "If that's not too much to ask."

"He died." I didn't want to get into the details. I'd shared them with Wes. He was one of a handful of people who knew the ins and outs. And the fact that it had seemed natural to tell him should probably have clued me in to how much I was falling for him.

"I'm sorry." Jenna reached for her latte and tipped it up, draining the last drops.

Silence settled over our table. It didn't feel awkward. To me, at least. Hopefully not to Jenna, either.

I'd nearly cleaned my plate when a shadow fell over the table.

"There you are." Whitney grinned and dragged one of the

chairs from a nearby table over, then sat. "I figured you'd gone off to find food."

"Sorry. I meant to text when we sat down." Jenna shot Whitney a sheepish look. "Glad you found us."

"It didn't take long. You left the sliding door open, too." Whitney shook her head. "Honestly, it's like having Beckett around."

"How old is he?" I'd heard him mentioned a few times— enough that I knew he was a child. But not much beyond that.

"Five. He'll start school soon. I can't believe it." Whitney's eyes were shiny. She took a deep breath and straightened her shoulders. "But I'm not obsessing about it. At all."

Jenna laughed. "Right. Did you figure out what you're going to do for school?"

"I think so. There's a good private school that's not too bad of a drive, even during rush hour. Smaller classrooms, more personal attention. They go through high school, too, and their seniors have some impressive scholarships at Ivy Leagues." Whitney offered a half-smile. "I feel a little guilty not sending him to public, but the more we talked about it, the more this felt like a better solution. Especially from a security standpoint. There are political kids who go there, so the school is super careful. Unfortunately, with Scott's money, it felt like that mattered."

"Makes sense. What do Austin and Kayla say?" Jenna tossed her napkin on top of her empty plate.

"Kayla is actually the one who sent me their website. That's where she's looking when they get there." Whitney glanced at the buffet. "I'm going to go get food. Megan'll be out in a few. Kayla is still sound asleep."

"Is security something you all have to worry about a lot?" I hadn't really considered the downside of mega money.

Jenna waggled a hand from side to side. "They're smart

about it. But as you see, it's not as if they're dragging bodyguards around with them. It helps that none of them are flashy or famous."

I nodded. I'd known Wes had money because he was able to afford the solo yacht charter, not because of his clothes or mannerisms. Although, seeing his dive gear would've been another clue. He went top of the line all the way there. Of course, so did people who were dive fanatics. They just saved up instead of paying cash.

"I'm going to get another iced latte. You want one?" Jenna stood and picked up her glass.

"Sure. Thanks."

"No problem." Jenna snagged my glass and strode off toward the tiki bar.

I leaned back in my chair and watched the waves lap at the beach. Other than the chatter of conversation from other diners and the occasional couple or group that strolled through my view, it was a lot like being at home.

I dug my phone out of my pocket and hesitated, then opened a text to Wes.

> Good morning. Sitting on the beach at the resort with the girls. They're great. It's weird.

WES

...

WES

WES

...

WES

> It's weird that they're great? Because...I wouldn't have great friends?

> No. Those were separate statements. I'm not used to girlfriends, but they absorbed me. Like an amoeba.

WES

> Amoeba. Charming. I'll let the guys know they married bacteria.

> Not what I said! Maybe we should stick to email.

WES

> Oh no. This is too much fun. What will you do today?

I glanced over at the buffet line. Whitney was slowly—very slowly—making her way through it. Turning more, I caught a glimpse of Jenna still in line at the tiki bar, chatting with the men behind her.

> No idea yet. Maybe they'll want to dive.

WES

> Maybe. You should convince them if not.

I smiled. How well would that go over? What would it be like to dive with them just as one of the group and not the person in charge? It'd probably be a lot like diving with Wes. I missed him. My fingers hesitated over the phone, then I typed. *Wish you were here, too.*

I regretted it almost as soon as I hit the arrow to send it. Not because it wasn't true, but I wasn't great at laying my cards on the table like that.

WES

> Any chance you could come back with them?

My eyebrows lifted. That was...an invitation. And the immediate answer was maybe? There wasn't a good reason to say no. Zee would understand. She'd been pushing for me to take a longer break, after all. And she was a hopeless romantic.

It felt like a big step, though.

But maybe one I was ready for.

I texted back:

> I'll see what I can do.

I bounced on my heels in the terminal at the airport watching the clock. Why was it taking so long?

"You need to chill." Austin glanced up from where he sat, a book in his lap. "They'll be landing soon."

"I know. I just can't believe she agreed to come back with the girls." I rubbed a hand absentmindedly over my chest. My heart felt as though it was going to beat through my sternum any minute now. Then it would flop onto the floor and splash around for a few minutes while it continued to race until it exploded.

The mental image that came with the thought was a little gruesome, though it helped that it was a cartoony heart in my mind's eye, not an anatomical one. The shape probably matched what I pictured my pupils turning into when I saw Sunshine on the video calls she'd started making from the beach in the early hours of the morning.

It was the sort of wakeup call I could get used to.

Austin snickered. "From what Kayla says, she's pining just about as much as you are. So it was a foregone conclusion that she'd come."

I shrugged. Didn't feel like it. Then again, what did I know? Relationships for me had always been some fun dinners out and a show if there was something good, then they'd fizzle out when the woman realized I had the emotional depth of a teaspoon.

That was a direct quote from the last one.

I sighed and checked the time on my phone.

"Would you sit? You're making me nervous." Austin patted the chair next to him. "You really like this woman."

I moved to perch on the edge of the chair beside Austin. "I do."

I paused as those words left my lips. I wanted to say them to Sunshine. Preferably when she was wearing something fancy and white and I was there in a suit—no tux for me, thanks. No tie, either. Just the two of us, a minister, and the beach at sunrise. Was that getting ahead of myself?

I hadn't actually said the words "I love you" to her. Nor had she said them to me. We'd talked around them. I was pretty sure she loved me. I knew I loved her. But it was almost as if saying it point blank was going to shatter the illusion swirling around us.

What did that mean?

Austin nudged my arm and nodded toward the window. "That's our plane touching down."

I sprang out of my seat. "Finally."

Austin laughed. "They still have to taxi."

I shrugged. Standing was better than sitting right now. I glanced over at Austin. "Did you feel this way about Kayla?"

He tipped his head to the side. "Still do. It morphs a little, mellows. But it's still there."

Good. That was good. Wasn't it? I took a deep breath and watched the plane as it came our way. Private planes still used jetways at this airport, not the stairs like in Puerto Rico. The luggage would be brought in separately. But there, finally, the plane stopped and the jetway began to move to cover the door.

"They're here."

Austin nodded, closed his book, and stood. "I'll take everyone else home. I imagine you'd like some time alone with Sunshine."

"That sounds good."

"You'll bring her to church tomorrow? And lunch with the gang?"

Nerves curled in my stomach. The girls liked her. Austin had told me that. Kayla wouldn't lie, either. Would the guys? Did it matter? Of course it mattered. I didn't think anyone in our group would stick with someone that the group had a problem with. Maybe that was unfair, but at this point we might as well be family. "Yeah. Of course."

"Good." Austin slapped my shoulder then moved past me, arms open, as Kayla launched herself into him.

Whitney came next, rolling her eyes and glancing around. "No Scott?"

"Austin said he'd pick everyone up. But, well, I'm going to grab Sunshine." I cleared my throat. "If that works."

"Fine with me." Whitney chuckled.

Megan, Jenna, and Sunshine came together, clumped up and chattering. They might have said something to me, but I didn't hear it. I just saw her. She tipped her head back and laughed and I would've sworn a beam of golden light from heaven shone down on her when she did.

"You've got it bad." Whitney whispered in my ear, breaking the spell.

I looked at her. "Is that not okay?"

"I think it's great. We like her. Big stamp of approval from us." Whitney patted my arm. "I'll round everyone up and we'll get out of your way. Have fun."

True to her word, Whitney made short work of organizing

the bags as they were brought up and shooing Austin and the rest of the ladies—luggage included—toward the car.

"Hi." Sunshine clasped her hands behind her back.

"Hi back." I closed the distance between us and haltingly slid my arms around her. I believed she was open to it. I prayed I hadn't been reading this wrong all along.

She linked her arms around me and bumped my nose with hers.

I stared into her eyes, just letting myself get lost. She was here. In Virginia. And sure, okay, it wasn't permanent yet, but right now, it honestly felt like adding the "yet" on the end wasn't wishful thinking.

Her stomach rumbled.

Sunshine leaned back and laughed. "I'm sorry."

She lowered her head to my shoulder, still laughing. I couldn't help but join in. "You don't need to apologize. I take it you're hungry?"

"Lucky guess." She squeezed me tight then stepped back.

I didn't want to let her go, but I did. I trailed my hand down her arm and linked my fingers with hers. "Any sort of food you're particularly in the mood for?"

"Is it okay if I ask for takeout? I don't want to sit in a crowded restaurant and share you with all the people who are eating." Her cheeks pinked as she spoke.

"I can get behind that idea. The Italian place near my house will do curbside."

"Italian is good."

"Then Italian it is." I gave her hand a little tug. "Whitney took the luggage. You're staying with her?"

"That's what she said. Megan also offered. As did Kayla." Sunshine laughed. "And Jenna. Honestly, I was starting to worry they were going to fight over it, so I told them to just tell me. Last I heard, Whitney won."

Hmm. I'd double-check. In my mind, staying with Jenna made more sense. She was living in what would be her and Noah's house all by herself. With eight bedrooms. Or maybe six? Some ridiculous amount anyway. Whitney and Scott had a small bed tucked into the office bedroom across the hall from Beckett. It was not what I'd consider an ideal setup.

"All right. We can firm that up after food." We made our way through the little airport and out to the parking area. I clicked the unlock button, suddenly a little self-conscious about driving a BMW. I cleared my throat and opened the passenger door.

Sunshine shot me a grin before sliding into the seat. "You're going to have to let me drive. Just once. Maybe somewhere we can go fast?"

I laughed and closed the door, then rounded the car to get behind the wheel. "Did I know you were a speed demon?"

"You had to have an idea, right? It's not as though the yacht was pokey." She clicked her seatbelt into place and ran a hand over the leather on the dash. "This is a gorgeous car."

"Thanks. I like cars."

"What's not to like?" She leaned her head back against the rest. "I don't have one. No need on the island. But I've always enjoyed renting them. Or a scooter."

I flashed to the memory of being pressed against her on the scooter ride to and from church. "Hm. Maybe I should have known you liked speed after riding pillion."

"Do we need to call ahead or something?" Sunshine's stomach rumbled again.

I got out my phone and navigated to the restaurant's website. I offered it to her. "Here's the menu. Once you know what you want, I can order online."

"Perfect."

I turned on the car to get the AC going while Sunshine scrolled through the list of options. I didn't blame her for taking some time. They had a lot to offer. And everything I'd ever tried had been delicious.

"Baked ziti. Can we get garlic bread?" She offered me the phone back.

"Absolutely." I added the ziti, garlic bread, and after a moment's thought, chicken parm for me to the cart. "Do you like fried mushrooms?"

Her eyebrows lifted. "Those aren't Italian."

I shrugged. "They're still yummy."

"Sure. I'll give it a whirl."

I added an order. "Tiramisu or cannoli?"

"Leave the gun." She glanced over at me.

I grinned. "Got it."

"Oh good. I was worried that movie reference was going to sail over your head."

"Are you kidding me? It's a classic." I finished the order then twisted in my seat and reached for her hand. "That said, can we make a pact?"

"Maybe. What's the pact?" Wariness entered her eyes.

I frowned slightly and worked to keep my voice light. "I get that I'm younger than you. I do. But it doesn't bother me. I don't want it to bother you. If you make a reference or a joke and I don't get it? Explain it to me. But don't make it weird. I'll do the same. Okay?"

After a moment, Sunshine closed her eyes and nodded. "Okay. I'm sorry."

"Pfft." I waved that off. "These are things we work through. That's it."

I brought her hand up to my lips and kissed her knuckles.

Sunshine drew in a quick breath and I glanced over, a question in my gaze. She gave a tiny shake of her head.

I squeezed her hand before letting go so I could put my phone into its cradle, shift into drive, and get us underway.

It wasn't a long drive from the airport into Old Town. I pointed out the few things that I thought were interesting or noteworthy as we passed them, but it wasn't like we were seeing monuments or anything else that made DC exciting. Mostly it was the Potomac River and neighborhoods.

Once we reached Old Town, I maneuvered the series of one-way streets so I came down the correct side of the road to pull into one of the curbside spots the Italian restaurant had reserved. Then I reached for my phone to let them know we had arrived.

"Shouldn't be long. They're pretty on top of things." I'd barely gotten the words out when the door opened and a server wearing all black and carrying a large white bag with the restaurant logo came out.

I lowered the window on Sunshine's side.

"For Mr. Allen?"

"That's me."

Sunshine reached through the window and took the bag. She settled it between her feet on the floor. "Thanks."

"Have a nice night." The server waved and turned to head back to the restaurant.

"Ready?" I looked at Sunshine and wanted to pinch myself. She was here. Sitting in my car.

"Now that I can smell the food? I really hope you don't live far."

I laughed and clicked the button to raise the window, then, after checking for traffic, pulled out into the road. It wasn't far to my house, but it was Saturday night in the summer and Old Town was bustling. Groups thronged the sidewalk. They waited at corners or took their chances darting across the road when they saw an opening. Even though I only lived a few blocks from the main shopping area, it took close to twenty minutes between traffic and stop lights.

Finally, I pulled into the driveway behind my townhouse.

Sunshine leaned down and looked out the window. "It's cute."

"Thanks." I didn't love the word cute, but it probably applied. The whitewashed brick had been a major selling point for me. It was a contrast to the boring red brick that most of the other houses in the area used. Of course, a few doors down, one of the neighbors had painted their brick a sort of neon green. If nothing else, it gave me a landmark to tell people if they needed directions.

I pushed open my door.

Sunshine followed suit.

I wasn't going to tell her to sit and wait for me to come around. That seemed dumb. But I would have gone to open it for her if she'd stayed put. Did she need to know that?

I got out of the car and closed the door, then came around to her side and reached for the food.

"I've got it." She clutched the bag to her chest.

"Okay." I chuckled and closed her door, taking a moment to click the lock button on the key fob. I scooted around her so I could get to the door and unlock it. I held it open. "Welcome."

She flashed a grin at me as she slid past and stepped into the kitchen. "Thanks. This is nice."

"I like it." I gestured to the small island. "You can put the food down there. I'll get plates."

"Okay." Sunshine set down the food and moved through the kitchen to peek into the room where we played poker when I hosted.

I didn't leave the game table up. It was set up as a den. I had the big TV in there and my game console. I probably spent more time in there in the evenings than anywhere else.

"This is cozy." She crossed the room and peeked down the hall. "What's down there?"

"Living room and the front door. You want a tour first or to eat?"

"Oh, food. For sure." She came back into the kitchen. "How can I help?"

"Do you want to grab a soda out of the fridge?" I nodded toward the appliance as I transferred her food from the takeout container to a plate, then repeated the process with my own meal. I frowned at the garlic bread and mushrooms, then went back to the cupboards for bowls.

"This is quite the collection." Sunshine stared at the shelf dedicated to various sodas.

"I just had the guys for poker. I overbought." Although that was a bit of a lame excuse. I often ended up with the shelf looking like that. I enjoyed soda—probably a leftover from my days as a programmer. "I'll take something with no caffeine. There should be options."

"Orange or lemon lime?"

"Let's live dangerously and do orange." I wasn't the biggest fan. Why had I bought that? Oh, right. Noah was on a kick.

Sunshine carried two cans over to the small table that sat pressed against the wall. I set her plate down at one spot and mine at the other before returning to the island to grab the bread and mushrooms.

"Forks?" She pulled out her chair.

"Right. Duh." I chuckled and went to get them. Why were my palms sweating? We'd eaten together a lot on the boat. And the island. Basically the whole time I'd been with her, we'd had three meals a day together.

They just hadn't been a date.

And this definitely was.

I sat and reached for her hand. "Would you like to say grace?"

"Sure." Sunshine bowed her head. "Thank You, Jesus, for a

safe flight. For the fun time the girls and I had in the islands. And for this time I get to spend with Wes. Guide us and keep us in your will. Bless the food and the hands that prepared it. Amen."

"Amen." I tightened my hold on her hand.

"I need that to eat." She laughed and tugged on her fingers.

I grudgingly let go and picked up my fork and knife. "How long can you stay?"

"I don't have any firm date in mind. I thought I'd play it by ear. I don't want you to get sick of me though."

"Not possible." I looked up from cutting my chicken.

"We'll see." She shrugged. "Can I hang out at the dive shop with you during the day?"

"Absolutely." I took a bite and chewed. "In fact, if you want to help out with the beginning certification class that just started, I'd love it."

"That sounds fun. I haven't run an open water class in a while."

I reached for a mushroom. "You teach other classes though, right?"

"Now and then, yeah. I haven't had as many recently. My own fault, really, as I haven't been seeking them out." She shrugged and took a bite.

"I guess you needed a little break after the whole shipwreck thing."

She reached for a slice of bread and studied it. "Not really. Although Zee was pretty firm on making me. I just wanted time to brood, I guess."

I nodded. I could understand needing that kind of time. According to the guys, I'd done a bit of that myself. Of course, that was because I was missing Sunshine. I just hadn't been willing—or able—to put it directly into words.

I cleared my throat. "I'm guessing the girls mentioned I was buying the island."

"They did." Sunshine's eyes danced with laughter. "It's a bit of a kick to say I know someone who owns an island."

"It's surreal to be able to say I own one. Although I don't close until the end of the month. So I guess I don't. Yet." I cleared my throat. "Any chance you'd want to come down and walk through it with me and the general contractor to talk through our plans?"

"Yeah. Of course."

Her agreement eased some of the tightness in my chest. She was here, and that was step one, but I still wasn't sure—not really—if she was all in on a relationship with me. I didn't want to ask outright. It seemed pushy. And insecure.

Which, okay fine, I felt both of those things. But neither were particularly masculine, and I didn't want to send her running because I was being childish.

I felt her eyes on me and looked up from my food. "What?"

"I could ask you the same thing." She reached across and laid her hand over mine. "Are you having second thoughts?"

"What?" I laughed and shook my head. "No. Ha. Definitely no. I was sort of wondering if you were."

She shook her head. "I'm pretty sure I'm in love with you, Wes. No second thoughts."

I closed my eyes as my breath came out in a whoosh. "Thank goodness." I opened my eyes and leaned forward. "I'm pretty sure I love you back."

24

SUNSHINE

I stretched, luxuriating in the cloud-like sheets on the guest bed at Jenna's place. Wes and I had lingered over dinner, and then spent the evening curled up on the couch in his den. There'd been a movie on the TV, but I certainly hadn't caught much of it.

I couldn't stop the grin.

Who would've thought he could kiss like that?

The best part? I hadn't gotten trapped in my head, comparing things to Luca. Wes was different. He was Wes. And as much as I loved Luca—and always would—I was gratified to know there was room in my heart for someone else without it turning into a competition of memory.

I closed my eyes and snuggled back into the pillow, replaying the gentle, almost hesitant brush of his lips on mine the first time. And then the insistent hunger that exploded when I responded.

It was good that I had been expected at one of the girl's houses for the night. I couldn't swear I would have made myself leave. And that wouldn't have been fair to Wes. Luca and I had always had a tiny bit of regret that we hadn't stayed true to our faith before we were married. Oh, we had reasons. Excuses, really. But they had worked in terms of justification for both of us. At the end of the day, we'd gone along with the idea that everyone lived together before they were married. Only people caught up in some kind of fanatical religion didn't. Why pay two rents if we didn't have to? We were getting married anyway.

It was easy to dismiss the niggle of conscience when it tried to poke through. And, in the end, we had gotten married. And about a year after that, we'd had to sit down and take a hard look at ourselves and realize that while we'd said we were Christians, we weren't living for Jesus and hadn't been for a while.

The change that came in our lives after we made a conscious decision to truly walk with Jesus had made us stronger as a couple. And it had given me the strength to carry on after Luca died. Because it wasn't my strength that was carrying me. It was God's. So now? I wasn't going to make those same mistakes again. No matter how much my body might prefer I did.

There were a couple of light taps on my door and then Jenna called out, "Sunshine? You up?"

"I'm awake. You can come in." I scooted myself up so I was sitting.

The door opened and Jenna poked her head in. "Morning. You said you wanted to go to church with us. That still true?"

"Absolutely. Do I need to hurry? I don't take long to get ready." I'd showered the night before, so it was a matter of clothes and a ponytail.

Jenna shook her head. "Not really. We have about ninety minutes before we need to leave."

"Is there coffee?"

"At the risk of being rude, duh." Jenna chuckled. "I can bring some up?"

"Don't do that. I'll be down in a few minutes. Maybe ten. I can wait."

"Okay." Jenna paused. "Did things go okay with Wes last night?"

I thought of Wes's lips on mine and his hands in my hair and on my hips. Mmm. I fought the urge to clear my throat and aimed for a casual tone. "Yeah. We got Italian takeout. Watched a movie."

"Yeah? What'd you watch?" Jenna leaned against the doorframe.

Heat flooded my face and I started to laugh. "I have no idea."

Jenna blinked once then joined in laughing. "That answers my next question, I guess. It's good. Wes has been a little lost since everyone started pairing up. He tries to hide it, but I think you're good for him."

"I want to be." He was good for me. But it needed to be a two-way street. I wanted it to last.

"Then I think you will be." Jenna pushed off the wall and stepped back. "I'll see you in the kitchen when you're ready for coffee."

I nodded.

Jenna pulled the door closed behind her.

I listened as her footsteps receded down the hall. She'd shown me her room on the floor below. I could have had any of the guest rooms—but this one, with the pale blue walls and white bedding. had seemed so fresh and inviting, I'd opted for it. I also enjoyed the sense of being on my own instead of feeling like an imposition as a houseguest.

I tossed the covers back, threw my legs over the side of the bed, and stood. I took a couple of minutes to stretch out the final few kinks from travel before padding to my suitcase and flipping it open. I hadn't packed a lot. The girls had assured me that casual would work for everything I might do. But I had thrown in a couple of sundresses. Just in case.

Church felt like it might be sundress appropriate.

I bit my lip and considered the options. Which would Wes like best? No. That shouldn't be my deciding factor. This was church. It was about worshipping Jesus and learning, not impressing Wes. Not that impressing him was likely. I didn't tend to dress to impress when I was piloting a charter. I went for comfort. And diving? Again, the attire was dictated by the task.

I reached for the dress nearest—it was a simple, solid, pale yellow that Zee had insisted I buy. She said it personified my name. So okay. I'd go with that.

I stripped off the shorts and tank top that made up my sleepwear and dragged the dress over my head. I loved the way the ruffle at the bottom of the skirt floated around my calves. I smiled and adjusted the cap sleeves. Good enough.

A few minutes in the bathroom to pull back my hair, wash my face, and, after a moment of indecision, slap on minimal makeup, I was as ready as I was going to get. I picked up my phone—its case held my ID and credit cards, because someone out there understood that women didn't always want to be lugging a purse around—and headed downstairs.

The stairs in Jenna's house—or, well, Noah's house—were gorgeous. Oval and open, they were the kind of stairs that demanded to be used as a grand entrance to a ball. I could imagine sweeping down them in some fabulous gown in the dim light of evening to a swarm of well-dressed men and women sipping cocktails and laughing.

I couldn't have explained why I pictured it as a masquerade —complete with feathered masks on long sticks, but I could go with it.

At the bottom of the stairs, I paused and tried to remember the directions Jenna had given me last night when we arrived. It was a blur. I tried the doors on the right and shook my head as they opened to reveal a cozy game room. There was a pool table.

Another table covered in felt. For cards? Probably. A giant TV with a console underneath full of equipment.

And it had no other doors, so it wasn't the pass-through.

I pulled the doors shut and crossed the large foyer to the set of doors on the other side. *There we go.* This room was also fabulous—which worked, because that was definitely the word I would use for the entire house—but more of a formal entertaining space.

Formal might be overstating a little. The furniture looked comfortable. Like you could curl up and read or just hang out with friends and chat for hours. It was a good room.

Doors on the adjacent wall were open. I crossed the room and headed through the doors into a grand dining room. The table could easily seat twelve. Or more. And the cabinet on the far wall needed to be filled with glimmering crystal and fine china. Maybe Noah and Jenna would do that after they married.

I continued through the open doorway down a hall, past a bathroom, and finally into the kitchen.

"You found it." Jenna looked up from where she sat at a small table against the wall.

"I did." I tilted my head to the side. "I missed these stairs though."

Jenna chuckled. "They're at the far end of the hall—you have to turn the corner to the shorter leg of the building."

I closed my eyes and tried to envision what she meant, then nodded once. "Okay. I'll keep that in mind. Although I love the main stairs. They're like something out of a movie."

"Right?" Jenna started to stand. "It's why I want to have our wedding here. Noah's not convinced."

"Sit." I waved Jenna back into her seat. "I can get my own coffee."

"There's chopped-up fruit in the fridge, if you want something to eat. I also have oatmeal packets. And probably a granola bar or two."

"Perfect." I crossed to the coffee pot on the counter and reached up to open the cupboard door just above.

"One more to the right."

I shifted my hand and opened the door Jenna indicated. I smiled at the mugs. No fancy mugs here. They all had cartoons or funny sayings. I snagged one with a narwhal on it and filled it.

"Do you have milk or cream or something?"

"Fridge. And sugar—just the real stuff, sorry—in the bowl there. Or one of the creamers is hazelnut and already sweetened." Jenna sipped her coffee. "That mug is one of my favorites."

"I've always liked narwhals. Any ocean creature, really. But the chances of diving with narwhals is slim, so I just have to admire them from afar." I opened the fridge and got out the flavored creamer. I added a generous splash to my coffee and returned it to the fridge door. I studied the shelves, finally spying the fruit. I took that container and shut the door.

"Bowls are in the cabinet you went for initially." Jenna frowned. "Would you mind bringing one for me? Now that I see the fruit, I'm hungry."

I chuckled and reached for two bowls. I balanced the fruit on top of them and picked up my coffee with my other hand and carried the whole pile to the table. After setting everything down, I turned back to the cabinets. "Where would silverware be?"

"Oh. Helpful, yes. Drawer to the left of the sink."

I crossed the kitchen and pulled open the drawer. "Fork or spoon?"

"Fork." Jenna didn't say "duh" but her tone did.

I grinned. "Just making sure."

I brought two forks back over to the table and sat, then slid one over to Jenna. "Thanks for putting me up."

"No problem. I'm glad I was able to convince the others that this made the most sense. They have guest rooms, sure, but I have the most space." Jenna stabbed some melon and scooped it into her bowl.

I sipped my coffee while I waited for her to get her fruit, then filled my own bowl. We chatted about inconsequential things while we ate, then Jenna excused herself to go finish getting ready. I sat in the kitchen, lingering over a second cup of coffee. I liked this house. I could see why Noah had wanted it. And the renovation or remodeling or whatever he'd had done was fabulous. I could still tell it was old—without needing to read the historic marker on a pole outside by the sidewalk—but it also felt modern and comfortable. A hard balance to achieve.

I took a few minutes to let Zee know I was doing well. That things with Wes were going great and that she shouldn't worry. Then I carried all the dishes over to the sink. There was a dishwasher on the right. I opened it and looked at the dishes inside. Jenna must be a rinser, because I couldn't decide if they were clean or dirty.

I closed the dishwasher and settled for rinsing everything in the sink and stacking it neatly. If there had been a drying rack, I would have gone ahead and just washed them, but I didn't see one handy.

Which was fine. I just wanted to be a good guest. I needed Wes's friends to like me. I got the sense that this group wouldn't put up with a significant-other that the rest of them didn't like. It was a good thing. Just a little stressful for the person auditioning to join the group.

"Ready to go?" Jenna strode back into the kitchen. She had to duck a little to get through the doorway since she'd added heels to her outfit.

"I am. But you look fancy. Am I too casual?"

"Not at all. You look great." Jenna brushed at her dressy slacks. "I was trying to match your energy, not show you up. Realistically, everyone else is going to be in shorts. Maybe jeans."

"Okay." I picked my phone up off the table. "I appreciate you going the extra mile so I'm not the only fancy one."

Jenna laughed. "Come on."

We exited through the kitchen door and crossed the expansive back garden to the detached garage.

I climbed into the passenger seat. "Why doesn't Noah want to get married here?"

"Hm? Oh." Jenna clicked her seatbelt into place and looked over her shoulder as she reversed out of the garage. "I think he's worried it won't hold everyone. But I don't think we'd end up with hundreds coming anyway. Megan and Cody had more people at their wedding than I want, and I think Megan said their guest list was right at eighty."

I pictured the space in the foyer. "Would you just put two rows of seats along each of the long foyer walls?"

"That's an idea. I was thinking of making short rows with an aisle between. I'm pretty sure we could get four chairs on either side with enough room for people. And probably eight, maybe ten rows." Jenna slowed and flicked on her turn signal.

"That's a good number. Maybe you should show him what you're thinking? You're an architect? I think that's what Wes said."

Jenna nodded and turned.

"So draw it up in CAD. Let Noah see that you've thought it out. Where would you hold the reception?"

"In the back. Heated tents. I really want to get married New Year's Eve. Noah's also not sure about that, but how great would it be to have a built-in reason to celebrate every year? Plus, it's an easy out for declining party invites that we don't want. 'Oh, so sorry. It's our anniversary.'"

I laughed. "You've thought this through."

"I have. I guess Noah's worried I'm going to be upset if I don't have a big church thing. But that's not really my style. I love church, and Jesus and the marriage covenant will definitely be the focus of our ceremony, but I think we can do that without being in an actual church building." Jenna slowed at a stop sign. "Plus, as much as I like our church? The sanctuary is stuck in the nineties."

I fought a grin. Redecorating was expensive. I'd always wondered why churches didn't take that into consideration and choose more timeless palettes when they finally worked up the money to change things.

"You'll see." Jenna turned again and then pulled into a parking lot in front of a brick building.

It was obviously a church. I didn't need the white sign out front or the cross on the steeple to tell me. But it was also charming. "We don't have churches that look like this on the islands. Or, not usually."

"I wouldn't imagine architecture there runs to colonial brick."

"Fair." I waited for Jenna to stop the engine then undid my seatbelt.

We both got out of the car and crossed the parking lot to the main doors. I glanced around, hoping to see Wes's car. How hard would it be to spot a BMW? Turned out, in the northern Virginia area, BMWs weren't as rare as I imagined they would be.

"He's here." Jenna turned and pointed to one of the cars I'd missed in my scan. "That's his."

"How do you keep it straight?"

"His license plate."

My gaze drifted down to the white-and-blue Virginia plate and I laughed as I read it. DVWM3. "Dive with me? Is that what it means?"

"You really are made for each other. None of us got it until he explained it." Jenna shook her head and pulled open the door to the church. "Come on. I bet he's already staked out our row."

I walked in behind Jenna and took in the foyer. Stairs led down and up over to the left. More doors stood straight ahead. And there was Wes.

"Or not." Jenna waved. "I'll go find Noah. I think you're in good hands."

"There you are." Wes crossed the foyer, expertly dodging groups that were chatting, and pulled me into a hug. "I was beginning to wonder."

"Are we late?" I eased back and shifted to hold his hand. I could PDA with the best of them, but in church? That seemed... not quite right.

"No. Not really." Wes stepped closer so our arms touched from shoulder to wrist. "I just missed you."

His breath on my cheek set delicious shivers through my body. I swallowed. My voice was a hoarse whisper. "We're in *church*."

Wes pressed a quick kiss just below my ear and I thought I might burst out of my skin.

"Quit it." I stepped away, breaking all contact except our hands. I shot him a warning look.

"Your smirk suggests you don't really mean it." His eyes danced. "But I'll try to behave. For now."

"Thanks." I needed to get myself under control. He needed to get himself under control. Good grief, neither of us were teenagers. "Should we go find your friends and sit?"

"We can do that. They're your friends too, you know."

I nodded. I could actually agree with that, even though I

hadn't known them long. At least the women were. The guys? Well, I guessed we'd find out what they thought of me after today. I took a deep, steadying breath. I could do this.

I would do this.

I tucked a stray strand of hair behind my ear and followed Wes as he led me into the sanctuary and down the side aisle to the row where I spotted Jenna and Megan already standing and chatting with the rest of the guys.

"Relax. They'll love you." Wes paused and met my gaze. "Even if it's only because I do."

I squeezed his hand, bolstered by his words. "I love you, too."

He flashed a grin and took the final steps to the aisle where his friends were gathered. "Hey, guys."

Everyone looked over.

I had one of those moments that usually only happens in dreams—where it feels like you're standing onstage in front of a packed audience with the bright, hot spotlight burning down from above and you realize you never got your copy of the script. My stomach knotted and it sounded like everyone talking was underwater.

"You all right?" Wes whispered and nudged me with his elbow.

I smiled, but it felt sickly. Hopefully, it didn't look that way to everyone else. "Yeah." I lifted a hand in greeting to the group.

Jenna shot me two thumbs up. The tension in my shoulders eased. My smile relaxed.

"Hi. It's nice to meet you all." I squeezed Wes's hand.

After a moment, he squeezed back. A couple of times. Oh. I loosened my grip.

Wes met my gaze and mouthed, "Ow."

"Sorry," I muttered.

"Looks like they're about to start." Wes nodded toward the platform where the worship band was moving into position.

Everyone in the sanctuary seemed to notice the cue. Conversations quieted and rows filled up with congregants.

I was grateful to have the aisle seat with only Wes beside me.

I enjoyed the service. It was a lot like the church I usually attended—minus the tropical temperatures. Most of the songs were the same, though some of the tunes were different. The pastor gave a good sermon on faith from Luke chapter seventeen. It left me with a lot to think about. So many people used the mustard seed in their sermons—or their inspirational faith memes—but I appreciated that the pastor focused more on how we weren't meant to have faith in our faith, but that we were to put our faith in Jesus and be obedient to Him.

I saved the notes I'd taken in my app and flipped my phone cover closed so I could stand with Wes for the benediction. When it finished and an upbeat Christian song began to play, he turned to me.

"What'd you think?"

"I liked it. A lot. I see why you chose it." I reached for his hand.

"Are you nervous?" Wes's eyebrows drew together. "We can skip lunch with the crew if you want."

I shook my head. "No. We don't need to do that. In fact, I think that would be a bad idea. I want to get to know them. I—they'll be my friends, too. Like you said."

Wes leaned forward and kissed my forehead. "Thanks."

"Where are we eating?" Megan bounced on her toes.

"Someone decide fast." Kayla was already unwrapping a granola bar. "The pregnant lady is starving."

"Uh-oh." Austin gave a mock shudder.

"Quiet, you." Kayla glowered at him and took a huge bite.

I smiled as the group bantered their way to a restaurant decision. It didn't take long, but it was clear they had a list of favorites that they worked through. Before too much time, everyone was on their way down the aisle and out the doors.

We paused when we reached the pastor.

"Wes, good to see you. Who's your friend?" He turned his gaze on me.

"This is Sunshine King. She's visiting from the Caribbean, but I'm hoping to persuade her to relocate." Wes beamed at me.

I shook the pastor's hand. "He's not going to have to work too hard."

Wes looked at me, pleased surprise on his face. "Yeah?"

One corner of my mouth quirked up. "Yeah. I want a future with you. And you live here. I don't have anything holding me in the islands anymore. At least nothing with a stronger pull than a life with you."

Wes chuckled. "That was easier than I thought it would be. Now I just have to convince you that we don't need a long engagement."

The pastor smiled. "Feel free to call my office this week to set up premarital counseling sessions."

"I might do that." Wes glanced at me.

My mouth went dry and my heart beat a rapid, island rhythm. "I...it's a good idea. I may have to do some virtually."

"We can make that work." The pastor looked between the two of us and nodded once. "Keep me posted."

"Sure. Thanks." Wes tugged my hand. "Have a good afternoon."

My mind was spinning as we walked down the steps from the church and into the parking lot toward Wes's car. "What just happened?"

Wes stopped and turned to face me. He rested his hands on my hips and his forehead on mine. "You have to have known this was where I was headed. We don't have to get married today. But

I want that. Soon. Maybe love at first sight doesn't happen to most people, but I can't laugh it off as impossible. Not anymore."

I closed my eyes. His words swam around in my mind and I absorbed their meaning, and the sincerity behind them. And it felt true. And right. "Neither can I."

25

WES

Her words pierced every part of my soul and let in light that I hadn't realized I was missing. I pulled her in and held her tight against me before lowering my mouth to hers. I didn't count heartbeats or seconds or minutes. As far as I was concerned, time could stop and I would just live in this moment.

A car horn blared and a voice shouted, "Get a room."

I broke away and whipped my head around, scowling.

Noah hung out the side window of Jenna's car laughing like the moron that he was.

"Don't give him the bird in the church parking lot."

Sunshine's laughing voice pulled me out of the dark thoughts of murder that I'd been thinking toward Noah.

I snickered. "Probably not the best idea."

"Come on, guys. Kayla's hangry. I don't want to be responsible for her deciding to wreak havoc on the unsuspecting." Jenna leaned over and called through Noah's open window. "You can make out later. Promise."

Heat flamed across my cheeks worse than the worst sunburn I'd had. I cleared my throat. "Thanks, Mom."

"Pfft." Jenna flicked her fingers at me and drove off.

"I don't really want to see the wrath of Kayla. She's pretty fierce when she's normal." Sunshine tugged my hand and dragged me the last few feet to my car.

"Reasonable." I opened the door and held it for her, then snuck a quick kiss on her cheek as she slid past me to sit.

Sunshine laughed. "Stop."

"Can't." I grinned and shut the door before circling the car to get in on the driver's side. I fastened my seatbelt and started the engine, then glanced over at Sunshine. "Would you be opposed to swinging by a jewelry store on the way home from lunch?"

Her face paled. "For...?"

I cocked my head to the side. Had I misunderstood? "A ring? For you. An engagement ring for you."

Sunshine blinked at me, then began to chuckle. The chuckle turned into full out laughter and she actually had tears leaking out of her eyes.

I frowned and backed out of the parking spot, heading toward the restaurant on the river we'd decided on. "What'd I miss?"

"Nothing." Sunshine took a deep breath and made several attempts to quell her laughter before she succeeded. "You didn't miss anything. I just—"

She broke off. I glanced over. "You just?"

"I feel like I need to preface this by saying it's about Luca."

I reached over and took her hand. "You can talk about him. He was a big part of your life. I don't ever want you to feel like I'm...I don't know, jealous? I'm not. And if I ever am? That's my problem, not yours."

"Okay." She blew out a breath and nodded. "Okay. Well. Luca never actually proposed, either. I was just thinking it was hilarious that I was going to be married twice and neither time would I have that moonlight-down-on-one-knee experience."

I bit my lip. "I'm sorry. I should have thought—we can do that. I'll surprise you later."

"Don't you dare." She glared at me. "We're engaged and I want a ring."

"You're a confusing woman sometimes, do you know that?" I shook my head, but I couldn't stop the grin that formed. "So you're okay with the jewelry store after lunch?"

"I absolutely am. But no diamonds."

"What? Why not?"

Sunshine wrinkled her nose. "Too flashy. They get caught on things. I want something I can wear when I dive and not worry about it."

I nodded. That made sense. Diving was a big part of her life, just like it was in mine. "I'll agree to the last part, but I'm not willing to rule out diamonds yet. Let's at least look. Do I need to remind you money is no object?"

She snickered.

I was glad she'd caught the tease. "Deal?"

"Deal."

I pulled my hand back to make the tight turn into the parking lot. It was crowded. No big surprise, seeing as it was a warm, summer Sunday. "I hope we can get a table."

"I don't mind waiting. As long as we can get Kayla a bread-stick or something."

"I imagine we can do that. They know us here. Ha." I spun the wheel quickly to angle into a parking spot that was hidden by a big truck. It took a little maneuvering to get in—and the truck was going to have to work to get out—but I did it. And, when I opened my door to double-check, I was in the lines. So any issues weren't on me.

Sunshine pushed open her door and climbed out. I did the same and met her at the back of the car. I took her hand and gave our arms a swing as we crossed the lot and climbed the steps leading to the deck at the front of the restaurant.

Megan greeted us. "They had a big table on the back deck. I called on our way over and they reserved it for us. Good thing, too, because another big group is gathering but they have to wait until everyone's here to be seated."

"Nice." I opened the door for the ladies and followed Megan and Sunshine through the crowded inside seating to the doors leading to the outside tables. A breeze blew off the river, bringing cooler air to move around the humidity, but also the little whiffs of the Potomac that were oh-so-different than the ocean freshness.

"Glad you could join us." Noah smirked over the top of his menu.

Jenna rammed her elbow into his side.

"Ow. What was that for?" He frowned at her.

"Be nice." Jenna shook her head. "I apologize for my immature fiancé."

"We're used to it." I pulled out the chair for Sunshine and then took the seat beside her. "Or, at least, I am."

"Oh, yeah. Cause you're so mature all the time." Noah made a face at me before hiding behind his menu.

"What's good here?" Sunshine flipped open her menu, her eyes widening at the multiple pages.

"I've never had anything I didn't like." Whitney dragged a wriggling Beckett onto her lap and kissed his hair. "Beckett likes the mac and cheese."

Sunshine laughed. "Always good to have a backup plan."

"I've always thought so." Noah exchanged a lovey dovey look with Jenna.

I fought the urge to make a gagging motion. I probably couldn't do that when everyone got gooey now that I had someone to be gooey with and about myself. My gaze flicked over to Tristan.

He heaved out a sigh. "Guess I need to get serious about finding a girlfriend now that Wes has one."

"Oh, but I don't." I shook my head and slipped my arm around Sunshine's shoulders. "I have a fiancée."

"What?" Megan practically jumped out of her seat, but Cody pushed her back down. "When did this happen? How? Let me see the ring!"

Sunshine chuckled. "We're going shopping after lunch."

"And the rest?" Tristan shot me a cool, measuring gaze.

What was his problem? I met his gaze steadily. "Sort of happened organically while we were talking to the pastor. Although it was something we've talked about—or around —before."

Kayla frowned. "That's not very romantic."

"I'm fine with it." Sunshine took my hand. "That's all that matters, really."

Tristan turned his gaze on Sunshine.

I bristled. "Leave it alone, man."

"I assume you'll be fine signing a prenup?"

I glared at Tristan. "I said to—"

"It's okay." Sunshine squeezed my hand. She looked at Tristan. "If that's what Wes wants? Absolutely. I'm not after his money. I do fine on my own. Maybe not to the level you all do, but I have a house. A boat. A job that gives me an income when I want it and freedom when I don't. I'm giving up a lot to move here. And I'm fine with that, too. Because Wes is enough. And I'll be sad if me loving him causes a problem with your friendship, but I won't walk away because of it. That'll be for you and Wes to fix."

Tristan cocked his head to the side and nodded once before opening his menu.

"Hear, hear." Whitney shot Sunshine a supportive grin. "Congratulations, you two."

I leaned close to Sunshine and lowered my voice as the rest of the group chattered with one another at a volume that suggested they were going out of their way to be cheerful. "I'm sorry."

"No. Don't be." She leaned in and kissed me. "I love you, not your bank account."

I swallowed the lump in my throat and closed my eyes. I rested my forehead on hers and sent up a silent prayer of thanksgiving for bringing her into my life.

"Are we ready to order?" The server's cheerful greeting cut through the conversation.

Lunch passed quickly. The food was good and the conversation wasn't as stilted as I'd worried it would be after Tristan's little hissy fit. He wouldn't make eye contact with me. Hopefully that meant he knew he'd crossed a line.

Yes, we'd skipped to engaged quickly, but it felt right. It was right. I'd been praying about our relationship. I believed that Sunshine had been as well. Had I planned on proposing during her trip up here? Not really. I wouldn't have been opposed, but I definitely hadn't thought it would come from a conversation with the pastor.

I smiled slightly at that memory and waved over the server.

"Yes?"

"I'll take the check, no need to split it."

"Okay." The server drifted off to another table.

"Wes." Whitney must have overheard me. "You don't need to do that."

I shrugged. "We'll call it an engagement party."

"That's for your friends to throw, not you." Whitney frowned. "Let me—"

"Stop. It's fine. I want to do this."

"Well. Thank you." Whitney smiled.

"Mama? Can we go home yet?" Beckett tugged on Whitney's sleeve.

She glanced at Scott. "What do you say, hon?"

Scott nodded. "I'll just get the check."

"I've got it." I waved him off. "Go home. We'll catch up later."

Scott studied me a moment. "Okay. Thanks."

"You bet." A couple of minutes later, the server brought the check. I handed her my card after a quick glance at the total. The other couples made their excuses, thanked me for paying, and left. When the server returned with my card and the slip, I added on the tip, signed it, and put my card away.

Only Tristan was left. He stood at my elbow with his hands in his pockets. "I apologize."

It didn't sound as though he meant it. His voice was stiffer than his posture. I wasn't sure how to respond.

"You don't need to." Sunshine scooted her chair back and stood. "You're looking out for your friend. And it seems reasonable that there might be something sketchy in a woman so much older, a widow at that, who's getting her hooks into your friend."

Tristan winced. "No. It's not reasonable. And no one else has a prenup, I know this. I don't have an excuse. Again, I'm sorry. Maybe Kayla wasn't the only one who was hangry."

I raised my eyebrows. "You're pregnant too? Congrats, man. Didn't know that was possible."

Tristan snorted and shoved my shoulder. "You're such a jerk sometimes."

"It's why we're friends. We're a lot alike."

"Yeah, yeah. I said I was sorry."

I nodded. "I think the second time you even meant it."

"Harsh. Also true. I'm gonna head home. Maybe hit the gym."

"Probably a good plan. Maybe it'll help your mood some."

Tristan shrugged. "Can't hurt, right?"

Sunshine stepped over to Tristan, arms out. "In the islands, we hug."

Tristan glanced at me. I nodded. He let Sunshine wrap her arms around him and he patted her shoulders awkwardly.

She stepped back. "Needs some work, but we'll get there. I appreciate that you love your friends. They're lucky to have you."

"Thanks." Tristan lifted his fingers in a casual wave. "Later."

I watched him walk off and frowned, then turned back to Sunshine. "You're awfully forgiving."

"No reason not to be." She shrugged. "I'm not sure how I'd feel in his position. When you look at us from an outside perspective, it's easy to jump to the same conclusion."

I stood and slid my arm around her waist. "He's wrong. I know it. You know it. So it doesn't matter. Let's go find you a ring."

"I'd like that. A lot."

When we got to the car, the truck had managed to leave the spot next to us without scratching the paint. I was grateful for that. I was even more grateful that the car that had taken its place was considerably smaller. I opened Sunshine's door for her.

She smiled up at me. "We should probably call your parents, too."

I froze.

Sunshine got in the car. On automatic, I closed the door and went around to get behind the wheel. She was right, of course. And Mom would be thrilled. The General would be The General. But Dad?

"What's wrong?" She held her gaze steady.

"Can we skip my dad? He and I are kind of not speaking right now." Had I told her about him hitting me up for money? I couldn't remember.

"Okay. It's the same with my family. I'll send an email. Eventually. They won't care."

I heard the hurt in her voice and wanted to do something—anything—to make it better. "You know what? Let's call Mom now. Because she's going to explode with joy."

I didn't wait for her to answer, just started the car and waited the couple seconds for my phone to hook up to the Bluetooth before calling Mom.

"Hi, sweetie. This is a nice surprise. You're finished with church?"

I shot a side-eye look at Sunshine, but if she picked up that it meant Mom had no clue about how long church lasted, she didn't show it. "And lunch, too. I have Sunshine here, I thought you might like to meet her."

"Oh! She came up to visit. How wonderful. Hi, dear. It's lovely to meet you. I wish we could do it in person. Soon, I hope."

"Hi Mrs. Allen."

Mom chuckled. "It's Pendergrass. Wes's father is the Allen. Hold on and let me get The General."

Sunshine's eyebrows lifted.

"I told you everyone calls him that."

Sunshine nodded.

"Hello? Wes? And Sunshine, I hear? Good to meet you."

"Thank you, sir. It's nice to get to say hello." Sunshine looked at me with a plea for help.

"Actually, the reason we called—is Mom there, still?"

"I'm here, honey."

"Great." I cleared my throat. Maybe the best way to go about it was to just spit it out. "We're engaged."

"You are? That's wonderful. Congratulations!" Joy pumped off each of Mom's words. "Now I really want to meet you in person. Is there any way you could make the trip while Sunshine's in town? At least, I'm assuming she'll have to go back and wrap things up."

I bit my lip. "Maybe? We'll talk about it and see if we can make it happen. I've been away from the shop a lot this summer, though, and classes are starting up."

"We could come to you." The General's no-nonsense voice made it sound like a done deal. "I'll look for tickets this afternoon."

"I'll send the plane. Let me know when you want to leave and I'll make arrangements." That was definitely easier. Mom and The General never asked—unlike Dad—so it was nice to be able to do something. And them coming here definitely was easier than trying to leave the shop again right now. "You can stay at my place. You know I have the whole basement suite. You'll have privacy for downtime."

"All right. I've always enjoyed your home, but I didn't want to presume. We'll chat and get back to you with dates. How long are you in town, Sunshine honey?"

I winced. Mom loved to call people dear and honey. I wasn't sure if Sunshine was going to be okay with it. It could come across as patronizing, but Mom never meant it that way.

"I haven't decided yet. I have flexibility in my schedule. So I'll be sure to stay long enough to spend a few days with the two of you." She twisted her fingers in her lap.

"Text me dates, Mom. We need to go. Love you."

"Love you too, honey. I'm so excited! Thanks for calling to let us know. Bye now."

The call ended and I looked over. "Do I need to apologize?"

"No." She smiled and shook her head. "I forgot to mention I'm not great with parents."

I laughed. "You did fine. Let's go get you a ring."

Sunshine leaned over and pressed her lips to mine. I cupped her cheek in my hands and dove in. It was several minutes before we got around to hitting the road.

I don't think either of us minded.

26

SUNSHINE

"It's good to have you home." Zee eyed me from behind the desk. "Although, is this still home?"

I smiled slightly. "It'll always sort of be home."

"You know what I mean."

"I do. And no. I told you."

Zee made a "come here" gesture with her fingers. "Let me see that ring."

"I think you'll approve." I laughed as I crossed the space between us and held out my left hand to show off the wide band of inset stones. There were some diamonds, Wes had won there, but there were also sapphires. The blue and white sparkle made me grin every time I saw it.

"He has good taste." Zee squeezed my hand. "I'm happy for you. And proud of you. And a little sad for me."

"I'll see you, Zee. He owns an island." I rolled my eyes. I still couldn't wrap my head around the idea of being married to someone who owned a whole island. Or a business, for that matter. I'd been content to work for other people. Luca had always wanted us to go out on our own, and I would have with him. Now, I guessed I was doing that with Wes.

Zee nodded. "You'll be busy. Living up in the States, flying down to dive."

"I'll make a point of visiting." I drew an X over my heart. "You can come up, too. You know that right?"

"No thank you. I like it right here. Maybe you can talk me into your island, when you get the guest houses with indoor plumbing set up."

I chuckled. "Got it. Creature comforts only. Thank you, Zee. For everything. I'm not sure I would have been brave enough to give him a shot without you."

"Girl, I know you wouldn't. How hard did I have to kick you to get you to call him? And then you emailed instead? Pfft." She shook her head. "You nearly ruined it. Good thing for you he has a smart head on his shoulders."

"Yes. He does." I leaned forward and kissed her cheek. "You approve?"

"He makes you happy. So of course I do." Zee patted my hand. "Now you get your ugly boat out of my slip and go back to your cottage. What will you do with it?"

I sighed. "Not sure yet. Maybe rent it. I don't think I can sell it. Not yet."

"You'll figure it out. Now you go on home. I'll miss you."

"I'll miss you, Zee. Thanks for everything." It was bittersweet to walk out of the charter offices, knowing I wouldn't be going back as an employee. And really, the only reason to go back would be to visit Zee, which the boss would want us to do on our own time. So maybe it was the last time ever.

I stopped on the sidewalk and looked back at the squat building. I had a lot of good memories tied up there. And some that weren't so good. But that was life. Lots of good, a little bad. The mixture made it work out.

I turned back to the water and strode quickly out to my boat.

This, at least, I wouldn't have to sell. We'd leave it at the island. It was a good boat for diving off. Not as fancy as the yacht Wes had chartered, but we wouldn't be going as far either. Day trips into the water surrounding his island. This would work perfectly for that.

After my checks were complete, I cast off and headed toward home. Was this the last time I'd make this trip, too?

I shook my head. Too many lasts. I shouldn't focus on them. I wouldn't. There were firsts ahead, too. I'd be better off focusing on those rather than dwelling on the others.

I let my mind drift as I steered across the water. Wes's mother was a delight. She'd had a moment when she realized my age and the relative impossibility that we'd be giving her grandchildren. She'd recovered quickly, but it had caused me to panic. And Wes had talked me down and then kissed me thoroughly to ensure I understood it wasn't a problem. Mom—she insisted I call her that—had followed up later with a hug and an apology.

The General was a big, gruff teddy bear. I loved him instantly. He grumbled some about everything, but his eyes were almost always glinting with humor. I was pretty sure he just liked getting a rise out of everyone.

And Wes. Oh my goodness. That man. I'd loved Luca fiercely. I hadn't believed it would be possible to love someone like that again, but Wes made it easy. He loved the ideas I'd given him for his classes—and he asked for more. He was always looking to learn, he said, and then told me I was the best teacher he'd ever had.

I grinned.

I didn't know what made the time fly, but soon enough, I was pulling up at the marina in town. I secured the boat and jumped off. My bike was there, no worse for wear, though sand clogged a few of the tumblers on the lock. I blew on them and gave the lock a bang against the rack, then tried again. This time they spun.

I straddled the bike and, after a moment, headed into town. I'd grab food first. There was nothing to eat in my cottage except canned food. And I didn't feel like cooking right now, anyway.

I waved to folks as I passed them and pictured news of my return spreading through the town. Joys of a tight-knit community. Was it something I'd miss? Maybe.

Probably not.

I parked my bike by Clara's door and strode in.

"Well, well. Look what the cat dragged in." Clara fisted her hands on her hips. "About time."

"Hi, Clara. What's the special today?"

"That's it? What's the special?" Clara grinned and came out from behind the counter, her arms open wide. She pulled me into a tight hug. "For you, the special is whatever you want, because I owe you."

"You do?" I eased back. Clara wasn't someone I would normally consider demonstrative. "Why?"

"Bennie, that's why."

As if summoned, Bennie came out of the kitchen, whistling. "Mi amor." He stopped when he spotted me and pointed. "Sunny!"

Bennie danced out from behind the counter and hugged me before putting an arm around Clara and kissing her cheek. "She finally gave in. I didn't let her have time to think and got the pastor to marry us right away."

Clara's face turned red and she sniffed. "Got tired of you nagging me. Hanging out at a table looking all sad."

Bennie laughed. "Good try, but no. Sunny, go sit. I have spicy pork tacos today that you will adore. Make her one of those fancy coffees she loves."

"Go cook." Clara sighed and watched Bennie head back into the kitchen.

"You're happy."

"I am. Surprisingly."

I chuckled. "He's a good man."

"He is. You have one, too." She nodded at my left hand before she took it and spun the ring on my finger. "With good taste."

"So everyone keeps saying."

"You don't agree?" Clara arched an eyebrow.

"Oh, I do." I paused, frowning as a thought occurred to me. "Does Bennie still do property management?"

"Sure. I don't need him here all the time. He only comes in on his light days. Why?" Clara tsked and raised a finger. "Your cottage. Yes, absolutely. I'll send him out and you can talk. I know how to fix his tacos. Go sit."

Clara shooed me toward the tables and hurried back to the kitchen.

I hadn't firmly decided a vacation rental was the right way to go, but with Bennie looking out for it, my cottage would do fine. Couples, maybe even small families, looking for a quiet beach retreat would love it.

I sat and watched the other patrons while I waited. It didn't take long for Bennie to appear, laptop under his arm.

"Clara says you want to rent your cottage. So smart. You'll leave the furnishings?"

I nodded. I wouldn't need them. Wes had a fully furnished townhouse in Old Town. Thankfully, I loved it. I probably would change a few things—there were some elements that screamed "I'm a bachelor!" but I could wait on that until he was ready.

"Do you want to do long term or just vacation?"

"Uh. I don't know. You're the expert. Advise me." I leaned

back as Clara approached the table with a plate. She set it in front of me and the spicy scent made my mouth water.

"I'll be back with your coffee." Clara nodded once.

"She seems happier than ever." I watched Clara. She stopped to chat with the other customers, not something she normally did.

"We make each other happy. Even when we make each other angry." Bennie grinned. "I think you know what I mean."

I did. I'd had that with Luca. Now I was getting a second chance with Wes.

I ate while Bennie explained the pros and cons of including the possibility of long-term rentals instead of just focusing on the vacation market. Ultimately, we decided to try for the best of both worlds. Long-term rental from May to September. Maybe October if the renter needed it. Then vacation rental only during the high season. If someone wanted to rent for a whole year, the rent would be higher than the long-term summer rate, but not as high as if they booked multiple weeks of vacation time.

It sounded like a good plan, but I made sure Bennie knew he had the authority to tweak it if it didn't work. When I finished my meal, I headed back out, climbed on my bike, and rode out to my cottage as the sun started to set.

I spent some time dusting and swapped out the bed sheets, leaving the old ones on the line to air out overnight. Then, I sat on the front step and buried my toes in the sand and called Wes.

"There you are." Wes's voice held a smile.

"Is it weird that I miss you?" I looked out over the water. The moon was rising on the horizon.

"I hope not, because I miss you, too. Maybe if it is, we can just be weird together."

I chuckled. "Deal. When do you close on the island again?"

"Thursday. I wish you could have stayed longer. I would've been able to come down with you."

"I know. But I have things to settle here. And with your parents gone, we lost our chaperone." We really needed that chaperone. I wasn't sure how to convince Wes that we should get married now. We'd done all but two of the premarital counseling sessions the pastor had outlined. He'd been convinced we probably didn't need the final ones, but he was open to doing them virtually if we wanted. "Did you set up the video conference with the pastor?"

"Yeah. Tomorrow still works, right?"

"Yep." I didn't have anything on my plan. Saturday was as good as any day. "Why aren't you at poker?"

"The couples wanted date night. I have a strong suspicion they're talking about us."

"Don't be paranoid." I shook my head. "Megan must have found an employee to take the Friday night shift. That's probably why."

"Probably. I still think they're talking about us."

I shrugged even though he couldn't see it. "So what? Let them."

He sighed. "I guess. I don't remember being like this with any of their girlfriends."

"You knew them longer. And they aren't older. It doesn't bother me, don't let it bother you. At least we got Tristan to get over himself."

"True. I think it was your ceviche that did that, honestly."

I grinned. I'd been pleased with the fresh fish at the supermarket near Jenna's house. I'd worried some about that—living on an island, I had high standards when it came to seafood. "That did turn out well."

"What do you say we get the pastor to finish up the counseling tomorrow? Then we can nail down a date."

"I'm for that." I pulled my toes out of the sand and brushed them off before I stood and climbed back to my deck. I brushed my feet off on the mat before walking inside and sitting on the sofa. "Can't we just get married when you come down to look over the island?"

"On Thursday?"

"Why not?"

Wes was quiet. I could hear him breathing, but he didn't speak.

A worm of worry wriggled through me. "Unless...are you having second thoughts?"

I wouldn't blame him if he was. This whole thing had moved incredibly fast. We'd known each other three months. And there was absolutely that camp of people who harped on the "when you know, you know" train. On the flip side, friendship was a necessary foundation to any marriage. I thought we had one. Maybe he wasn't there yet.

"No." His answer was fast. "No, it's not that. I don't know how anyone could get to the island."

Ah. "I didn't think about that. I don't have anyone here who would be slighted if they weren't invited. I was picturing you, me, a minister, the beach."

"Oh. Hmm." He cleared his throat. "I've had that same sort of picture. I didn't think..."

"We could have a party when we get back home. Honestly, you could let your mom run with that. Set it up however she wanted."

Wes laughed. "You're devious. But that would assuage her feelings, for sure. Maybe if I told her to involve the girls."

"Absolutely." I held my breath. I wanted this more now that I'd given voice to the idea. I couldn't imagine living in Virginia near Wes and waiting another six months or a year for a wedding. I would do it, if that was what he wanted, but it would be torture.

"Let me call Mom. You have a pastor there who would do it?"

"I think so. Especially if I get him in touch with yours to chat about the counseling." I was a pretty regular attender at our local church. Unless I was on a job. I was reasonably sure he'd be happy to do it. "If you stopped here on your way, we could take care of the license. That has to be done in the city, not my little town. I can meet you there."

"Why do you know that?" He chuckled.

"Well, first, because I looked it up. But also because I remembered needing to do it before."

"Right. I forgot."

"Does it bother you?"

"No. I told you that. Without him, without your life before now, you wouldn't be the woman I love."

I closed my eyes. I believed he meant it. I also had a feeling that we'd end up talking over, around, and through Luca for the rest of our lives. It was okay. I was committed to making things work with Wes. And he was with me. "I love you too."

"Let's do it. I'll bring a suit. No tux. No tie. I'm firm on that."

I laughed. "No shoes. I'm firm on that."

"Okay. Can we do Wednesday? Then we can fly to the island together Thursday."

My heart sped up as the reality crashed down. Wednesday. Less than a week. I was marrying Wes in less than a week. I wiped my sweaty hands on my shorts. "Wednesday it is."

"I should call my mom, make sure I'm not ticking her off."

"If she objects—really hates it—we can figure something else out." I didn't want to, but I also didn't want to cause problems between Wes and his family. Marriage was hard enough without adding in-laws that disliked you into the mix.

"Plan on Wednesday unless I get back to you. I'll call you tomorrow. I love you."

"Love you back. Good night." I ended the call and breathed out. *Is this the right thing, God? It feels right. Make it clear if we need to wait. But please...don't ask us to wait.*

I scrubbed hands over my face and then pushed up off the couch. I needed to get online and see about a dress. I didn't need, or want, a big silk ballgown, but I needed something a little fancier than a linen sundress.

I just needed it to be able to get here by Tuesday.

27

WES

I stood on the sand just out of reach of the water that was in the process of going out. Sunshine's pastor stood beside me, holding his Bible, and grinning widely. The sun was beginning to paint colors on the clouds as it sank into the horizon.

The slap of a screen door made me turn.

My breath caught. She was beautiful. Her dress glowed in the sunset, the white setting off her persistent tan perfectly. A breeze caught the edge of her skirt and I got a glimpse of her long legs.

I swallowed.

Sunshine crossed the sand in long, steady strides.

Music. There should have been music. Although, maybe the swish of the waves and the call of the birds was enough.

I reached for her hand. She laced her fingers through mine and we turned to face the pastor.

"Marriage is hard."

I chuckled at the pastor's opening words.

"It is." He opened his Bible. "But it's worthwhile and good as well. Every morning, wake up and choose to love your spouse. Choose to forgive your spouse. Choose to choose your spouse."

I listened as he transitioned into reading First Corinthians chapter thirteen. I met Sunshine's gaze and held it.

The pastor closed his Bible and nodded to Sunshine.

"Wes, I love you. The pastor is right that marriage is hard, but I promise to choose you and our life together every day. More than once a day if necessary. I'll be with you when it's easy and when it's hard. Through sickness and health. And if poorer happens, I'm not walking away. I'm yours, for as long as we both shall live."

I swallowed the lump in my throat and blinked as tears burned the back of my eyes. I absolutely was not going to cry at my wedding. If the guys found out, I'd never hear the end of it. "Sunshine, your name is fitting because it's what you bring to my life. Even when things get dark, I will choose you and work with you to make it light again. I love you with everything I am and am grateful that God brought us together. I am yours, for as long as we both shall live."

The pastor looked at Sunshine. "Do you have a ring?"

Sunshine pulled one hand free from mine and slipped it into the pocket on the side of her dress. The light glinted off the shell inset in the circle of platinum as she slid it onto my finger. "With this ring, I thee wed."

I savored each word as she said them. Then it was my turn. Her engagement ring was more like a wedding band, but I'd found a skinny circle of diamonds that would be the perfect addition.

I slid it onto her finger. She gasped.

The pastor chuckled.

I finished the words that went along with the ring exchange and held Sunshine's hands while the pastor prayed a blessing over our life together. Then, finally, the words I'd been waiting for all day.

"You may kiss your bride."

I didn't need a second invitation. I stepped forward and pulled her into my arms. Our lips met and my fingers curled, bunching up the waist of her dress.

Sunshine chuckled and eased away as she began to laugh. "Easy there, cowboy. We have our whole life ahead of us."

The pastor cleared his throat. "If you want to get the license, I can sign it and I'll get out of your way. I promise to get it filed tomorrow."

Sunshine reached into her pocket again and pulled out a folded piece of paper. The pastor opened it, skimmed it, and signed it before tucking it into the pocket of his suit coat.

"Have a good night. Congratulations, Wes. And you, Sunny. I think Luca would be pleased."

I glanced sharply at Sunshine, but she just smiled and slid her arm through mine.

She waved. "Thank you."

I watched the pastor make his way across the beach to his car. I looked down at Sunshine—my wife!—and leaned in for another kiss.

This time, she didn't push me away so quickly. After a while, she stepped back and took my hand and started walking toward her cottage. She glanced over her shoulder with a sultry smile. "Why don't we go inside?"

I jogged a few steps and scooped her into my arms, then took the steps to the porch in one stride. I nuzzled her neck as I worked to open the screen door and get us inside. "Mrs. Allen, I believe that's the best idea you've had yet."

EPILOGUE

Tristan

Well, he'd done it. Wes had gone off and married Sunshine on Wednesday. All by themselves on a beach, apparently. I'd checked the laws of the island Sunshine called home, and it was legal that way. Thursday, Wes and Sunshine had gone to his island to sign the final papers. The lawyer I'd found for him through various connections had reported that it all went smoothly.

So had Wes. He'd texted the group.

I sighed and pushed away from my desk.

I should be happy for Wes. For all of them. Most days, I was. But some days, like today, it caught up with me.

Everyone teased me about needing to get out there and date, but they didn't understand it wasn't that simple.

"Whose fault is that?" I muttered.

Great. The talking to myself thing was getting out of control. I should look into getting a dog. A cat would make more sense. I didn't exactly live a dog-friendly life with my work hours. But I ran my own office. I made my own rules. I could bring the dog to work with me.

If I had a dog, when I needed to talk to myself, I could pretend I was talking to him. Definitely a him. A big, manly Labrador maybe. Or a golden retriever. No, too much hair. I didn't need to add hours of grooming to my daily list of chores.

I pulled up the animal shelter website and navigated to the list of dogs they had available. There were a couple of possibilities. I checked the time. If I left now, and if traffic was kind, I could make it before they closed. I packed up my laptop and the stack of files I needed to look over this weekend.

"Heading out?" The part-time assistant-slash-receptionist looked over the top of her reading glasses.

"Yes, ma'am. Why don't you go ahead and head out early as well?"

She studied me a moment before she nodded. "You're the boss."

It didn't take her long to shut down the computer and transfer the main phone line to the answering service. Most of my clients had my cell number, but the service was an expense I didn't mind paying since it guaranteed I didn't miss an important call.

I held the door for her and then locked up behind myself. "Have a good weekend."

"You, too." She lifted a hand and scurried to her car.

I texted the guys that I wasn't going to make poker, then muted the chat so I didn't have to deal with all the pestering. Because oh boy, there would be pestering. Maybe the dog was a dumb idea. But now that I'd started down that road, I felt like I needed to see it through.

Traffic was brutal. Had school started already? Was that why there were so many people out clogging up the streets? I banged on the steering wheel as yet another traffic light turned yellow, then red as I approached.

I glanced at the clock. There was no way I'd make it before the shelter closed now. Not when it had taken thirty minutes to get four blocks and I wasn't even quite to the interstate. I turned my steering wheel and flipped on my signal, then squeezed between two cars when the light changed so I could turn down a side street and start making my way back toward the waterfront and my condo.

Rain started to fall. The sprinkle turned to a drizzle and then to a full-on deluge. My wipers could barely keep up. By the time I made it home and inside, a headache had taken up residence and was blasting away like a frat party in my head. And because of course that was the way today was going, the elevator stopped on every floor on the way up.

I finally got off and stalked down the hallway. I wanted aspirin like I wanted my next breath. And then some kind of takeout. Maybe Chinese.

Someone stood in front of my door, knocking.

"Who are you?" The words came out harsher than I meant them.

The person whirled and crossed their arms over their chest.

I tipped my head to the side but the person—woman?—wore a baseball cap and long hair and big glasses obscured her face. I cleared my throat and tried to gentle my voice. "I think you have the wrong door. Who are you?"

After a moment, she straightened, jutted her chin, and reached up to take off her glasses. "It's me, Tristan. Your wife."

Continue reading in The Billionaire's Wife.

ACKNOWLEDGMENTS

I had such high hopes of getting this book out sooner than it's arriving. But life is a funny thing and as much as I love that writing is my job, it's not my number one job. That is, and will always be, my family. I'm so grateful that I have the opportunity to be a wife and mom and I will never begrudge the need to be present and active there. Even when it means my writing time gets pushed aside here and there. And it provided me with another opportunity to see God move in my life, because He gave me two weeks with long stretches of writing time and I wrote the bulk of this story in those two weeks. It was amazing to see the words flow!

I'm grateful to God for the words. For my family. And for reminding me what my priorities should be.

I'm also, as ever, grateful to my writing squad - Valerie, Stephanie, Jess, Kendra, Mandi, and Hannah - y'all rock. Thanks go to my beta readers for catching the typos that my amazing editor, Lesley McDaniel, and I miss. And thanks go to my readers for ignoring the ones that made it through all those eyes. I know they're in there somewhere.

I can NOT wait to hear what Emma Faye and Joel Simler do with the audio for this story. Every book's audio version gets better and I'm going to be sad when we reach the end of the series if only because it means an end to working with them. Unless, of course, they want to keep going with whatever's next.

Thank YOU for being a reader. For reading my stories -

whether this is the first of mine or you're a devoted fan - please know, I appreciate you and never, ever take for granted that you spend your time on me.

WANT A FREE BOOK?

If you enjoyed this book and would like to read another of my books for free, you can get a free e-book simply by signing up for my newsletter on my website.

OTHER BOOKS BY ELIZABETH MADDREY

Billionaire Next Door

The Billionaire's Nanny

The Billionaire's Best Friend

The Billionaire's Secret Crush

The Billionaire's Backup

The Billionaire's Teacher

The Billionaire's Wife

Postcards, A Novel

So You Want to Be a Billionaire

So You Want a Second Chance

So You Love to Hate Your Boss

So You Love Your Best Friend's Sister

So You Have My Secret Baby

So You Need a Fake Relationship

So You Forgot You Love Me

Hope Ranch Series

Hope for Christmas

Hope for Tomorrow

Hope for Love

Hope for Freedom

Hope for Family

Hope at Last

Peacock Hill Romance Series

A Heart Restored

A Heart Reclaimed

A Heart Realigned

A Heart Redirected

A Heart Rearranged

A Heart Reconsidered

Arcadia Valley Romance – Baxter Family Bakery Series

Loaves & Wishes

Muffins & Moonbeams

Cookies & Candlelight

Donuts & Daydreams

The 'Operation Romance' Series

Operation Mistletoe

Operation Valentine

Operation Fireworks

Operation Back-to-School

Prefer to read a box set? Find the whole series here.

The 'Taste of Romance' Series

A Splash of Substance

A Pinch of Promise

A Dash of Daring

A Handful of Hope

A Tidbit of Trust

Prefer to read a box set? Get the series in two parts! Box 1 and Box 2.

The 'Grant Us Grace' Series

Wisdom to Know

Courage to Change

Serenity to Accept

Pathway to Peace

Joint Venture

Prefer to read a box set? Grab the whole series here.

The 'Remnants' Series:

Faith Departed

Hope Deferred

Love Defined

Stand alone novellas

Kinsale Kisses: An Irish Romance

Luna Rosa (part of A Tuscan Legacy)

For the most recent listing of all my books, please visit my website.

ABOUT THE AUTHOR

USA Today bestselling author Elizabeth Maddrey is a semi-reformed computer geek and homeschooling mother of two who lives in the suburbs of Washington D.C. When she isn't writing, Elizabeth is a voracious consumer of books. She loves to write about Christians who struggle through their lives, dealing with sin and receiving God's grace on their way to their own romantic happily ever after.

- facebook.com/ElizabethMaddrey
- instagram.com/ElizabethMaddrey
- amazon.com/Elizabeth-Maddrey/e/BooA11QGME
- bookbub.com/authors/elizabeth-maddrey
- youtube.com/@ElizabethMaddreyAuthor